ARKAN

CW00938059

A History o...

Richard Cavendish was born in Henley-on-Thames, the son of a clergyman, and studied medieval history at Brasenose College, Oxford. After publishing three novels he wrote *The Magical Arts* (Arkana 1984), on the European magical tradition. He subsequently edited *Man, Myth & Magic* and *The Encyclopedia of the Unexplained* (Arkana 1989). He is also the author of books on the history of magic, the Tarot pack and the Arthurian legends and has edited encyclopedias of mythology and legends. His guidebook to prehistoric England was published in 1983, and until 1987 he edited the magazine *Out of Town*.

A HISTORY OF
MAGIC

Richard Cavendish

ARKANA

ARKANA

Published by the Penguin Group
27 Wrights Lane, London w8 5tz, England
Viking Penguin, a division of Penguin Books USA Inc.
375 Hudson Street, New York, New York 10014, USA
Penguin Books Australia Ltd, Ringwood, Victoria, Australia
Penguin Books Canada Ltd, 2801 John Street, Markham, Ontario, Canada l3r 1b4
Penguin Books (NZ) Ltd, 182–190 Wairau Road, Auckland 10, New Zealand

Penguin Books Ltd, Registered Offices: Harmondsworth, Middlesex, England

First published in Great Britain by Weidenfeld & Nicolson 1987
Published by ARKANA 1990
1 3 5 7 9 10 8 6 4 2

Frontispiece: One of many artistic interpretations of Anthony's encounters with demons

Printed by Clays Ltd, St Ives plc

CONTENTS

Prologue

Magic is as old as man. It is found as far back as evidence of human existence runs and has influenced religion, art, agriculture, industry, science, government and social institutions. The western tradition of magic was born in the Roman world at about the same time as Christ, but its ultimate ancestry is veiled in the mists and cloudbanks of prehistory. The same type of thinking links the primitive hunters who created the superb cave paintings of prehistoric Europe with the modern magician, drawing his circle and evoking his gods in the clatter and bustle of London, Paris or New York.

Magic is an attempt to exert power through actions which are believed to have a direct and automatic influence on man, nature and the divine. It is impossible to isolate the history of magic completely from the history of religion or science. The religious, scientific and magical attitudes to experience are distinct from each other in theory. The religious impulse is to worship, the scientific to explain, the magical to dominate and command. But in real life attitudes are not kept in separate compartments and the distinctions are frequently blurred. In the distant past everything strange was magical, or religio-magical, and this was true of human beings as well as the environment. In Homer, for example, 'all departures from normal human behaviour whose causes are not immediately perceived, whether by the subjects' own consciousness or by the observation of others, are ascribed to a supernatural agency, just as is any departure from the normal behaviour of the weather or the normal behaviour of a bowstring'.[1]

Magic tries to control these mysterious agencies. It is far more concerned with what 'works' than with why or how things work. In magic, if the right procedure is followed, the desired result will occur: if it does not, then the correct procedure cannot have been followed. The correct procedure is the one which experience associates with the desired result. Ceremonies were held every year in ancient Egypt to make sure that the Nile would flood. They were held at the time when the Nile was due to flood in any case. Similarly, primitive societies which conduct rain-making ceremonies hold them at the beginning of the rainy season, not in the middle of the dry season. The ceremonies are man's contribution to the right order of things, which includes the seasonal renewal of rainfall. To omit them would be to disturb the right order, and the rains might not come.

Against this background, the simplest reason for believing in magic is that it works: not always, but often enough to inspire confidence. The Nile normally does flood, the rains usually do fall. And confidence in magic can cause it to work. When a spell is cast to heal someone who is sick, and he believes in it, his belief may help him to recover. When a spell is cast to murder a man, and he believes in it, his belief may kill him. A case was reported from Australia a few years ago of an aborigine who was dying, though there was nothing physically wrong with him, because he knew that a medicine-man had put a death spell on him. When he was taken to hospital and placed in an iron lung, he became convinced that this magic was stronger than the medicine-man's and he recovered.

Because of this psychological mechanism, belief in magic helps to bind the members of a community together and give them strength, not merely by warding off supernatural evil which they fear but by inspiring positive confidence. The prehistoric cave paintings are examples of magic in this role. The people who produced them lived by hunting, fishing and gathering. Animals were painted in sanctuaries deep inside caves to give man control of the species. Pictures of animals wounded by weapons were probably meant to help the hunters wound and kill them in real life, and would have helped them on the most practical level by giving them confidence. Or some of the 'wounds' and 'weapons' may have been sexual symbols intended to promote the fertility of the species and so secure an adequate supply of game

Delineation in pictures is part of the magical technique of mimicry, which works on the principle that if something is imitated with sufficient concentration and vividness it comes into being in reality. In some of the caves there are pictures of dancers in animal costume. Hunting peoples wear animal masks and skins to stalk game, imitating their prey to get close to them. It is likely that in imitative dances, disguised as an animal and mimicking its cries, movements and courtship, prehistoric magicians felt that they became the animal and so controlled the species. They may also have identified themselves with gods or spirits imagined in animal or partly animal and partly human form, for rites of this kind induce a sense of being filled with a power that is more than human. Later, certainly, the attempt to become superhuman or divine is the ultimate aim of magic in the entire western tradition.

The most famous prehistoric example is the figure sometimes called 'the dancing sorcerer' in the Trois Frères cave in the south of France. It is a man wearing an animal's skin and tail, with an owlish-looking mask and the antlers of a stag. It is in the deepest part of the cave, above a high rock ledge twelve feet up from the cave floor. It may represent both a god and the medicine-man of the tribe: 'some kind of prime – or indeed divine – teacher of magic; and his representative, the "current" sorcerer, would have mounted the same high pulpit under the picture to officiate, before the elders of the tribe, at ceremonies aimed at ensuring hunting luck and animal fertility'.[2]

The medicine-men, or shamans, of prehistoric tribes are the distant ancestors of the modern magician. Some rare individuals possess unusual abilities which seem superhuman: the power to glimpse the future, for example, or to be aware of what is happening at a great distance, or to go at will into trance and assume a different and eerily impressive personality. In any given case, these abilities may be genuine or cleverly faked or, perhaps often, a mixture of both. They mark their possessor out as a magician and all sorts of marvellous feats are credited to him.

Shamanism still exists in Siberia. In the past it influenced an arc of territory from Scandinavia to Indonesia (and much more recently, modern occultism has drawn directly on the shamanistic practices of North American Indians). A shaman is a specialist in the sacred who is gifted with uncanny powers. He can put himself into trance, in which he is believed to escape from his body, travel to far-off places and observe events there, and penetrate the world of spirits. He ascends to the sky and descends to the underworld. He can restore the dead to life. He can levitate and fly, and is seen simultaneously in different places. He can see into the future, make himself invisible, and kill at a distance. He is skilled in healing, divination and the lore of animals, plants and stones. He communicates with animals and birds, is aided by spirits in animal forms and can turn himself into an animal. He knows the myths and history of the tribe and the names and concerns of gods and spirits. He is a master of poetry, chants and spells. He is a man of power and many of his characteristics descended to the holy men and magicians of the ancient world.

With the development of agriculture and cattle-breeding and the rise of civilizations in the Near East, magic was applied to the fertility of farmers' crops and herds. Kings and priests inherited the functions of tribal magicians. The growth of specialized crafts gave industry a magical mystique. Craftsmen's skills and trade secrets, denied to ordinary men, seemed to mark them off as possessors of supernatural knowledge and power. Smiths, in particular, gained a lasting reputation as dangerous magicians. Magic continued to be used for the general prosperity and safety of the community. Jumping and leaping, for example, is an old piece of magical mimicry to make crops grow tall and animals thrive, and again induces a state of excitement in which the performers feel that they are imbued with superhuman force. An ancient hymn to Zeus, discovered in Crete, calls on the god to 'leap' for flocks and crops, cities and ships, observance of the laws, trade and peace and security. The word for leap is a pun, meaning both 'jump' and sexually 'cover' the female, to impregnate her. The hymn was sung by young men performing a jumping dance and in their ecstasy identifying themselves with the divine power they summoned.

Ecstatic techniques not only kindle subjective excitement but can generate abnormal physical powers which appear superhuman and magical. The maenads, the women worshippers of Dionysus in Greece, ran wild on the hillsides at night, wearing masks and fawnskins and wreathed with ivy. Some held snakes in their hands or twined them in their hair. Dancing, tossing their heads and crying out in rising frenzy, they reached a peak of abandon at which they tore live animals to pieces and ate them raw.

Originally, the climax of the rites had probably been the rending and cannibal devouring of a man. The maenads believed that they were eating Dionysus himself, so that they became possessed by the god and were freed from the normal restrictions of human nature. They saw visions and they claimed to be immune to wounds and able to handle fire without being burned; and judging from parallels elsewhere these claims may have been true.

Sex is a component of magic to promote fertility and vitality because of its ecstatic, power-filled qualities and because magic works by analogy. The kings of Babylon went through a 'sacred marriage' each year with the great goddess Ishtar, representd by a priestess. This was considered essential for the fertility of the land and the prosperity of the community. The custom of sacred prostitution in the East had the same rationale. Prostitutes crowded the temples of fertility goddesses in Mesopotamia, Asia Minor, Syria and Egypt, and their activities contributed to abundant harvests in theory and the temple treasuries in practice.

In the East the king was a focus of magic for the well-being of his country. As the embodiment of the state and its people, he had to be protected from hostile influences. Persian kings ate their meals behind curtains, to shield them from magic directed at them while they were susceptibly swallowing food. The names of Egyptian pharaohs, when written in inscriptions, were enclosed in a protective cartouche or oval ring. Kings were guarded against threatening omens, and in one case in Assyria a mock king was substituted for the real one for a hundred days and then killed to preserve the real king from the effects of a fatal omen.

But the king also exercised powerful magic himself, through the divinity that hedged him. For thousands of years the rulers of Egypt were treated as deities walking the earth. Pharaoh was the god Horus in his lifetime and the god Osiris after his death. He personified the right order of things and he was magically responsible for his people's welfare, and specifically for the annual Nile flood. He was thought to control rainfall and several pharaohs acted as water-diviners when new wells were dug in the desert. This power over water was inherited from prehistoric tribal chieftains who were rain-makers. They may have been put to death when their powers began to fail, perhaps by drowning or dismemberment (both motifs occur in the myth of Osiris, the prehistoric king who became a god), and replaced by a younger successor. Later, pharaoh was ritually rejuvenated and his coronation renewed at the Jubilee Festival. The medicine-man's costume of the prehistoric chiefs was also inherited by the pharaohs, who on ceremonial occasions wore the beard of a goat and an animal tail and carried the goatherd's flail and crook.[3]

In Babylon, during the New Year festival, the king was formally humiliated. He was stripped of his regalia and struck in the face by the high priest of Marduk, the Babylonian supreme god and god of magic. This may again have been a watered-down version of an earlier custom of killing and replacing the king because the prosperity of the country depended on the magic of his virility.

Another ceremony at the Babylonian New Year festival was the recitation, and probably the acting out, of the myth of creation, which told how the powers of chaos had been vanquished and civilized order established in the world by Marduk. This was an important magical builder of confidence for the coming year. It subdued the menace of disorder and guaranteed peace and security by repeating, and so renewing, the original events. Similarly in Egypt, a common magical technique was to repeat words which a god had relied on in some mythical incident. By imagining himself as the god and reciting the words, the magician expected the same success.

Language, like mimicry, is an instrument of power. In the first chapter of Genesis, God is described creating the world by expressing commands in words: 'And God said, "Let there be light"; and there was light.' According to the creation myth of Memphis in Egypt, the world was made by the god Ptah, who thought of all the things that exist and then stated his thoughts in words, which caused everything to materialize. Long ago, as language developed, men evidently felt that words gave them a firmer grasp on reality. This is suggested by the old belief that everything has a 'real' name, which is its identity. To know the real name of a thing is to control it, and 'names of power' are used in incantations as magical sources of energy.

The invention of writing added another weapon to the magician's arsenal. It was believed that the gods must have devised this marvellous way of capturing speech and giving it tangible form. The fact that most people were illiterate and writing largely the preserve of priests added to the reputation of letters and alphabets as containers of mysterious wisdom and power. Words and phrases written on clay, stone, parchment, metals or jewels were used for protection against hostile forces and to obtain good luck and success. The Egyptians called the picture-writing which they used in temples and tombs 'the speech of the gods', and the Greeks called the Egyptian letters hieroglyphs, 'sacred carvings'. The hieroglyphs have retained a powerful magical aura ever since.

Everywhere in the ancient world magic was used to secure a happy afterlife for the dead. The Egyptians regarded a physical body as essential for this, and by about 2400 BC the corpses of pharaohs were being mummified in a rough and ready way to prevent them decaying. Mummification later became extremely elaborate and efficient, and spread from the royal house to the Egyptian aristocracy. The process was believed to be a repetition and renewal of the rites which had rescued Osiris from death. The mummy was given life by priests through the magic of language and gesture in the ceremony of 'the opening of the mouth', which resembled the ritual used to animate the statues of the gods. It was then placed in a coffin covered with magic texts and symbols and pictures of protective deities.

Paintings in Egyptian tombs show people eating and drinking, dancing and playing games, making love, fighting, hunting and fishing, as illustrations of the afterlife but probably also as magic to invigorate the dead man. To save him from having to do forced labour in the afterworld, small figures of servants and workmen were placed in the tomb, inscribed with spells expressing their readiness to do the work for him.

Besides its positive role as a means of maintaining confidence and attempting to secure prosperity and success, magic is a mechanism of defence against natural and supernatural evil. All sorts of methods, ranging from elaborate rituals to spells, amulets and minor superstitions are employed against the hostility of the elements, the prevalence of bad luck and the malice of demons and ghosts. They are also used to counter the machinations of sorcerers and witches.

Magic is double-edged and the popular distinction between white magic and black magic rests in the eyes of the beholder. The medicine-man who puts a curse on an enemy of his tribe is working white magic from his own people's point of view, but black magic from the enemy's. And magic is not practised only by authorized professionals – the medicine-man, the king or the priest. It is also worked by private individuals, some of whom set up as unlicensed professionals, and protection against them is needed. In Meso-potamia, for instance, specialist priests treated those who were suffering from the unwelcome attentions of sorcerers and evil spirits, which frequently took the form of diseases, and a common way of dealing with a hostile magician was to make a small figure to represent him and then burn it.

At more sophisticated levels, the distinction between white and black magic becomes a distinction between legitimate magic (often not classified as magic at all), which is authorized by tradition and conducted by approved officials for public purposes, and illegitimate magic, which is worked privately by unlicensed practitioners for personal gain. Accusations of sorcery, and the actual practice of sorcery, are fostered by the existence of two roads to power in a society.

On the one hand, there is *articulate* power, power defined and agreed upon by everyone (and especially by its holders!): authority vested in precise persons; admiration and success gained by recognized channels. Running counter to this there may be other forms of influence less easy to pin down – *inarticulate* power: the disturbing intangibles of social life; the imponderable advantages of certain groups; personal skills that succeed in a way that is unacceptable or difficult to understand. Where these two systems overlap we may expect to find the sorcerer. . . .[4]

The sorcerer need not, of course, actually exist in order to be blamed. Human beings have a primitive and persistent reluctance to believe that things happen by chance and, where everything strange is magical, harmful events are readily put down to evil magic. In the ancient world magic was credited with extraordinary powers over nature. A Greek treatise on epilepsy, *The Sacred Disease*, doubtfully attributed to the famous physician Hippocrates (fourth century BC), mentions magicians who claim to know how to bring the stars down from the sky, darken the sun, make the ground barren, and cause storms or fine weather, rain or drought. There was an old Roman law against using magic to transfer crops from one farmer's field to another's, and witches were still being accused of doing this in the seventeenth century in Europe.

From the seventh century BC Greek rationalism made inroads into magic's territory by looking for natural explanations of what had previously been considered supernatural. The Roman world, however, experienced a resurgence of interest in magic comparable to the modern occult revival. In the melting-pot of the Roman Empire influences from the East, Greece, Rome itself and the barbarian cultures of western and northern Europe mingled and fused together to form the western magical tradition.

1
Rome and the East

The Roman world resembled the modern West in several ways. Progress in science and a decline of traditional religion were followed by an upsurge of interest in the occult, to the alarm of conservatives and rationalists. The scientific spirit of earlier Greek thought failed to satisfy human needs and by the second century AD confidence in rational means of gaining knowledge had waned. Strange sects and cults flourished, as they do today. There was a lively interest and belief in magic, witchcraft, ghosts, spiritual healing, fortune-telling and lucky charms, and in self-development by way of meditation, trances and altered states of consciousness. Astrology had a grip on educated minds which it has recently begun to recover. At one time a new golden age was expected to dawn, which we hear of again now as the Age of Aquarius. Modern Spiritualism has parallels in classical theurgy.

There was an awed respect for the older civilizations of the East, which had been opened up to western exploitation. Alexander the Great conquered Syria, Egypt, Mesopotamia and Persia, and fought his way into India, before his death in 323 BC. He was succeeded in command of the East by Greek dynasties and then by the Romans. Flooding back into the West came tides of oriental religion, magic and astrology, channelled principally through Hellenistic and Roman Egypt: 'all the rivers – Assyrian, Babylonian, Anatolian, Persian, Jewish – met in Egypt as in a reservoir, and from Egypt flowed out to water the earth'.[1]

The Roman world experienced the same dissatisfaction with both rationalism and orthodox religion which is familiar in the modern West. Greek rationalist and agnostic philosophies created anxiety by turning the gods into abstract and distant figures, remote from earthly life and its problems. They cast doubt on whether the gods existed at all and indeed whether any proposition of human importance could be established with confidence. The public worship of the Olympian gods and the agricultural rites of the countryside were considered essential to the fabric of the state and were kept up, as services are held in churches and synagogues now. They still commanded some genuine devotion, but in the late centuries BC the grip of the official gods had weakened in times of war, revolution and turmoil, which they seemed powerless to prevent.

There were other important factors, especially at middle-brow intellectual levels. Rome swallowed up independent cities and states, making the individual a smaller fish in a much larger pond. Urbanization cut many people off from the country-side and its settled rhythm of life and worship. Increased social and physical mobility, cosmopolitanism and the slackening of family ties contributed to rootlessness, anxiety and what is now called an identity crisis: a situation in which many people feel uncertain of who they are, where they belong and what their role is.

The result was a demand for a more direct, personal and certain relationship with the divine than the state cults could supply, for unofficial and private ways to truth, salvation and psychological security. The demand was met by new religions, mystery cults, esoteric groups and 'men of power' – holy men, sages, prophets, healers, magicians, astrologers. Some of them received official backing, but the proliferation of swarms of unlicensed pro-fessionals was inevitably distrusted by authority and disliked by conservatives. Private groups were suspect as anti-social, hard to control and a danger to the state, and many of them bore the double stigma of novelty and foreignness.

High Magic

The Greek and Latin words for magic, *mageia* and *magia*, imply that magic was foreign. They originally meant the arts of the Magi, the Zoroastrian priests of Persia, who had a reputation for profound secret wisdom and supernatural power. The Magi presided over religious ceremonies, interpreted omens and dreams, and studied astrology. They were the advisers of kings and took charge of the education of royal princes. The three wise men from the East, who brought gifts to the baby Jesus, were Magi, and Magus is a title of high rank in modern occult societies.

In reality, much of the magic of Greece and Rome was native and not foreign at all, but Greek and Roman writers lumped all magic together as an importation from the alluring but dubious East. Throughout its subsequent history, magic is normally a pejorative term. An accepted, traditional magical practice is not classified as magic but as part of religion or respectable folk custom. 'Magic' is something illicit and alien.

Since magic was linked with the Zoroastrian priests, its founder was naturally identified as Zoroaster himself. By the first century AD, when Pliny wrote his *Natural History*, the Persian prophet was renowned as a great sage and numerous books on religion, magic and astrology were credited to him. Pliny worked out a rough (and highly inaccurate) family tree of magic, starting with Zoroaster. From him magic descended to the Magi and in particular to Osthanes, a wizard who accompanied the Persian king Xerxes on his unsuccessful invasion of Greece in 480 BC. Osthanes, Pliny says, wrote a book on magic which infected the Greeks with a mania for the subject. Pythagoras, Plato and other philosophers went to the East to learn magic and taught it in secret on their return. A second and later branch of magic was the Jewish variety, deriving from Moses, Jannes, Lotapes and others. Jannes was traditionally one of the Egyptian magicians defeated by Moses and Aaron in the contest before Pharaoh. Lotapes is a corruption of Iotape, which is a variant of Yahweh, the name of the God of the Old Testament himself.[2]

Zoroaster and Moses were both founders of religions who claimed to be divinely inspired, which gave them a potent esoteric mystique; and Zoroaster had claimed a knowledge of the powerful demonic forces at work in the world which made him especially qualified to be the founding father of magic. There were no comparable figures elsewhere in the East. However, there were Persian Magi in Babylonia, or Chaldea as it was often called, after the country became part of the Persian Empire in the sixth century BC. There were also native Babylonian priests and astrologers with an old reputation for secret wisdom. Chaldea was another foreign source of magic and 'Chaldeans' became a label for astrologers, fortune-tellers and wizards in general.

Many classical writers recognized that the principal fountainhead of foreign magic arts was Egypt. The immemorial antiquity of its civilization, the splendour of its temples and pyramids, its intriguing animal-headed gods, the mysterious hieroglyphs, the rites for the dead and the divine aura of the pharaohs gave Egypt a compelling glamour which, for the occultly inclined, it has never lost. The Sphinx of Gizeh was regarded as a symbol of esoteric wisdom and great Greek thinkers were believed to have gone to Egypt to learn the secrets of the Egyptian priests.

All four of the peoples principally associated with magic – the Egyptians, Persians, Chaldeans and Jews – had powerful specialist priesthoods. The Indian Brahmins and the Celtic Druids, who were also regarded as master magicians, were again specialists in the sacred. Greek and Roman priests, with rare exceptions, were not. They served as priests only for a limited time. They were not expected to give up their ordinary secular activities while in office and, as priests, they had little political importance. By contrast, the priesthoods of the East, in lifelong contact with the divine, counsellors of kings, carefully trained as professional mediators between men and the gods, acquired in Greek and Roman eyes an aura of supernatural knowledge and power. It repelled Pliny, who called magic 'the most fraudulent of arts', but others were attracted.

There is a useful rough distinction between high magic and low magic. High magic is an attempt to gain so consummate an understanding and mastery of oneself and the environment as to transcend all human limitations and become superhuman or divine. This was the magic which Pythagoras and other philosophers were supposed to have learned in the East, and it was associated with the acquisition of superhuman powers like the ability to control the weather or to be in two places at once. Low magic is comparatively minor and mechanical, undertaken for immediate worldly advantage, to make money or take revenge on an enemy or make a conquest in love. It tails off into the peddling of spells and lucky charms. The distinction between the two types is blurred in practice and many magicians have engaged in both.

Pythagoras is the most famous of the Greek high magicians allegedly trained in the East. Born in Samos, he emigrated in about 530 BC to the Greek colony of Croton (modern Cotrone) in southern Italy, where the people identified him as Apollo. He founded a secret society there, open to men and women who could pass the initiatory tests and ordeals, and submit to a strict discipline of purity, vegetarianism, silence and searching self-examination. They observed various curious taboos, including one on beans and another on putting the left shoe on before the right. Perhaps not surprisingly in the circumstances, they disapproved of immoderate laughter.

The disciples of Pythagoras avoided using his name and referred to him as 'himself' or 'the divine one'. He believed in reincarnation and the transmigration of souls, ideas which may have spread westwards from India. It was said that he remembered many of his own past lives, and that he once recognized a dog as a former friend of his. He thought that numbers held the key to understanding the universe, and his followers had a formative influence on numerology in the West. In the spirit of high magic, he evidently regarded understanding the universe not as a mere intellectual quest but as the way of salvation.

There was a revival of Pythagoreanism in the first century BC and by this time a mass of stories had gathered round the Master. As a young man, he was supposed to have gone to Egypt, where he absorbed the wisdom of the priests, and to Mesopotamia, where he was taught the secrets of the Magi and the Chaldeans. He was also said to have travelled to India to learn from the Brahmins and to Britain to study with the Druids (or alternatively, one of his slaves went to Britain and taught Pythagoreanism to the Druids). He went down into the underworld through a cave in Crete and spent a year there. He was a great healer, using music and incantations in his cures, and he could predict the future and command the weather and the sea. He could also control animals and there are stories about him using magic words to summon an eagle from the sky, tame a bear, drive away several poisonous snakes and persuade an ox to give up eating beans.

An even mistier figure than Pythagoras is the Cretan holy man Epimenides, a poet and wonder-worker who seems to have lived about 600 BC. It was said that he remembered many previous lives on earth and that he could escape from his body and go about independently of it. He was a vegetarian, spent fifty-seven years asleep in a cave (probably the equivalent of Pythagoras's stay in the underworld), and lived to an immense age. Another miracle-worker was the Sicilian Greek poet and philosopher Empedocles, who was supposed to have studied magic in Egypt. In his poems he claimed to be a god in human form, able to cure disease, foretell the future and control the winds and the rain. He died about 433 BC, allegedly jumping into the crater of Mount Etna in the hope that his disappearance without trace would convince people that he was divine. He also remembered many reincarnations: 'For I have been ere now a boy and a girl, a bush and a bird, and a leaping dumb fish in the sea.'[3]

Mistier still, though he was probably a real person, is Orpheus, the great Thracian poet, singer and lyre-player of legend, whose music was so magically compelling that it drew animals, birds, trees and rocks to him. Rivers paused in mid-flow and mountains moved when he sang. His melodies so charmed the grim rulers of the dead that he would have succeeded in rescuing his wife, Eurydice, from the underworld if he had not fatally looked back at her at the last moment. He was killed by raving maenads, who tore him limb from limb and threw his head into the river Hebrus. It floated away down the river and out to sea, still singing. The Thracians built a tomb for him and the nightingales sang more sweetly there than anywhere else in the world.

Orpheus stood for the enchantments of music, and he also was said to have learned magic in Egypt. As a great poet, he was supposed to have written formidable incantations. Mystical poems on salvation from death were ascribed to him, some of them by the Pythagoreans, and so were hymns to the gods and books on astrology, the magic of gems and the properties of herbs.

The figure of the shaman looms behind these legendary magicians, with their superhuman abilities and healing power, their descents to the underworld and their rapport with nature and the animal kingdom. The Greeks had encountered shamanism in Scythia in the seventh century BC and probably also in Thrace, the homeland of both Orpheus and the orgiastic cult of Dionysus. There were still numerous shamanistic traits in Apollonius of Tyana, a Pythagorean sage of Asia Minor in the first century AD. His biography, written by Philostratus about 220, has been a significant influence on the western concept of the master magician.

At the moment when Apollonius was born, according to Philostratus, a bolt of lightning hung motionless in the sky for a moment and then disappeared. He was a vegetarian, dressed in simple clothes and home-made sandals, observed a vow of silence for five years, and abstained entirely from sex, thereby becoming 'master of the uncontrollable'. He immersed himself in Pythagorean philosophy, which enabled him 'to know his own true self'

He went to India to learn from the Brahmins and conceived a profound admiration for them, which they reciprocated. He also studied with sages in Egypt, by whom he was not impressed, and with Babylonian priests.

As described by Philostratus, Apollonius was a man of commanding and impressive personality. He travelled about, teaching and visiting temples. He descended into the underworld through the cave of Trophonius in Greece. He believed in reincarnation, remembered an earlier life of his own as an Egyptian ship-pilot and recognized a former Egyptian king in a tame lion which he saw on display. He was also a healer and once drove away a disease-spirit which had infected the city of Ephesus with plague. In a famous episode at Corinth, which inspired Keats's poem *Lamia*, he met a young man who had fallen passionately in love with a beautiful foreign woman and was just about to marry her. At the wedding feast Apollonius unmasked the bride as a vampire, intent on draining her husband's life by drinking his blood, and forced all her servants and furniture, which were magical illusions, to vanish like smoke.[4]

Apollonius could see into the future, had telepathic powers and could transport himself from one place to another in a flash. When he was put on trial before the Emperor Domitian, accused of murdering a boy so as to divine from his entrails who the next emperor would be, he miraculously vanished from the court. He later clairvoyantly watched the assassination of Domitian in Rome, while he himself was hundreds of miles away at Ephesus. He was suspected of being able to turn himself into an animal or a tree, but denied it. According to various tales, he did not die but mysteriously disappeared. One story was that he ascended bodily into heaven, but was seen on earth again after his 'death'.

Philostratus was anxious to defend his hero from the charge of being a magician, but whether Apollonius was a holy man or a sorcerer was a fiercely disputed question. The Emperor Caracalla built a temple to him, and Alexander Severus was said to keep four statues in his private shrine – of Orpheus, Abraham, Christ and Apollonius. But the enemies of Apollonius accused him of being a black magician, possessed by an evil spirit and driven by a cannibal hunger for children's flesh. Attempts were made to promote him as a pagan rival to Christ. As a result his name stank in Christian nostrils to such an extent that as late as 1680, when the first part of an English translation of Philostratus came out, there was an outcry against it as a threat to the Christian religion and publication of the rest was dropped.

Apollonius is the magician as outsider. He is the spiritual descendant of the tribal shaman, but in a society which has moved on from shamanism the magician has lost the shaman's social function. He works for himself and an exclusive coterie of disciples, not for the community as a whole. He is no longer inside the accepted religion and the apparatus of society, but outside it. He travels a lonely, forbidden road to holiness and power, and he is inevitably accused of black magic.

Perhaps the most telling remark in Apollonius's biography is the one about him discovering 'his own true self'. Belief in reincarnation and transmigration, the ability of a magician to penetrate non-physical planes of existence, to turn into an animal, to move from place to place in an instant and observe events hundreds of miles away, reinforced the idea of a self which could leave the body and survive death, which had magical powers and which was actually or potentially divine.

One reaction to the failure of the traditional gods to keep order in the world and look after their worshippers' interests was the deification of powerful human rulers who were more reliable. Alexander the Great was recognized as a god in his own lifetime. So were his successors in the East. An Athenian poet of the third century BC hailed Demetrius of Macedonia as a god who was present on earth in person, unlike the other gods who lived far away and seemed to have lost their ears and not to care about human beings. Augustus and the Roman emperors after him were deified at death. While each emperor was still alive, his *genius* was worshipped, that essential spirit or true self which inhabited his mortal body.

Numerous religio-magical cults and groups in the Roman world were dedicated to discovering the true self and becoming divine. The most prominent of them were the mystery religions, which reached the height of their influence in the early centuries after Christ. Details of the Mysteries were rarely revealed to outsiders, but they culminated in an overwhelming emotional experience in which the initiate identified himself with his god. He was 'reborn', free of the animal lower self which had held him down. He had conquered death and was sure of a happy immortality. He had solved his identity crisis in finding his eternal identity. This climax was achieved as much through the magical, power-inducing effect of dramatic ritual as through religious devotion to the god.

The most famous Mysteries were those of Demeter at Eleusis, near Athens, which originated in agricultural fertility rites and survived until late in the fourth century AD. Augustus and several other emperors were initiated at Eleusis, and so was Apollonius of Tyana. The Emperor Gallienus identified himself so closely with the Eleusinian goddess after his initiation that he styled himself in the feminine, Augusta Galliena, on his coinage. It was said that the holiest rites at Eleusis involved a 'sacred marriage', followed by the announcement that the goddess had given birth to a sacred child; and that the ultimate symbol revealed to the initiates was 'a green ear of corn reaped in silence'.

There were also Mysteries of Dionysus, Cybele and Attis, Isis and Osiris, and Mithras, all of which also stemmed from fertility magic. Fasting, chanting, prayer, contemplation of symbols, baptism in water or drenching in the blood of a bull, flagellation, torture and other ordeals were used to prepare for and induce the final ecstatic experience. The sanctuaries of Mithras, for example, were underground and candidates for initiation had to find their way through labyrinthine passages in darkness, seeking for the light.

The Orphic movement, which took its name from Orpheus, believed that there is a spark of the divine in man, which is imprisoned in the body as in a tomb. Asceticism and vegetarianism were ways of freeing the divine self from reincarnation in a succession of earthly bodies. The Stoic school of philosophy, founded by Zeno about 300 BC, gave an impetus to magic because it believed that the universe is ruled by one supreme power – which could be called Zeus or Nature or Destiny – which permeates everything that exists, including man. Magic is similarly pan-theistic, and the magician seeks to tap divine power in all phenomena – in letters and numbers, planets and stars, herbs, stones, metals, fire and water, bones and blood – and especially in himself.

The gnostic sects of the eastern Mediterranean also believed that a spark of the divine exists in man, where it is held captive in the body and the evil world of matter. It can be freed from its bondage while still on earth, to achieve its full divine potential. The means of liberation is the *gnosis*, or saving knowledge. This is not knowledge achieved by reason but 'the knowledge of the heart', gained through meditative visions in which the truth is revealed: or as a second-best, learned from those who have received the direct revelation. The *gnosis* is essentially the knowledge of one's true identity. In the system of Valentinus, an Alexandrian who taught at Rome in the second century AD, the *gnosis* is revealed to the initiate by his guardian angel, who accompanies him all through life and who is really his true, divine self. This concept has come to the fore again in the modern revival of magic.

The most formidable gnostic magician, in legend at least, was Simon Magus, a Samaritan of the first century, who was bitterly denounced by Christian writers as a dangerous opponent of the Church and the founder of heresy. Simon was worshipped as a god in Samaria because of his wonder-working powers. Attracted by the miraculous feats of the early Christians, he joined the Church, but he was swiftly expelled from it for trying to buy the power of the Holy Spirit with money (and so gave his name to the sin of simony). Then, it was said, he went to Rome, where he impressed everyone with his marvels. He had learned magic in Egypt and he cured diseases, made himself invisible, brought statues to life and made them laugh and dance, raised the dead and conjured up spirits. He manufactured a human being out of thin air, which he said was much more difficult than making a man out of earth, as the Creator had made Adam. He could turn himself into an animal or into any shape he chose. He claimed to be immune to wounds and fire, and able to fly, turn stones into bread and make trees grow and blossom. According to the Christians, these wonders were illusions, stage-managed for him by the Devil.

Simon claimed to be an incarnation of the Christian Trinity. He said that his mistress, a prostitute from Tyre, was a reincarnation of Helen of Troy and the bodily vessel of the Thought of God, through which the whole world was created. As Simon himself was God, she was his own Thought. Unfortunately for the magician, however, he was dogged by St Peter, who kept exposing his miracles as shams and performing more spectacular miracles of his own. Everywhere that Simon Magus went, Simon Peter was sure to go, and when the infuriated sorcerer conjured up giant spectral dogs to tear St Peter to pieces, the saint calmly made them vanish. Simon finally announced that he would put his godhead beyond all doubt by ascending bodily into heaven. He flew up into the air from the top of a tower specially erected in the Campus Martius, but was arrested in mid-career and brought crashing fatally to the ground by the prayers of St Peter. Simon is the first example of a magician from within the Christian Church who is driven by hunger for power to forsake God and cleave to the Devil, and his legend eventually merged with that of Faust.

The potential divinity of man is the central theme of the Hermetica, Greek texts of a strongly gnostic cast, which were written in Egypt in the early centuries AD:

If you do not make yourself equal to God, you cannot apprehend God, for like is apprehended by like. Outleap all body and expand yourself to the unmeasured greatness; outstrip all time and become Eternity; so shall you apprehend God. . . . Embrace in yourself all sensations of all created things, of fire and water, dry and wet; be simultaneously everywhere, on sea and land and in the sky; be at once unborn and in the womb, young and old, dead and beyond death; and if you can hold all these things together in your thought, times and places and substances, qualities and quantities, then you can apprehend God.[5]

This is a forceful statement of the goal of high magic and one of its principal techniques: escaping from the body and expanding consciousness in the imagination and in meditation, trances and visions. The Hermetica had a powerful influence on Renaissance magic and subsequently on the modern revival. The texts contain revelations attributed to various deities, but principally to Hermes Trismegistus, or Thrice-Great, a mythical sage who was identified with Thoth, the Egyptian god of wisdom and magic. Egypt at about the time of Christ was also the birthplace of alchemy, an attempt to manufacture artificial gold which turned into a quest for salvation and divine power, and became one of the main branches of the western magical tradition (see Chapter Two).

Gnostic and hermetic ideas are mingled with plentiful quantities of low magic in the Graeco-Egyptian magical papyri of about AD 100 to 500. The longer texts seem to have been handbooks, copied out and used by practising magicians. There are impassioned incantations in which the magician summons a god to him and identifies himself with the god: 'Come into me, Hermes, as children do into women's wombs ... I am thou and thou art I.' There are prayers to the gods and planets for help, frequently turning from supplication into command: 'You have to do it, whether you like it or not.' There are processes for making money, achieving success, casting out evil spirits and curing disease, killing or injuring enemies, forcing women to submit, finding lost property and reading sealed letters. The incantations include long strings of vowels and peculiar jumbled syllables, and they volley and thunder with words of power which are the names of Egyptian, Greek, Babylonian and Persian gods and spirits, titles of the God of the Old Testament and, less often, the names of Christ, the Holy Spirit, the Virgin Mary and the seven archangels of Jewish and Christian belief. Hellenistic syncretism, the mingling together of gods from different traditions, was used in magic to tap as many sources of power as possible.

There are also processes for summoning up spirits and demons, which may appear in plain view or show themselves shadowily in a bowl of ink or water, or in a crystal. Or they may take possession of a person and speak through his mouth. These spirits are powerful and highly dangerous. There are spells for keeping them under the magician's control and for forcing them to go obediently away when he has finished with them.

The existence of daemons, or lesser spirits, was accepted everywhere in the ancient world. Some of them were the nature spirits of hills, trees, streams, rocks and winds. Some were diseases and some were projections onto the outside world of unexpected ideas and impulses arising in human minds. They were the supernatural agencies to which anything strange was customarily attributed. They were readily blameable for things that went wrong, and were thought to be more easily controllable by magic than a great god would be. A text from the Hermetica, the *Asclepius*, discussing the statues of the Egyptian gods which were brought to life by magic, says that the rites did not really introduce gods into the statues but daemons. It was these daemons which gave the images the power to do good or evil, cause or cure disease and supply indications of the future.

The daemons were classified in groups according to the deity and the department of nature with which they were connected. There were spirits of Jupiter, spirits of Mars, and so on. Planets, stars, animals, plants, metals, colours and other phenomena were classified in the same way, so that there were chains of 'sympathy' or 'correspondence' running through the universe, which a magician could use. A herb corresponding to Venus, for instance, brought into play an influence linked ultimately to the planet and the goddess herself. A ring made of copper, the metal of Venus, would be powerful in love magic, and lead, the metal of Saturn, in a death spell. Links of this kind are used in the magical papyri and systematic correspondences between planetary deities, plants and precious stones go back at least to the time of Bolus of Mendes in Egypt, who wrote books on magic about 200 BC.

By the early centuries after Christ it was generally accepted that the universe was a set of nine spheres (or sometimes ten), one outside the other like the skins of an onion. The outer skin was the sphere of God as Prime Mover. Inside it was the sphere of the stars, and inside this again were the spheres of the sun, moon and planets, with the earth motionless at the centre. There was consequently a hierarchy of stages from the supreme God, or the One, at the summit, down through the lesser gods and the stars, planets and daemons to man and the animals, plants and material objects on earth. The spheres provided a ladder which man could climb to reach God. He could do this because he was a microcosm or 'little world', a miniature copy of God and the universe – the macrocosm or 'great world' – containing in himself all the levels of being. This view of the universe, which dominated western thought down into the seventeenth century, was vital to magic. It meant that everything in existence contained divine energy, which could be put to magical use. It meant that man could ascend into higher realms – as the shamans of earlier days had ascended into the sky – and ultimately attain supreme power.

The hierarchical universe was essential to Neoplatonism, which was the intellectual spearhead of pagan resistance to Christianity, but which also influenced Christianity itself. The founder of the school, Plotinus (205–70), was a mystic who detested gnosticism and condemned magic as an effective but egotistical misuse of power. Some of his successors, however, including Iamblichus (died 330) and Proclus (410–85), were far more sympathetic to gnostic and magical ideas and practices. Proclus, who taught at Athens, was a rain-making magician and a diviner. He was also an expert on theurgy.

Theurgy means 'acting on the gods', as distinct from theology or 'talking about the gods'. The word may have been coined by Julian the Chaldean (second century AD), a powerful magician reputed to have caused the 'miracle of rain', a thunderstorm which saved a Roman army under the Emperor Marcus Aurelius from destruction in 173. (The Church attributed the miracle to the prayers of Christian soldiers of the Twelfth Legion.) Julian wrote a poem in Greek, *The Chaldean Oracles*, which mingled material from Greek, Egyptian, Jewish, Syrian, Babylonian and Persian sources. It became the Bible of theurgy and Iamblichus and Proclus wrote commentaries on it. Only fragments of it have survived.

The last pagan emperor, Julian the Apostate, was an enthusiastic supporter of theurgy, but it was banned in the sixth century under the Christian Emperor Justinian. The theurgists claimed to bring statues of gods and spirits to life. This was done through incantations containing secret names of power, and through animals, herbs, gems, perfumes, letters and symbols corresponding to each god, which were placed inside his statue. The statue would then answer the theurgist's questions by moving or changing its expression, or by putting ideas into his mind while he was asleep, thereby refuting Christian sneers at pagans for worshipping lifeless images of wood and stone. The theurgists need not necessarily have been lying. Magical rituals tend to induce a state of heightened suggestibility in which a man sees what he hopes and expects to see.

The other theurgical method of communicating with the divine was to put a human medium into trance and conjure a god or spirit into him. The god would speak through the medium's mouth. Iamblichus said that young and rather simple-minded people made the best mediums, which has been the general experience ever since. Some of the peculiar occurrences associated with modern Spiritualist trance-mediums also happened at the theurgists' seances, including levitation of the medium, the appearance of mysterious lights, interruptions by evil or mischievous spirits which seized control of the medium and tried to disrupt the proceedings, and apparently the production of ectoplasm. The aim of theurgy was salvation through contact with the divine. The pagan theurgists were rediscovered during the Renaissance and the magic of bringing images of gods and spirits to life, which is also mentioned in the *Asclepius*, attracted excited attention as a way of communicating with powerful superhuman entities.[6]

Roman Religion and Magic

Although the Romans classified magic as a foreign import, it was also in fact part of their traditional religion. Most of their religious ceremonies centred on a sacrifice. This was a gift to the gods, but it was also a magical way of obliging a god to do something which he might not do otherwise. There was a strong feeling that a sacrifice ought to bring its benefits automatically, and if it did not, then the probable explanation was that it had not been performed correctly. The sacrificer said to the god, *do ut des*, 'I give so that you will give.' Then he would say, 'Be thou *macte* by this offering', *macte* apparently meaning 'strengthened' or 'increased'. Power demands recognition, for one to command another must obey, and although the worshipper needed the god, the god also needed the worshipper. Each had his place in the right order of things, which the sacrifice helped to maintain.

The magical strands in a religion always stand out most clearly in moments of danger. In 217 BC Rome was locked in a critical struggle with Carthage and the city was threatened by Hannibal, who had invaded Italy across the Alps. In this emergency the Senate consulted the Sibylline Books, a collection of prophecies and rules for averting disaster, kept in the temple of Jupiter. As a result it was announced that the offering which had been made to Mars, the god of war, had not been properly carried out and must be repeated on a more generous scale, and that a temple must be promised to Venus, games and a 'sacred spring' offered to Jupiter and a *lectisternium* celebrated for the twelve Olympian gods.

The *lectisternium* was a public banquet at which the gods were the guests of honour. They attended in the form of their statues, which were settled comfortably on couches and served with food. The 'sacred spring' meant the sacrifice to Jupiter of all the cattle, sheep, pigs and goats born during March and April. This was promised to the god if, and only if, he kept the Roman republic safe for the next five years. It was not easy to achieve, because it required the co-operation of all the people, who had to slaughter their animals, and because they might not all observe the correct procedure. On the magical principle that saying a thing is so makes it so, the chief priest therefore announced:

> Let him who shall make such a sacrifice do so at whatever time and by whatever rite he chooses; in whatever way he does it, let it be accounted correctly done ... if he unwittingly sacrifices on an unlucky day, let the sacrifice be deemed to have been correctly offered; whether it is done by day or night, by a slave or a freeman, let the sacrifice be deemed to have been correctly made. ...[7]

When Hannibal smashed the Roman army at Cannae in 216, anxiety in Rome was so intense that the Senate resorted to human sacrifice. After a further consultation of the Sibylline Books, 'a Gaulish man and woman and a Greek man and woman were buried alive in the Cattle Market, in a place walled in with stone'.[8] This is an extreme example of what the Romans called an *expiatio*, a way of restoring the right relationship between human beings and the mysterious powers at work in the world when that relationship had been disturbed. Any unusual and worrying event – ranging from an owl hooting at midday or the birth of a child with six toes to unseasonable weather, an eclipse or defeat in battle – showed that the proper order of things had been upset, and an *expiatio* of comparable scale was needed to put it right.

Magic also bulked large in dealing with death. In Italy, as in Egypt, a magical way of ensuring a happy afterlife for the dead was to represent it in pictures in tombs. The dead are shown enjoying the pleasures of paradise on Etruscan tombs of about 600 to 400 BC. Roman sarcophagi of the early centuries AD use various myths and symbols for the same purpose. Selene, the moon goddess, is shown approaching the sleeping Endymion, who represents the human soul which will wake from the sleep of death at her embrace. Variations on the same theme include the stories of Cupid and Psyche, Peleus and Thetis, and Bacchus and Ariadne, which turn on a deity's love for a mortal. The triumph of Bacchus (the Roman name for Dionysus) appears on some sarcophagi, with a procession of dancing maenads, satyrs and wild animals accompanying the god in his chariot, to show the paradise of erotic and spiritual delight which the soul will enter at death. Garlands and wreaths, supported by cupids or figures of victory, represent and so magically bring about the victory of life and love over death. The Romans put flowers on graves, especially roses, as symbols of life renewed. One of the characters in the *Satyricon* of Petronius, ordering his tomb, asks for a carving of himself with his dog at his feet, jars of perfume and pictures of every fight in the career of a famous gladiator of the day. 'Then, thanks to your good offices, I'll live on long after I'm gone.'[9]

Ceremonies celebrated regularly in Rome included one called the October Horse, in honour of Mars, who was concerned with agriculture and cattle-raising as well as war. A chariot race was held in the Campus Martius and one horse of the winning team was stabbed to death with a spear as a sacrifice to the god, to ensure good crops. Its head and tail were cut off. The head was garlanded with loaves of bread and fought for by men from two areas of the city. The winners carried the head off in triumph and fastened it up in their own quarter. Meanwhile, the tail had been taken by a runner to the Regia, the former palace of the kings of Rome, where it was hung up so that blood from it dripped on the hearth. Then the Vestal Virgins, the priestesses of the hearth goddess, collected the blood and kept it till the following April, when it was used in the ritual purification of cattle.

Ceremonies like this were performed long after the logic of them had been forgotten. When Ovid wrote a book about them, early in the first century AD, he frequently had to resort to guesswork to explain them. But they were kept up and were considered necessary for the safe preservation of the Roman state, because they 'worked'.

In Mars's own month of March there were horse races in his honour in the Campus Martius, apparently connected with the training of cavalry horses for the new campaigning season. The energy expended in the racing may also have been thought to benefit the spring crops. In the same month, and again in October at the end of the fighting season, twenty-four priests of Mars called Salii ('leapers' or 'dancers') went through the city, dressed in bronze armour, peaked caps and cloaks embroidered in red and purple. They carried spears and shields of antique design, shaped roughly like a figure eight. They danced a three-step and leapt vigorously up and down, beating their shields and singing a song to Mars and other gods. The song was so old that by the first century

BC very little of it could be understood. The ceremony was apparently a mixture of a war dance and a fertility dance, perhaps originally intended to frighten evil spirits away and to improve the growth of crops by leaping high.

Every year in February, young men went to a cave on the Palatine hill called the Lupercal, the Place of the Wolf, which was traditionally the lair of the she-wolf that suckled Romulus and Remus, the legendary founders of Rome. They sacrificed a dog and some goats and smeared themselves with the blood, which they wiped off with wool or goats' hair dipped in milk. Holding strips of goat's hide and naked except for girdles made of the skin of the sacrificed animals, they ran round the boundary of the old city, marked by a wall of stones in classical times, though Rome had already spread beyond it. They slapped everyone they met with strips of goatskin and this was believed to induce fertility in barren women and an easy delivery in childbirth.

Roman writers were puzzled by the Lupercalia, but usually explained it as a purification rite. The young men were popularly called 'he-goats', which are notorious for pugnacity and sexual vigour. What the human he-goats seem to have been doing was to re-draw the magic circle of the city's boundary, to keep good inside and shut evil out, especially the evil of infertility. Flagellation can be a way of working up sexual energy and also of driving out evil forces, and has long been used for both purposes in European folk customs.

In the Roman countryside, farmers and their families and labourers used to go ceremoniously round their boundaries once a year, in effect drawing a magic circle round their land. No work was done that day by man or beast, and the oxen all wore garlands on their heads. Each person taking part had to wash in running water and put on clean white clothes and an olive wreath. Anyone who had made love the night before was excluded from the ceremony. A male lamb was led three times round the boundary, followed by all the farm people in procession. Then it was sacrificed to Bacchus and Ceres, the corn goddess, who were asked to drive all evils away across the boundary, see that the fields and cattle were fertile and keep wolves away from the farm. Next, the lamb's liver and entrails were examined. If they were normal, then the gods had accepted the offering and would keep the bargain. Their share of the meat was then burned on an altar and everyone sat down to a feast.

Far more often than not the lamb's liver and entrails would be normal, and this is another example of magic's positive role in creating confidence and enhancing the solidarity of a group. The negative side appears in the rule that during the ceremony no one was allowed to use any ill-omened words. They could not say things like 'We ought to have a good crop this year if the weather holds up.' As a result everyone said as little as possible until the ritual was over. Both the Greek and the Latin expressions for 'to say good words' (*euphemein* in Greek, *favere linguis* in Latin) also meant 'to keep silent'.[10]

Pliny discusses whether words are effective in this way or not. Sophisticated people, he says, refuse to admit that they are, but the great majority believe it, consciously or otherwise. It is generally accepted that there is no point in sacrificing to the gods or asking them for advice unless the correct form of prayer is used, not altering or omitting a single word. It is also generally believed that the Vestal Virgins know a spell which arrests the flight of runaway slaves by rooting them to the spot, provided they are still within the boundaries of the city.[11]

A common way of using the magic of language against an enemy was to write a curse down and bury it in the ground, so consigning the victim to the powers of the underworld: 'I put quartan fever on Aristion to the death.' The curse would be written on a piece of pottery or metal, especially lead, and could be tied round with wire to make it additionally 'binding'. Or a nail might be driven through the victim's name: 'I nail his name, that is, himself.' 'May his tongue and his soul become lead that he may not be able to speak or act.' 'As this lead is worthless and cold, so may he and his possessions be worthless and cold.' To bury the curse in a tomb would give it a peculiarly murderous force. 'As the dead man who is buried here can neither talk nor speak, so let Rhodine who belongs to Marcus Licinius Faustus be dead and unable to talk or speak.'

Spells of this kind first seem to have become common in Greece in the fourth century BC. People heartily cursed in them include well-known politicians like Demosthenes. They were also used in love magic, in attempts to fix horse races by holding back the rival runners, and to muddle the tongues and scatter the wits of opponents in court cases. 'I bind Theagenes in tongue and soul, and the speech that he is preparing. I bind also the hands and feet of Pythias the cook, his tongue and his soul and the speech that he is preparing.' Two other hostile witnesses are similarly 'bound' and then the curse says, 'All this I bind, obliterate, bury, impale.' The spell seems to work gradually up to a high peak of ferocity, and it was probably the magician's own mounting rage and hatred, directed at his victims through the curse, which was believed to make it effective.

A curse written on lead with the words spelled backwards was thrown into the water at Bath, in England. 'May he who carried off Vilbia from me become as liquid as water.' Down to about 1850, a similar method was in use at the cursing well of St Elian, near Colwyn Bay in Wales. The procedure was to write your enemy's name on a piece of paper and put it in a lead box. You took it to the keeper of the well and paid him a fee. He recited the curse in a special voice and threw the box into the well. As soon as you had gone, he would probably hurry off to tell your enemy, who would pay him another fee for fishing the curse out of the water again.[12]

Classical writers condemned curses of this private, unofficial sort; but curses used officially for purposes of state were quite another matter. In Greece a curse could be pronounced by magistrates or priests against a criminal or a public enemy. The Romans consigned enemy armies to destruction in official curses. Chapter 28 of Deuteronomy contains a catalogue of maledictions against sinners, so comprehensive and appalling that Jewish congregations were frightened of hearing it read at all, in case it brought them on their heads. These official curses are the predecessors of the Christian ritual of excommunication. Much earlier, the first substantial evidence of the Egyptian claim to control Palestine and Syria comes from the 'execration texts' of the nineteenth century BC, which name various local chieftains as enemies of Egypt. They were written on vessels or figurines which were then smashed as a magical way of breaking the chieftains in reality.

Some official curses were intended to take effect only on stated conditions, as a way of ensuring that people met their obligations. When the Romans made a treaty in early times, the terms were read out to the representatives of both sides. Then the Roman spokesman, who came equipped with a pig, called on Jupiter to smite the Roman people if they intentionally broke the treaty, just as he now struck the pig, but harder. Saying which, he struck the animal with a rock of flint.

Curses and spells were used in the murder of Germanicus Caesar, adopted son of the Emperor Tiberius, in AD 19. Germanicus fell ill at Antioch of a mysterious disease and, according to Tacitus, sinister charms were found under the floor of his bedroom and behind the walls: 'the remains of human bodies, spells, curses, lead tablets inscribed with the patient's name, charred and bloody ashes, and other malignant objects which are supposed to consign souls to the powers of the tomb'. Germanicus died not long after this discovery and Tacitus believed that his fear of the evil magic which had been worked against him helped to kill him. Cnaeus Calpurnius Piso, the governor of Syria, and his wife, Plancina, were accused of murdering Germanicus by poisoning and magic. When Piso returned to Rome, he was nearly lynched by a furious mob and, protesting his innocence, he committed suicide. Plancina also killed herself, years afterwards when the accusation was renewed.[13]

Another way of harming an enemy was to make a doll of clay, rags, straw or wax to represent him and then pierce, torture and burn it, in the belief that the victim would suffer the same agonies. Image magic has been practised all over the world, for healing and in love spells as well as to kill, injure or drive insane. In Virgil's eighth eclogue a woman whose lover is unfaithful draws him back to her by incantations, chanting the refrain : *ducite ab urbe domum, mea carmina, ducite Daphnim*, 'bring him home from the city, my spells, bring Daphnis home'. She makes a wax doll to represent him and ties it round with three threads, 'the fetters of Venus', to bind him. Then she melts the doll in the fire to melt his heart with longing. The poem is fiction, of course, but it describes a type of magic which people believed in and were frightened of, and which might consequently be effective. As Gibbon said : 'the harmless flame which insensibly melted a waxen image, might derive a powerful and pernicious energy from the affrighted fancy of the person whom it was maliciously designed to represent'. But Virgil's poem itself makes a deeper claim. The faithless lover, Daphnis, does not believe in magic, but the spell compels him all the same.

Like curses, image magic was used in public ceremonies as well as in private sorcery. At Rome in May twenty-seven dummies in human shape, known as Argei, made of straw and dressed in old-fashioned clothes, were carried in procession to the oldest bridge over the Tiber, the Pons Sublicius, and were solemnly thrown into the river in the presence of the Vestal Virgins. Ovid thought that the dummies represented human victims who in the distant past had been sacrificed to the river. An alternative possibility is that they were meant to pacify the Tiber as substitutes for real people who would have been drowned trying to ford it if the bridge had not been built.

Healing, Dreams and Witchcraft

Though the Greeks made important contributions to accurate medical knowledge, magic and healing remained closely bound up together. Pliny mentions numerous magical prescriptions in his

Natural History. To do away with a headache, for instance, bind a hangman's noose round the temples. If you are feverish, mix the parings of your fingernails and toenails with wax and stick them on a neighbour's door during the night, which transfers the fever to the neighbour. For jaundice, simply stare earnestly at a curlew. This cures the disease because there is a 'sympathy' between it and the curlew, which attracts the disease to itself. The blood, bones and organs of a man who died prematurely, especially if killed by violence, were believed to carry a charge of unused life-energy which had magic power. Consequently, a way to soothe sore gums was to rub them with the tooth of a man who had been murdered or executed. A treatment for epilepsy was to drink water from the skull of a man who had died by violence. Another, singularly unpleasant cure for epilepsy was to suck the blood of a wounded or dying gladiator.

Herbs and drugs were naturally valued in medical treatment, sometimes for their genuine properties, but also because a traditional remedy inspires confidence and so may promote a cure even when in itself it is worthless. An army doctor named Dioscorides, about AD 60, listed hundreds of herbs in his *Materia Medica*. Few of them have the properties he attributed to them, but his catalogue was used for centuries afterwards and was the ancestor of the medieval and modern herbals.

Since herbs contained mysterious power, the professional herb-gatherers in Greece took magical precautions against the effects of handling them. They drew a magic circle round black hellebore and cut it facing east and saying prayers. A circle was drawn three times round gladwyn, it was cut with a double-edged sword and wheat-cakes were put in its place 'to pay for it', evidently to compensate the ground or the earth spirits for its loss. Three circles were drawn with a sword round the narcotic and poisonous mandrake, which was used as a pain-killer and aphrodisiac, and it was cut facing west. When cutting the second piece, 'one should dance round the plant and say as many things as possible about the mysteries of love'.[14]

One type of mandrake has a forked root, resembling human legs, and the Romans called it 'half-man'. There was a Jewish belief, mentioned by Josephus in the first century AD, that the mandrake screamed when it was drawn out of the ground. Later, in medieval Europe, this sinister semi-human plant was supposed to be gathered at dead of night. The operator stuffed his ears with cotton or wax against the mandrake's cry and tethered a dog to the plant with a piece of string. Then he stood well back and threw meat to the dog which, straining for the meat, pulled the plant out of the ground. The dog was killed by the mandrake's screech and was buried in its place. Witches were accused of using mandrakes as puppets in image magic.

In prehistoric times healing was presumably a combination of magic and medicine. Herbal remedies and physical treatments found effective would be administered to the patient while the medicine-man or shaman chanted, danced and cast spells. Cures would depend heavily on the patient's confidence in the doctor and the treatment, as in many cases they still do. It was probably believed, as it was later in Egypt and Mesopotamia, that a disease was an evil spirit which had entered the patient's body.

In ancient Egypt drugs and physical treatments were reinforced by incantations, in which a disease was harangued and ordered to go away. Healing amulets were hung on patients and spells were recited to enlist the help of the gods. Isis and Thoth were both powerful healers, but the specialist Egyptian god of healing was Imhotep, a high-ranking minister of Pharaoh Zoser (about 2650 BC) and the architect of Zoser's tomb, the Step Pyramid at Sakkara. He acquired a reputation as a powerful magician, wise man and healer, and eventually turned into a god.

Mesopotamian medicine was the preserve of specialist priests who again employed a mixture of medication, religion and magic. The priest, equipped in shaman's style with a copper drum covered with bull's hide, chanted incantations to drive the disease-spirit away. There might be an attempt to transfer it from the patient into an animal. For example, one text prescribes putting a kid in bed with the sick man. Then the patient is struck on the throat with a dummy wooden dagger and the kid's throat is cut with a copper knife. The kid is dressed in the sick man's clothes and treated as a dead human being, with lamentations and offerings to the goddess of the underworld. The disease and the death it carries with it have now been transferred to the kid and the sick man will recover.

In Greece and Rome, though some intellectuals had re-servations, it was popularly believed that diseases – especially mental and nervous illnesses which made people behave in alarmingly abnormal ways – were spirits. The most obvious and notorious example was epilepsy, whose name means literally in Greek that the patient has been 'seized on' by something from outside. All the Olympian deities had healing powers, and the equivalent of Imhotep was Aesculapius (Asklepios in Greek), who may also have been a real man, living about 1200 BC. His cult, which seems to have originated in Thessaly, became popular from about 400 BC on. In 292 BC, suffering from plague, the Romans sent for the god on the advice of the Sibylline Books. A sacred snake representing the god was fetched by boat from his temple at Epidaurus in southern Greece. It swam ashore on an island in the Tiber and disappeared. The plague stopped and a temple was built on the island for the god.

The principal shrines of Aesculapius in Greece and Asia Minor were a mixture of temple, hospital and health resort, equipped with a theatre, a race course, a library and a gymnasium. Some patients stayed at them for months or years. Drugs and special diets, emetics and purges, blood-letting, exercise and baths were used to treat patients, but the chief method was 'incubation'. This meant sleeping overnight in the temple to obtain a dream or vision in which the god would appear and either cure the patient there and then or give a prescription. Records of the cures were kept at Epidaurus, which has been called 'the Lourdes of Greece'. A woman who was blind in one eye recovered her sight after dreaming that the god cut her eye open and poured ointment into it. A man with paralyzed fingers dreamed he was playing dice and the god jumped on his hand and straightened it. A man infested with lice was freed of them by a dream in which Aesculapius swept him down with a stiff broom. Many patients may have gone away disappointed, but it seems clear that some were genuinely cured.

Incubation was not confined to shrines of Aesculapius or to healing. It was also used to obtain information and instructions from a god about any important matter. Usually the enquirer was ceremonially purified beforehand and had to fast or go on a special diet. In the temple he sacrificed an animal and in some cases, apparently, he took a drug. He then lay down on the animal's skin and either went to sleep or went into a trance. The procedure was likely to induce a state of mind in which he saw what he expected and wanted to see, which in turn would reinforce his confidence in the vision or dream, and this confidence might cure him or enable him to cope with the problem about which he had consulted the god.

Dreams were treated with respect in the ancient world as indicators of the future and channels through which supernatural beings communicated with man, though it was recognized that not all dreams were significant. According to Greek tradition, the old oracle at Delphi was consulted through dreams, before it was taken over by Apollo. In the Old Testament God speaks to people in dreams, either directly or through subordinate spirits. The dreams of Jacob, Joseph, Pharaoh, Nebuchadnezzar and others are described and interpreted. Solomon went to the sanctuary at Gibeon, offered sacrifice and burned incense, and then went to sleep, perhaps in the hope of inducing the dream he had, in which God appeared and stilled his anxieties.[15]

The most important people naturally dreamed the most important dreams, which could justify decisions of state. According to Herodotus, three dreams persuaded Xerxes to invade Greece, rather against his better judgment. But there was also growing interest in the dreams of private individuals. The oldest surviving textbook of dream interpretation is Egyptian, the Chester Beatty Papyrus, dating from about 1350 BC. It frequently relies on the same type of associations and plays on words used in explaining dreams in modern psychoanalysis. It also contains incantations for warding off dangers revealed in dreams. In one, the dreamer first identifies himself with the god Horus, then calls on his mother, Isis, for help, and finally·announces in her voice that she has come to protect him.[16]

Texts in the library of the Assyrian king Assurbanipal (seventh century BC) deal with the meanings of dreams, and books on dreams appeared in Greece from about 400 BC. The most influential of all dream manuals, the *Oneirocritica* of Artemidorus, was written about AD 140. Artemidorus lived in Asia Minor and travelled about collecting dreams. He drew on earlier Greek, Egyptian and, possibly, Assyrian material and he has been plundered by the compilers of popular dreambooks ever since. He also wrote a book on palmistry, the *Chiroscopica*, which has not survived.

Much of the material on witchcraft, from the ancient world and later, has a dream-like atmosphere which suggests that so far as it represents the experiences of real witches it is based on hallucinations. The classical witch, however, is largely a nightmare literary creation. Greek and Roman writers associated witches with night and darkness, eerie moonlight and the powers of the underworld who ruled the land of the dead. Witches could kill or injure people and cattle, drive their victims mad, ruin crops, stir up storms, provoke lust or hinder love. They were skilled poisoners and makers of perfumes and love potions. They could tell what was happening at a distance. They summoned up the dead and forced them to reveal the future. They had a malicious sense of humour and liked to play unpleasant practical jokes. They reversed all normal and decent values, revelling in evil, blood and dirt.

Witches worshipped the moon goddess – Hecate, Diana or

Selene – and Persephone or Proserpine, the queen of the under-world. These were not fertile mother goddesses but virgins or hags, barren and baneful, rulers of darkness. The moon is linked with female mysteries through the connection between the lunar month and the menstrual cycle. One of the feats frequently credited to witches was drawing down the moon (which modern witches take to mean drawing down the goddess into the human personality). They could change shape, as the moon does in the sky, turning themselves into owls, dogs, weasels, mice or flies, and they could also transform their victims into animals.

Witches worked their magic through the power of their goddess, but they might also possess innate powers of their own and many of them were believed to have the evil eye. They used incantations and images, herbs, poisons and all sorts of materials which had magic force in proportion to their peculiarity and repulsiveness. The witch Pamphile in the *Golden Ass* of Apuleius is equipped with incense, metal plates engraved with secret symbols, the claws and beaks of birds, gobbets of dead men's flesh and the blood, skulls, noses and fingers of murdered men and executed criminals. She turns herself into an owl, to fly into the bedroom of a young man she lusts for, by smearing herself with ointment and muttering a long incantation. Pamphile is a literary invention, but the use of ointments which apparently induced hallucinations of flying was later part of the pattern of medieval witchcraft.

The owl as a nocturnal bird of prey was closely connected with witches and *stria*, *striga* or *strix*, 'screech-owl', was a common term for a witch. Ovid mentions 'screech-owls' which attack small children in their beds at night, tearing their flesh and drinking their blood. He says they may be real birds or witches transformed into birds by spells. The witch Canidia in one of Horace's poems makes a concoction of eggs smeared with frog's blood, a screech-owl's feather, bones and poisonous herbs to compel a rich elderly lover to come to her. When her magic fails to work, she assumes that he is protected by a rival witch. She kidnaps a young boy and plans to bury him in the ground up to his chin and leave him to starve to death, so as to use his hungering marrow and liver in a more powerful charm.[17]

Like magicians, witches were credited with extensive powers over nature, and in some authors their feats become absurdly high-flown. They can make the sea boil on a windless day, stop waterfalls in mid-flight, arrest the flow of rivers or throw the earth off centre. Running through accounts of these extraordinary powers is the theme of witches reversing the natural order of things. 'There are witches', says a character in the *Satyricon*, 'and the ghouls go walking at night, turning the whole world upside down.' Sophisticated authors were not as sceptical about witchcraft as might be expected. St Augustine quoted seriously as an example of what magic can do a passage from Virgil's *Aeneid* about a priestess whose incantations could stop the flow of rivers, turn the stars back on their courses and make trees walk. He was also uncertain whether Apuleius, the author of the *Golden Ass*, had really been turned into a donkey by witchcraft or had merely made the story up. [18]

The two most famous witches of classical legend and literature are Circe and her niece, Medea. In the *Odyssey*, 'the beautiful Circe, a formidable goddess' lives on the island of Aeaea. She is the sister of Aeetes, the wizard-king of Colchis, owner of the golden fleece. Her house is in a forest clearing and she sings in a captivating voice as she works at her loom. The wolves and lions which prowl the clearing are men who have been transformed into animals by her magic potions. With a powerful drug and a stroke of her wand she turns Odysseus's men into pigs, though they retain their human minds and emotions. Odysseus becomes Circe's lover and persuades her to restore his crew to human form and help him on the next stage of his voyage. [19]

Circe is a prototype of the great superhuman enchantresses of later legends and romances, beautiful, ruthless, dominating, sexually fascinating, able to put men under a spell and hold them in thrall, to turn them literally or metaphorically into animals. Medea, though also regarded as a goddess by some classical writers, is usually a stage nearer to the ordinary human witch. Her name means 'the cunning one' and she is the daughter of Aeetes by his wife Eidyia, 'the knowing one'. She falls in love with Jason when he goes to Colchis, helps him to steal the golden fleece, runs away with him and murders her own brother to delay pursuit. She knows the lore of herbs and poisons and the use of wax images, and she can make a warrior proof against wounds and an old man young again. When Jason finally rejects her for another woman, Medea kills her rival and her own children by Jason, and flees in a chariot drawn through the air by dragons.

Other witches in classical literature are human and mortal, though endowed with uncanny skills. Horace's witch Canidia seems to have been based on a real woman. He describes her and another witch, Sagana, prowling barefoot through the cemetery on the Esquiline hill by moonlight, with dishevelled hair. They tear a black lamb to pieces with their teeth and pour the blood on the ground to call up the spirits of the dead. They have a doll made of wool and another of wax, which they melt in a fire, and they howl invocations to Hecate, goddess of magic, ghosts, graves and terror.[20]

The witch is sexually voracious and is often described working magic to ensnare men she desires. She also casts spells for clients, frequently in connection with sexual matters. The mother-in-law of the Emperor Honorius, in the fifth century, was said to have hired a witch to prevent him from consummating his marriage with her daughter. In the following century, Antonina, wife of the famous general Belisarius, was rumoured to have gained his love with spells and charms that had been handed down in her family.

Somewhere between the real, human witch and the superhuman enchantress of legend is Erichtho in Lucan's *Pharsalia*, 'a horror-comic witch' as Robert Graves called her. How seriously Lucan took this gruesome creature it is hard to say, but he presumably expected her to give his readers a shudder down the spine. She lives in Thessaly, a region in north-eastern Greece which was notorious for its witches and its magic herbs, planted there originally by Medea, so the Thessalians said. Old, gaunt and loathsome, Erichtho squats in tombs and eats corpses. She forces the dead to speak and reveal the future by taking a recent corpse and pouring into its breast a mixture of warm menstrual blood, the guts of a lynx, a hyena's hump, the froth of a mad dog and other poisons. Then she chants an incantation which mingles the howl of a wolf, the hoot of an owl and other animal cries with a gloating invocation to Proserpine and the dark powers of the underworld.[21]

The distinction between magic and witchcraft in classical literature is one of sex. Witchcraft is feminine magic and it is almost always evil magic. The witch has the mysterious knowledge and secret, deadly power attributed to the female by men. Her close association with herbs and poisons may be a legacy from much earlier times when gathering and cultivating plants was women's work, while the men were responsible for hunting. The elements of fear and hatred in the attitude to women in male-dominated societies focus on the figure of the witch, who reverses the 'natural order' of male dominance. She becomes a wildly exaggerated stereotype of the woman who does not stay dutifully at home, obedient to her menfolk. She roams the night, sexually aggressive, hobnobbing with the dead, harming children, giving rein to her anarchic impulses and calling on her baleful female deities.

Astrology and Divination

In a fierce diatribe against the female sex, written about AD 100, Juvenal comments on the mania of women for having their fortunes told. Fashionable ladies, he says, will not drive a mile or scratch an itch without first consulting a textbook of astrology to make sure that the moment is propitious. They run to some old Jewish hag to interpret their dreams. They listen awestruck to an Armenian or Syrian fortune-teller, who examines the lungs of a freshly killed dove and promises them a youthful lover or a handsome legacy: 'he will probe the breast of chicken, or the entrails of a puppy, sometimes even of a boy. . . .' The Chaldeans command even greater confidence, and women do not stop at asking about the future but take steps to influence it. 'One man sells magical spells; another sells Thessalian charms by which a wife may upset her husband's mind. . . .'[22]

Juvenal was exaggerating for effect, but it was accepted in the ancient world that events cast their shadows before them. All sorts of occurrences were omens of the will of the gods and the trend of the future, generally not as signs of what was bound to happen but of what was likely to happen. A good omen was an encouragement and inspired confidence. A bad omen might be a sign that the gods did not favour a project, a warning of danger in the offing or a signal that the right relationship between gods and men had been disturbed. An omen might occur spontaneously in the ordinary course of events or it might be deliberately provoked. At Pharai in Greece, for example, where Hermes had a shrine, an enquirer would pay a fee to be allowed to whisper a question into the ear of the god's statue. Then he would put his fingers in his own ears until he had left the shrine, when he took the first chance remark he overheard as the answer to his question.

The queen of the divinatory arts is astrology, which in the Roman world was called *mathesis*, 'the learning', the pre-eminent branch of knowledge. It owes its prestige to the awe which the starry sky inspires and to the fact that the indicators it uses, the planets and stars, behave in an orderly and predictable way. Mesopotamian priests connected the sun, moon and planets with gods and goddesses, which meant that each of them acquired its own character and sphere of influence. Mars, for instance, was linked with the god of war and plague, and Venus with Ishtar, the goddess of love and fertility. Greek philosophers, including Plato and Aristotle, believed that the stars were divine and the Greeks and Romans substituted their own deities for the

Mesopotamian ones. Astrology, Franz Cumont said, 'has exercised over Asia and Europe a wider dominion than any religion has ever achieved'.[23]

Astrology goes back to the observation of omens in Babylonia, where events in the sky – the movements of planets and stars, comets and eclipses, rain, hail and the behaviour of clouds – were carefully recorded by specialist priests and matched with events subsequently occurring on earth, so that they could be interpreted as portents affecting the king and the well-being of the community. For example, the disappearances and reappearances of Venus from behind the sun were observed and treated as omens in the time of King Ammisaduqa of Babylon, who died in 1626 BC. The *Enuma Anu Enlil*, a collection of sky omens, was gradually put together over hundreds of years and completed in about 1000 BC. Babylonian star-gazing laid the foundations of scientific astronomy, but its principal purpose was to enable the royal government to react intelligently to the trend of events. 'If the moon and sun are seen together on the thirteenth day, it betokens unrest, trade and commerce in the land will not prosper, the foot of the enemy will be in the land ... if the moon and the sun are seen together on the fourteenth day, it betokens prosperity, the heart of the land will be of good cheer. ...'[24]

Omens were also drawn in Mesopotamia from the behaviour of animals and birds, the liver and entrails of sacrificed animals, earthquakes and floods, abnormal and multiple births, dreams, the fall of lots, the shape formed by oil or flour poured into a bowl of water, and the shape and movements of smoke rising from a censer. A person's physical peculiarities, mannerisms of speech and walk, the colour of his hair, the shape of his nails and the positions of moles on his body were regarded as indications of his character and probable future. There were also priests and priestesses who specialized in delivering spoken prophecies, apparently in trance.

Assurbanipal of Assyria, who died in 627 BC, collected a substantial reference-library of omen texts, including sky omens. Mesopotamian methods spread to Syria, Egypt, Greece and India. The Babylonians identified the circle of the zodiac, divided into twelve equal sections or 'signs', and the Egyptians followed suit.

The invention of natal astrology, the casting of horoscopes for individuals based on the planetary positions at the time of birth or conception, came comparatively late. Herodotus seems to have encountered it in Egypt in the fifth century BC. The Greek astronomer Eudoxus reported it from Babylonia in the fourth century and said that he did not believe in it. A few Babylonian

37

horoscopes of this period have survived. 'The position of Jupiter means that his life will be regular. He will become rich and will grow old. The position of Venus means that wherever he may go it will be favourable for him. Mercury in Gemini means that he will have sons and daughters.'[25]

Berosus, a priest of Marduk, founded a school on the island of Cos, about 280 BC, where he taught Babylonian astronomy and astrology. Other Chaldeans emigrated to the West and Greeks went to study in Babylon. But the main pipeline through which astrology flowed westwards ran from Egypt. For example, Mesopotamian omen material was included in a book written in Greek in the second century BC, supposedly by an Egyptian priest named Petosiris for his master, the mythical Pharaoh Nechepso. It was picked up from this source by Ptolemy, the Alexandrian astronomer and geographer of the second century AD, whose books circulated all over the Roman world.

The Stoic philosophers accepted astrology and other forms of divination, which fitted satisfactorily into their picture of the universe as a coherent design, linked together by chains of sympathy or correspondence between its parts. The Syrian philosopher and polymath Posidonius (died 50 BC), who taught at Rhodes, thought that astrology, divination, oracles and visions depended on the action of daemons which communicated with man, apparently in a way akin to telepathy.

Posidonius proved the connection between the tides of the sea and the phases of the moon, which was a stock example of a 'sympathetic' rapport between the heavens and the earth. 'The moon, too', Ptolemy wrote, 'as the heavenly body nearest the earth, bestows her effluence most abundantly upon mundane things, for most of them, animate or inanimate, are sympathetic to her and change in company with her; the rivers increase and diminish their streams with her light, the seas turn their own tides with her rising and setting, and plants and animals in whole or in some part wax and wane with her.'[26] This concept has remained alive in astrology ever since, and in the 1930s it was reported that French peasants customarily sowed seed at the new moon and pruned trees and picked vegetables while the moon was waning, so as to be in harmony with the rhythms of nature.

Like magic, astrology had its 'high' and 'low' registers. At one extreme it was part of a noble pagan creed which saw in all events the hand of the divine, which taught that man should willingly accept what Destiny decreed for him, and which believed that after death the souls of the just would ascend among the immortal stars. At the other, since the invention of natal astrology, it provided a living for horoscope-salesmen and peddlers of amulets. In the middle it brought some sense of order and stability to people who felt themselves adrift on uncertain waters.

Augustus, Tiberius and several other Roman emperors consulted astrologers. Nero, on astrological advice, warded off the threat of a comet which presaged the death of an important personage by having a number of prominent people murdered. Domitian had the horoscopes of leading citizens analyzed for seditious tendencies. Although authority used astrology, it was highly suspicious of the art in private hands. A prediction that he would succeed to the throne might embolden an ambitious man to try, and might gain him support. Unsuccessful attempts were periodically made to expel astrologers from Rome.

In AD 371, in the time of the Christian Emperor Valens, a group of conspirators were tried for treason because they had attempted, probably quite innocently, to find out who would succeed him : not through astrology, but with a device resembling a modern ouija board. It consisted of a tripod of laurel wood, on which was a round metal plate with the letters of the Greek alphabet engraved on its rim. Above this was suspended a ring on a linen thread. After incantations to a god, probably Apollo, the ring was set swinging from letter to letter, spelling out words. When asked who the next emperor would be, it spelled out THEO. They took this to mean Theodorus, one of the imperial secretaries. Theodorus was executed, and so were they, but the ring had been right all the same. When Valens died in 387, he was succeeded by Theodosius.[27]

Another divinatory device, dating from the third century AD, has been discovered at Pergamum in Asia Minor. It consists of a three-legged bronze table, engraved with images of Hecate, a circular dish divided into sections in which are various symbols, and two rings. Apparently it worked like a roulette wheel and the rings would come to rest on symbols which were interpreted as a message from the goddess.

Prophecy and politics are old bedfellows. An early example of a calculated and postdated political prediction is an Egyptian one ascribed to Neferti, a prophet of about 2600 BC.

A king shall come forth from Upper Egypt called Ameni, the son of a woman of the South. . . . Be glad, ye people of his time! The son of a highborn man will make his name for all eternity. They who would make mischief and devise enmity have suppressed their mutterings through fear of him. . . . And Right shall come into its own again and Wrong shall be cast out.

The Ameni of this prophecy is Amunemhet I, who seized the throne in about 1990 BC, and the 'prediction' was intended to justify his action and smooth his path.[28]

In Greece and Rome, as in the East, divination was originally a department of religion, presumably as a legacy from the medicine-men of prehistoric tribes. There were official Roman augurs who observed the flight and cries of birds – including eagles, vultures, owls, ravens and woodpeckers – to discover whether a course of action was pleasing to the gods. Sulla, Pompey, Cicero, Julius Caesar and Mark Antony all served as augurs in their time. Roman armies took sacred chickens with them on campaign, and the birds' behaviour was watched before deciding to join battle. The college of augurs kept records of all cases, but the rules of interpretation became so complicated with the accumulation of data, and the suspicion of political bias in many of the findings grew so strong, that augury fell out of use. Haruspicy, drawing omens from the liver and other internal organs of animals, came to Rome from the Etruscans and lasted longer, into the late fourth century AD. The *haruspices* also interpreted lightning, meteors, abnormal births and other unusual occurrences.

The old rites of *expiatio*, intended to restore the right order of things when an alarming omen showed that it had been upset, were killed by the rise to power of Christianity. This dismayed pagans like Ammianus Marcellinus, the historian, who records that in 359 a 'horrible portent' occurred in Daphne, a suburb of Antioch. It was the birth of:

... an infant with two heads, two sets of teeth, a beard, four eyes and two very small ears; and this mis-shapen birth foretold that the state was turning into a deformed condition. Portents of this kind often see the light, as indications of the outcome of various affairs; but as they are not expiated by public rites, as they were in the time of our forefathers, they pass by unheard of and unknown.[29]

Apollo was the principal divine patron of trance-mediums, as at his oracles at Delphi and elsewhere. His priestess at Delphi, the Pythia, put herself into a trance in which the god took possession of her and spoke through her mouth in obscure and riddling words which were interpreted by trained priests. The oracles also fell victims to the advance of Christianity, but already by Plato's time there were private, unofficial mediums who discerned the future and gave advice, like the modern clairvoyant. St Paul was followed about by one at Philippi in Macedonia. She was a slave girl and her owners, who charged for her services, were not pleased when St

Paul decided that she was possessed by an evil spirit and drove it out of her.[30]

Apollo was believed to have inspired the Sibylline Books which, according to tradition, emanated from a sibyl or trance-medium at Cumae, near Naples, and were acquired by the Etruscan kings of Rome. They were kept by priests, who alone were allowed to consult them and then only when ordered to do so by the government. In 18 BC Augustus edited the verses to suit his own political requirements. So far as is known, they were last consulted in 363, and were burned not long afterwards. Forged Sibylline prophecies were manufactured by Jews and Christians for propaganda purposes. They were ascribed to a Jewish sibyl, who acquired a respectable position as a divinely inspired prophetess in Christian art.

Though pagan official forms of divination were swept away by Christianity, many private methods which flourished in the ancient world survived in more or less Christianized form in medieval Europe. So did the use of lucky charms, which again is probably prehistoric in origin. The prehistoric figurines representing a goddess which have been found in Europe and the Near East are likely to have been amulets, worn for good luck and prosperity, and to keep harmful forces at bay. The Greeks made faces at evil, literally, by carving glaring heads of gorgons, with tusks and lolling tongues, to frighten off hostile influences. Another, pleasingly simple Greek method of defence against evil spirits was to write above the door of a house, 'Hercules lives here'. The numerous Egyptian amulets included the *ankh*, the symbol of life, which has recently come back into vogue, and figures of Bes, the dwarfish god of good luck, were worn or carried as charms.

Amulets were frequently used for protection against illness, especially diseases of the eye, digestive and gynaecological disorders, sciatica, consumption and hydrophobia: 'Flee, demon hydrophobia, from the wearer of this amulet.' Pliny says that a man named Mucianus, who was three times consul, carried a live fly wrapped in white linen as a charm against ophthalmia, and another man guarded himself against the same complaint with the Greek letters *rho* and *alpha*, written down and wrapped in white linen, which he hung round his neck. The makers of amulets tried to harness the power of gods and symbols from different traditions. One found at Welwyn in England has on its two sides figures of Isis and Bes, a lioness, a key with seven wards, a scarab-beetle, a snake devouring its own tail, an invocation to a spirit named Ororiouth, and three different versions of the name of the God of the Old Testament.

Some believers in astrology, divination and luck denied human free-will altogether and said that all events were determined by inexorable fate. Others thought of divination as a way of finding out what was likely to happen, but not inevitable. Most people, then as now, probably did not trouble themselves with logic and believed simultaneously in both fate and free-will. The philosopher Alexander of Aphrodisias remarked in the third century AD that:

Those who maintain energetically in their discourses that Fate is inevitable and who attribute all events to it, seem to place no reliance on it in the actions of their own lives. For they ... never cease to pray to the gods, as though these could grant their prayers even in opposition to Fate; and they do not hesitate to have resource to omens, as though it were possible for them, by learning any fated event in advance, to guard against it.[31]

This comment seems equally applicable to the new paganism of today, when conflicting ideas about free-will, fate and luck, confidence in lucky charms, a feeling for omens and premonitions, and a hope that appeals to God may serve in desperate situations, are all jumbled together into a mixture found necessary in a society where both rationalism and religion are felt inadequate.

2
Christianity
and the Middle Ages

Christianity was at first only one of several oriental cults which promised initiates the discovery of their true identity, salvation and a happy life after death. It was particularly offensive to conservatives because Christians were intolerant of non-believers, scorned the pagan gods and the Roman state religion, which they regarded as an engine of the Devil, and cherished dangerously egalitarian social ideals. Garbled reports of their beliefs and ceremonies contributed to the impression that Christians were anti-social and anarchic. Because Christian men and women called each other brother and sister, held services together and exchanged the kiss of peace, they were accused of revelling in promiscuous and incestuous orgies. In the Mass they were rumoured to sacrifice a child and feast on his body and blood. The oldest picture of the Crucifixion that has survived is a scrawl on the wall of a house in Rome showing a Christian worshipping a crucified donkey.

The primitive determination to see malevolent design behind disasters caused Christians to be held responsible for plagues and catastrophes. Tertullian said that whenever anything unusual and alarming happened, the Christians were blamed. If the Tiber flooded or the Nile did not, if the earth moved or the sky stayed still, if there was famine or pestilence, the cry went up: 'the Christians to the lion'. Ironically, in course of time the same instinct drove Christians to tar heretics, Jews and witches with the same brush.

Christ himself was attacked by some pagans as a magician, and Celsus, who wrote a polemic against Christianity in about 180, suggested that Jesus had learned his magic in Egypt. The life of Christ, as described by Christian writers, lent some semblance of colour to the charge. The miraculous birth of Jesus, accompanied by the portent of the star and the homage of the Magi; the portent at his baptism in the Jordan; the miracles of healing, calming the wind and sea, walking on water and providing supernatural quantities of food and drink; the ability to restore the dead to life; the portents at the Crucifixion, his mysterious disappearance from the tomb and his reappearances after death; the story of his descent into the underworld; these marvels, which helped to persuade Christians that Jesus was divine, could be represented as the achievements of a magician. His power to cast out evil spirits had caused his enemies among the Jews to accuse him of black magic.

But attacks on Christ as a magician failed because to many potential converts possession of supernatural powers was not a liability but an attraction. The opening chapter of St Mark, the earliest of the gospels, stresses the effect of Jesus's feats of healing and exorcism in drawing excited attention to him and his teaching. The magic of Christ and the Church was an important factor in Christianity's success and all through the Middle Ages one of the principal functions of the Church was to provide a bastion of magic protection against evil, infertility, insanity, disease and misfortune.

The Magic of the Church

From the beginning of the Church's history, Christian success in healing and exorcism impressed pagans and made converts. By the time of Jesus, there were plenty of private specialists in casting out spirits from 'possessed' patients. St Paul met a group of itinerant Jewish exorcists at Ephesus and a Jewish exorcist named Eleazar demonstrated his skill before the Emperor Vespasian. In the second century Lucian mentions a celebrated Syrian specialist who charged high fees in return for expelling demons from lunatics.

Jesus commissioned his disciples to heal the sick and the possessed, without fee, and they continued to do so with inspiring effect after he had left them. When St Peter brought a dead woman back to life at Joppa, 'it became known throughout all Joppa, and many believed in the Lord'. When St Paul cured a cripple at Lystra in Asia Minor, the crowds thought he must be a god and a priest brought oxen to be sacrificed to him. At Ephesus, Paul's handkerchiefs and aprons were taken to the sick, 'and diseases left them and the evil spirits came out of them'.[1]

As the Church gained ground, specialists in exorcism were appointed and had many successes. The name of Christ, the sign of the cross and the presence of persons of formidable spiritual force were frequently effective. According to Bede, the mere approach of St Cuthbert, a notable healer who was Bishop of Lindisfarne in the seventh century, expelled from a woman a demon which had thrown her into convulsive fits. In the Middle Ages patients continued to be cured by exorcism, and some by contact with the relics and tombs of saints, like the man who remained insane for three years until he touched the sepulchre of St Francis of Assisi. There is no reason to doubt the truth of many of these stories. 'Possessed' patients tend to be highly suggestible and abnormally responsive to external influences.

Possession is a good example of the way in which magic 'works'. The strength of the possession hypothesis as an explanation of mental and hysterical illness was that, on the face of it, it made sense. A possessed person did behave as if an alien intelligence had taken control of him. When he was exorcised and it was commanded to come out of him, it very often did and he recovered. This reinforced belief in possession and confidence in the Church's apparently magical ability to deal with it. Conversely, the fact that the belief was so firmly established caused people in disturbed, hysterical and highly suggestible states of mind to accept that they were possessed by demons and to behave accordingly.

Ecstatic and visionary experience was as important in early Christianity as in the competing pagan and gnostic cults. Seven weeks after the Crucifixion a group of Jesus's disciples, perhaps about a hundred of them, met in Jerusalem on the day of the Jewish feast of Pentecost. 'And suddenly a sound came from heaven like the rush of a mighty wind, and it filled all the house where they were sitting. And there appeared to them tongues as of fire, distributed and resting on each one of them. And they were all filled with the Holy Spirit and began to speak in other tongues, as the Spirit gave them utterance.' An astonished crowd gathered and St Peter had to explain that the Christians were not drunk – he pointed out that it was much too early in the day for that – but imbued with divine power.[2]

The descent of the Spirit, in which the believer became possessed by God, occurred wherever the gospel was carried in the early days. The gifts which the Spirit brought included apparently magical healing power and prophetic power as well as speaking in tongues. The peculiar ecstatic behaviour associated with the experience offended persons of conservative temperament, but it was infectious, convinced others that the Christians were indeed god-possessed, and made converts as it has done during sporadic 'enthusiastic' revivals ever since. For the Christian it was the sign that he was 'God's temple', as St Paul said, inhabited by the divine. 'For God's temple is holy, and that temple you are.'[3]

Later, the Church's attitude changed. People convinced that they are God's temples are not easy to deal with. The value of religious enthusiasm is hard to assess and St Paul himself was dubious about it. The larger the Church grew and the more efficient an organization it built up, the more suspect ecstatic prophecy, speaking in tongues and the display of startling psychic abilities became. They might be marks of sanctity or of something quite different. In the Middle Ages they were taken as evidence of demonic possession.

Meanwhile, however, in a world in which many people felt hopelessly lost, Christian holiness and power was attractive. This appeal was strengthened by the fact that the Church had turned the pagan daemons into demons. For Christians, the pagan gods were masks worn by Satan and the lesser spirits were evil intelligences under his command, enemies of God and man. It was their machinations which accounted for the otherwise inexplicable resistance and hostility which the Church encountered and the otherwise inexplicable infestations of heresy which plagued it. The Christian conviction of living in a world full of sinister and threatening forces satisfied the mood of the age, while at the same time the Church provided a defence against the armies of evil. The Christian 'man of power' – the martyr, saint or ascetic – who rejected the wicked world and was divinely inspired to defeat it, was an admired and compelling figure.

In 325 the Council of Nicaea forbade Christians to castrate themselves, which some of them had been doing in rejection of the world and for the increase of holiness. In the fourth and fifth centuries ascetics swarmed into the Egyptian and Syrian deserts, to wrestle with evil and acquire supernormal powers. The victories of St Anthony of Egypt (died 356) over hordes of ferocious demons, which attacked him in animal and grotesque forms, supplied a theme for artists for centuries afterwards. In the mountains outside Antioch the doyen of the pillar saints, St Simeon Stylites (died 459), lived for forty years on a small platform at the top of a column sixty feet high. People came to gape up at him and ask for spiritual counsel, others wrote him letters, governments consulted him as an oracle, and he performed miracles of healing and was responsible for numerous conversions. His disciple, St Daniel Stylites (died 493), who spent thirty-three years on top of another pillar, was consulted by emperors and bishops, and the sick were brought to him to heal.

Christianity grew up in a pagan world and converts naturally brought pagan religio-magical beliefs and customs with them. The custom of putting models of diseased limbs and parts of the body in churches, in the hope of a cure or in thanksgiving for one, was also common in pagan temples, especially those of Aesculapius and Isis. The pagan method of curing disease by incubation spread to Christianity and patients were taken to spend the night in churches with a reputation for healing. Christians in Egypt turned the *ankh* into the cross of their faith. In the West, the early Christians used the same kind of magical funeral art as pagans, and sometimes the same motifs and figures, including Cupid, Psyche and Orpheus, who was a symbolic type of Christ. The raising of Lazarus was often depicted in the Roman catacombs, as an aid to the soul's resurrection. Noah saved from the Flood, Jonah cast up onto dry land by the whale, and Shadrach, Meshach and Abednego safe and sound in the fiery furnace had the same function.

The Christian bishop's gesture of benediction originally represented the blessing and protection of the sun. The birthday of the sun at the winter solstice, taken to be 25 December, which was also the birthday of Mithras, was adopted as Christmas by the Church in the fourth century, apparently because so many Christians already celebrated the sun's festival in any case. About 450, Leo the Great complained that Christians on their way up the steps to worship in St Peter's turned round and bowed to the sun before going in.

In Asia Minor at one time Easter was celebrated at the spring equinox on the day of the resurrection of the fertility god Attis. The constellation of ideas and imagery which had gathered round the dying and rising gods of fertility also clung to Christ. Just as the dead Osiris had been depicted in Egypt with corn sprouting from his corpse, so Christ was sometimes shown crucified on a flowering and fruit-laden tree. All over Europe, pagan festivals and customs intended to promote fertility and prosperity became part of the Christian year, but inevitably retained much of their pagan and magical feeling. Christianity's lack of a bountiful and protective mother goddess was largely repaired by the cult of the Virgin Mary, who acquired many of the characteristics of the pagan fertility goddesses.

There was a rivalry between Christian and pagan magic, the flavour of which comes through in a story from the life of St Hilarion of Gaza (fourth century), written by St Jerome. A Christian charioteer, due to race against a pagan, found that his opponent had bewitched his chariot and horses. He hurried to St Hilarion who, though reluctant at first, agreed to help for the honour of the faith. Hilarion gave the charioteer his drinking cup with some water in it. The charioteer sprinkled the water on his horses and chariot and won the race easily. The win was hailed by the spectators as a victory for Christ.[4]

During its first four centuries Christianity moved across the frontier from the wilderness of dubious and illicit cults to conquer the territory of accepted public religion and the state. Its magic was one of the reasons for its success, but the Church itself, like pagan authorities before it, used magic as a pejorative term. Theologians did not accept the popular distinction between white and black magic. All magic was bad magic. Magic which was part of the practices of the Church was not classified as magic.

Once the Church had suppressed paganism, the magician was necessarily no longer a wicked pagan but a renegade Christian (or a Jew, the only outsider left). It was not to be imagined that a man could work wonders by himself. If he was not a saint, whose miracles were performed by God, then his marvels must be worked by Satan and his legions of fiends, and he must be in league with them. This was believed to mean that, explicitly or implicitly, he had made a pact of allegiance with them, abandoning his faith, renouncing his baptism and with it his Christian identity, and signing his soul away to the Devil. Stories about people who had done this began to circulate widely from the sixth century onwards. The consequence was that any form of magic of which the Church disapproved, even if it was beneficent in intention, carried with it a dangerous stigma of trafficking with demons.

People continued to rely on the Church's own magic, however. The veneration of martyrs and their relics, for example, had magical as well as religious purposes. Some of the faithful carried fragments of martyrs' bones about with them as amulets, and demands for help were scrawled on walls near their graves: 'Lord Crescentio, heal my eyes for me'; 'Peter and Paul, protect your servants.' There was so much pressure to be buried near a martyr that the Church had to remind its flock that salvation was obtained through imitation of a martyr's virtues, not through physical proximity to his corpse. The Empress Constantia asked Gregory the Great for the head or some other portion of St Paul. The Pope declined, and sent her filings from the chains the apostle had worn in prison instead. St Augustine had earlier criticized travelling-salesmen who traded in bits of martyrs' bodies, but it became the accepted practice to dig them up and dismember them because, following a ruling in 787, each church had to possess a holy relic. [5]

Objects associated with Christ, the Virgin Mary and the saints were also venerated and though most theologians regarded relics as channels through which God might choose to work miracles, many ordinary Christians thought of them as objects which contained magic power in themselves. In the Middle Ages churches, monasteries and private collectors built up substantial hoards of relics. Trier Cathedral held Christ's seamless robe, the body of St James the Apostle at Compostella in Spain attracted throngs of pilgrims, and Glastonbury Abbey in England owned a piece of the table of the Last Supper and one of the stones which Christ had refused to turn into bread, as well as the bodies of St Patrick and other saints. 'Outside England, the more surprising relics included a feather from the wing of the angel Gabriel; a jar full of the darkness inflicted on Egypt by Moses; rays from the Star of Bethlehem; samples of the Virgin's milk; and a whole wardrobe of her chemises.' [6]

The faithful made pilgrimages to famous relics and shrines, for healing and spiritual merit. They took home with them, as powerful talismans, cloths or keys which had been placed on the graves of saints, oil from lamps burning at the tombs, flowers from the altars. Images and icons of Christ, the Virgin and the saints were also frequently believed to cure disease, ward off misfortune and bring success. The Byzantine icon of the Virgin in St Mark's, Venice, known as 'Our Lady of Victory', was believed to assure triumph in war.

Other holy symbols and rituals gave an impression of being

magically effective. In part of France in the fifth century, for instance, many pagans were converted during an outbreak of cattle disease, when cattle belonging to Christians either escaped infection or recovered from it. This was put down to the Christians' use of the sign of the cross. The famous hymn known as the Breastplate of St Patrick ('I bind unto myself today the strong name of the Trinity') was valued as a powerful protective incantation. According to an author in the seventh century: 'Every person who sings it every day with all his attention on God shall not have demons appearing to his face. It will be a safeguard to him against sudden death. It will be a protection to him against every poison and envy. It will be an armour to his soul after his death.'[7]

Innumerable medieval folk remedies employed Christian magic. According to an Anglo-Saxon medical book of the tenth century, a cure for snakebite is to drink holy water in which a snail has been washed. A complicated cure for bewitchment, recommended by Hildegard of Bingen in the twelfth century, involves cutting a cross into a loaf, reciting incantations and nibbling away the loaf round the cross. John of Salisbury said it was useful to repeat the Lord's Prayer and the names of the four evangelists when gathering and administering medicinal herbs. The Agnus Dei, a figure of a lamb in wax, specially blessed by the Pope and immersed in holy water, was believed to assist women in childbirth and protect its wearer against enemies, evil spirits, lightning, epilepsy and sudden death.

Medieval Christians crossed themselves and their children, houses, cattle and crops, to keep misfortune away and in self-defence in moments of danger. They wore amulets inscribed with the cross or with verses from the gospels. In the early fourteenth century it was apparently a common, though highly unorthodox, practice for priests to rebaptize people in the belief that this would keep them in good health. In 1458 Nicolas Jacquier said it was the custom to take holy water home from church every Sunday for protection. Some of it was sprinkled on the beds each evening to ward off night-stalking demons and ghouls.

The Roman Catholic priest, as a specialist in the sacred, acquired a magical mystique. A clear division between clergy and laity had grown up by the end of the second century, with the clergy being ordained by a bishop through the laying on of hands. The result was a belief that the clergy had supernatural power, and some of them traded on it. In 363 the Synod of Laodicea condemned priests who dealt in magic, astrology and the manufacture of amulets. The Council of Arles in 506 threatened priests who used the Bible for fortune-telling with excommunication. Charlemagne forbade the same practice again in 789. There was a widespread belief that priests were uncanny and that it might be ominous to meet one, which must have been a singularly irritating superstition for the Church to bear. It is not entirely extinct even yet.

A major factor in creating the mystique of the priesthood was the Mass, which over the centuries gained the most formidable magical reputation of all Christian ceremonies. A rite in which bread and wine were transformed into the flesh and blood of God – through repetition, and so renewal, of the words and gestures used by Christ at the Last Supper – and were then consumed to unite the worshipper with God, was bound to give the impression of being a magical ritual of awe-inspiring force. The impression was driven home by the Church's doctrine that a priest could say Mass effectively even if he was in a state of sin, had evil intentions or was a heretic. The Mass seemed to have an independent power of its own, regardless of the spiritual condition and motives of those who used it.

Christians accordingly turned the ceremony to all sorts of purposes. The Gelasian Sacramentary, which contains Roman material of about the sixth century, includes Masses said privately for rain, for fine weather, for the sick, to ward off diseases of cattle, to obtain children, for the safety of someone going on a journey and for the souls of the dead. Saying Mass over cattle, farm implements and fishing boats and nets, to bless them and make them productive, was common in the Middle Ages and still occurs today.

The Church's use of the Mass in this way led inevitably to its employment in black magic, and eventually to the Black Mass in honour of the Devil. The Council of Toledo in 694 condemned priests who said Mass for the dead, naming not a dead man but a living man, with the intention of killing him. Giraldus Cambrensis, who died about 1220, said that priests were doing this in his time, and some would say Mass over a wax image of the victim placed on the altar, cursing him. The University of Paris condemned the use of the Mass in magic in 1398, and a fifteenth-century treatise, *Dives and Pauper*, again complained of priests using the Mass for the dead in murderous sorcery. The authorities were constantly instructing priests to keep the hosts and the holy oil under lock and key, to prevent people from stealing them for use in sorcery, love charms, medicines and poisons.

Runes and Druids

Medieval folk magic mingled Christianity with survivals from the older pagan world. Roman customs have a parallel in later ceremonies of 'beating the bounds', which are still held in some places in Europe in the spring. A procession led by the clergy carrying crosses went round the boundary of the village or town, in effect drawing a magic circle round it. At intervals on the way prayers were offered to Christ, the Virgin Mary and the saints for a good crop and to keep away storm and blight. Young men and women might be whipped at certain stations along the boundary: to help them remember how it ran, it was said, but this was probably an attempt to explain away a custom whose original purpose had either been forgotten or was considered unduly redolent of pagan fertility magic.

Jumping up and down was for centuries a magical way of improving the growth of crops in Europe, as it had been in Greece and Rome. The leaps of Morris dancers are an example. In Belgium people danced round bonfires and jumped over them for good crops. In one area of Switzerland, usually at midsummer, groups of masked men went from village to village, clashing their cudgels fiercely and leaping to make the corn grow tall. In Germany and elsewhere people jumped over bonfires at Easter and through another imitative link this was connected not only with fertility but with Christ's resurrection from the grave. In Latvia and Macedonia on the morning of Easter Day girls rigged up swings and swung as high as they could; and down into the nineteenth century in England women were lifted up high in the air three times in succession on Easter Monday.

Customs of this kind in western and northern Europe go back ultimately to the pre-Christian Germanic and Celtic tribes. Germanic deities were sometimes carried through the countryside in procession to bring prosperity and good fortune, and in medieval times this was practised all over Europe with images of Christ, the Virgin and the local saints. According to the *Germania* of Tacitus, written late in the first century AD, the Earth Mother of the tribes in Denmark and Schleswig-Holstein was taken round the land in a cow-drawn cart, in which her sacred image was concealed. When she returned to her home, in a grove on an island, her image and cart were cleaned by slaves, who were drowned immediately afterwards because they had seen and touched her. Later in Scandinavia, the fertility god Freyr made similar progresses in a wagon or a ship and human sacrifices were offered to him. This is apparently the origin of the medieval Scandinavian custom of carrying a ship round the fields to bless them, which survived into modern times.

Tacitus described German methods of taking omens from the cries and flight of birds and the neighs and snorts of sacred white horses. The Germans also cast lots by dropping strips of wood marked with different signs onto a white cloth. The signs developed into the runic alphabet, which was surrounded with an aura of magic and mystery. Rune comes from a word meaning 'secret', surviving in the modern German word *raunen*, 'to whisper'. The runes gave magical effect to what was stated in them and were used for healing, to protect a warrior in battle or calm the waves on a sea-voyage. They were cut on tombstones to put a curse on anyone who stole or destroyed them, and engraved on swords to make them irresistible in war. When Christianity conquered the North, the runes were banned as devilish. As late as the seventeenth century in Iceland people found in possession of runes were burned to death.

German, Scandinavian and Celtic kings in pre-Christian times bore the same magical responsibility for the fertility of the land and the well-being of the people as the pharaohs in Egypt. Sacrifice was extensively employed to secure fertility, and success in war. Classical writers were repelled by the human sacrifices which the Germans offered to their gods – prisoners taken in battle were hanged on trees – and astounded by the dedicated wastefulness with which the spoils of war, horses, weapons, armour and ornaments, were thrown into swamps and rivers as offerings to the war god. The Celts, who were head-hunters, drew omens from the death throes of men knifed in the back, shot with arrows or impaled. They also offered human sacrifices by drowning, suffocation, stabbing, hanging, burning or a combination of methods. Julius Caesar described the Celts in Gaul as 'extremely superstitious' and said:

... persons suffering from serious diseases, as well as those who are exposed to the perils of battle, offer or vow to offer, human sacrifices, for the performance of which they employ Druids. They believe that the only way of saving a man's life is to propitiate the god's wrath by rendering another life in its place, and they have regular state sacrifices of the same kind. Some tribes have colossal images made of wickerwork, the limbs of which they fill with living men; they are then set on fire and the victims burnt to death.[8]

When a Roman army attacked the Druid stronghold of Anglesey in Wales in AD 61, they were confronted not only by the enemy warriors but by women in black robes with dishevelled hair, brandishing torches. 'Close by stood Druids, raising their hands to heaven and screaming dreadful curses.' The spectacle 'awed the Roman soldiers into a sort of paralysis'. After they had recovered and defeated the enemy, they demolished the sacred groves of the Druids. 'For it was their religion to drench their altars in the blood of prisoners and consult their gods by means of human entrails.'[9]

The Romans suppressed Druidism in Gaul and Britain, though not in Ireland, which the Romans never reached and where the Druids survived until the Christian conquest. Druids probably also survived until Christian times in Scotland. They were part of the Celtic specialist priesthood, or more broadly of the class which the Irish called 'men of art', including priests, scholars, bards, ovates or diviners, and skilled craftsmen, all of whom had a magical mystique. Druidism may have been pre-Celtic and taken over by the Celts in Gaul and Britain from the earlier inhabitants, and there was probably a shamanistic strain in its ancestry. According to Irish traditions, the Druids were powerful magicians and could change themselves into any shape they chose. The chief Druid of the King of Ireland is described on one occasion wearing the hide of a bull and the head and wings of a bird. The Druids practised incubation, eating the flesh of a cat, a dog and a pig, and then going to sleep on a bull's hide to induce meaningful dreams.

The Druids were custodians of traditional lore and wisdom, including knowledge of the gods, natural science, astronomy and the calendar, herbal medicine and healing, and tribal law. This knowledge was not written down but preserved in verses, memorized and passed on from generation to generation. It was said to take twenty years' training to become a Druid. According to Pliny, the Druids venerated the oak and the mistletoe, which they used in magic and which was ceremonially cut with a golden sickle and caught in a white cloak as it fell from the bough. They also used magic eggs, supposedly made of the spittle of snakes.

Some classical accounts of the Druids are steeped in a misty, romantic awe which has reappeared in the modern Druid movement. As wise men and specialists in the sacred, they were compared to the Magi, the Egyptian priests and the Brahmins. They were credited with Pythagorean beliefs about reincarnation and the significance of numbers and were said to be masters of astrology. At the same time, they acquired a sinister aura through their predilection for human sacrifice and their connection with sacred groves and sanctuaries in the dark depths of forests. Lucan described one of these holy places near Marseilles, a clearing among trees spattered with human blood, and studded with rough, uncanny wooden images of gods, pallid and rotten with age.

As Christianity consolidated its hold on western and northern Europe, the Church prohibited pagan religion, sacrifices and the veneration of standing stones and springs. But much of it survived under a Christian veneer. Sacred springs and wells continued to be regarded as holy and magically healing as well as luck-bringing, but were now put under the patronage of Christian saints. The great Celtic festivals of Beltane and Samain turned into May Day and Hallowe'en. Primitive and pagan rites and customs kept their vitality for centuries, because they promoted confidence and communal solidarity and because they 'worked'. Some of them have lasted down to the present day and many were revived or recreated in the nineteenth century.

The Jewish Tradition

The western tradition of high magic is heavily indebted to Jewish influences. Magic and divination are condemned in the Old Testament but, as usual, it is private and unauthorized magic which is meant. Authorized magic was worked by prophets and priests who were instruments of God, like Moses and Aaron routing the Egyptian magicians in the contest before Pharaoh. Moses parted the Red Sea with his magic wand and struck water from a rock in the wilderness, but the marvels were God's doing. From an outside point of view, especially an Egyptian one, Moses was a powerful and distinctly sinister magician. From an Israelite point of view, he was a holy man and a servant of God.

Israelite religion included sacrifices and other ceremonies with a magical tinge. One of them was the ritual on the Day of Atonement each year, when the sins of the people were expelled from the community by being loaded onto the head of a goat, which was driven out into the wilderness. There were authorized methods of divination, through approved indicators like dreams; the Urim and Thummim, which seem to have been lots inscribed with symbols; and the utterances of prophets in trance or ecstasy, in which they were believed to be mouthpieces of God. But as always, there were also unauthorized magicians and diviners. Deuteronomy condemns 'anyone who practises divination, as a soothsayer, or an augur, or a sorcerer, or a charmer, or a medium, or a wizard, or a necromancer'. Isaiah disapprovingly mentions 'the mediums and wizards who chirp and mutter'. These mediums and wizards were people who communicated with the dead. They possessed or were possessed by a spirit (in Spiritualism nowadays called a 'control') which spoke through them. The word now rendered 'medium' was in older translations 'witch' and texts from the Old Testament provided scriptural justification for the killing of witches in medieval Europe.[10]

The well-known story of the woman of Endor shows both sides of the situation. King Saul had attempted to drive all the mediums out of the country, but as a battle against the Philistines drew near he needed supernatural reassurance and advice. The prophet to whom he would have turned, Samuel, had recently died. Saul consulted the approved indicators, but could obtain no answer. In desperation he found a medium at Endor and persuaded her to summon up Samuel from the dead. She did so, and told Saul that she saw an old man wrapped in a robe coming up out of the earth. Saul, who evidently could not see the apparition himself, accepted that it was Samuel and asked what he should do, only to be told that God had doomed him to destruction.[11]

Jewish magic, supposedly founded by Moses, but in reality a mixture of Jewish, Mesopotamian, Egyptian and Greek ingredients, had a substantial reputation in the ancient world. Its most brilliant legendary figure was King Solomon, whose fame as a master magician lasted for centuries. The Old Testament, which says that God gave him riches, honour and wisdom surpassing that of all other men, 'even all the wisdom of Egypt', laid the basis of his renown. The real Solomon (tenth century BC) was in fact the most powerful of Jewish kings and the Bible's description of the Temple in Jerusalem, which he built, magnificently adorned and equipped, produced an indelible impression of his wealth and grandeur. The story that the Queen of Sheba visited him and asked him perplexing riddles, all of which he answered, supported his reputation for sagacity. His appetite for foreign women and strange gods gave his character an intriguingly unholy cast. In folk tales he became a type of the man who, in his devouring ambition to know and master everything, challenges the prerogatives of God and ensures his own downfall: the theme of the story of Adam and Eve in Genesis, and later the core of the Faust legend.

Solomon was believed to have owned a magic ring, given him by God, with which he controlled all nature, all men and all spirits. He used it to subdue the demons which were hindering the construction of the Temple and he forced them to work on it for him, which was why it took only seven years to build. He understood the languages of animals and birds, he explored the world, the sky and the depths of the sea, flying on the wind or on a magic carpet of luxurious design.

The most famous western textbook of magic is the *Key of Solomon*, and the sage's ability to control spirits made him the supreme authority on this type of magic especially. Legend had it that magical texts written by Solomon, or by the demons under his control, were banned by King Hezekiah of Judah, about 700 BC. In the first century AD Josephus mentions a book of incantations for summoning spirits, attributed to Solomon and used by the exorcist Eleazar. Magical textbooks were also attributed to Moses, and the *Eighth Book of Moses* or *Key of Moses* seems to have emanated from the Jewish community in Alexandria.

The Jewish belief in angels, which Christians inherited, gave magicians good spirits to command as well as evil demons. The *Testament of Solomon*, in Greek and possibly dating from the second or third century AD, describes the physical appearance and individual functions of the fifteen principal demons and reveals the divine and angelic names of power which subdue them. It also provides a catalogue of the thirty-six spirits of the decans (Egyptian divisions of the zodiac), which are demons of disease, and gives spells against them. The names of the angels and demons come from Jewish, Graeco-Egyptian, Mesopotamian, Persian and Christian sources. A later version of the *Testament* has a different list of spirits, with their 'characters', the hieroglyphic symbols through which the magician can summon and control them.

The *Sword of Moses*, of the tenth century or earlier, has close affinities with the Graeco-Egyptian magical papyri. It claims that by using it, 'every wish is fulfilled and every secret revealed, and every miracle, marvel and prodigy are performed'. It supplies a long prayer for the magician to recite, asserting that God will give him power over all angels and spirits. The names of the spirits, through which their energy is tapped, come from the same mixture of sources as in the *Testament*. The miracles, marvels and prodigies to be performed include striking people blind or dumb, walking dryshod through water, murdering an enemy through an image of him made of mud, freeing captives from prison, speaking with the dead, catching a lion by its ear, blackening one's neighbours' reputations and sending them dreams, forcing a woman to submit in love, catching fish, appointing and deposing kings, finding out all mysteries and secrets, and curing the sick. The mixture of 'white' and 'black' magic and of momentous and trivial goals is typical of the whole genre.

A Byzantine writer of the eleventh century, Psellus, mentions a book by Solomon on demons and the properties of precious stones. The *Speculum Astronomiae*, probably written by Albertus Magnus in the thirteenth century, refers to the *Almandel* of Solomon. A Greek *Key of Solomon* in the British Museum has been dated to the twelfth or thirteenth century and Roger Bacon knew of books attributed to Solomon which contained rituals for summoning up demons and offering them sacrifices. A *Livre de Solomon*, with instructions for invoking demons, was burned about 1350 on the orders of Pope Innocent VI. A *Clavicula Salomonis* (Key or Little Key of Solomon) and a *Sigillum Salomonis* (Seal of Solomon) are mentioned in a pamphlet of 1456, addressed to the Duke of Burgundy, and from the sixteenth century onwards numerous Solomonic textbooks were in circulation in a variety of languages (see chapter three).

The *Key of Solomon* and its variants and relatives are primarily Jewish in tone, with Graeco-Egyptian, oriental and, rarely, some Christian material blended in. Devout prayers to God and a stern insistence on chastity, fasting and cleanliness as prerequisites for success, are mingled with operations 'to bring destruction and to give death, and to sow hatred and discord', or 'for preparing powders provocative of madness'. Divine energy is tapped automatically through prayers, conjurations and names of power, regardless of the magician's motives. In massive incantations, drawing extensively on the Old Testament, the magician musters all his reserves of will and force to compel powerful spirits to appear and obey him.

We then, by the just judgment of God, by the Ineffable and Admirable Virtue of God, just, living and true, we call ye with power, we force and exorcise ye by and in the Admirable Name which was written on the Tables of Stone which God gave upon Mount Sinai; and by and in the wonderful Name which Aaron the High Priest bare written upon his breast, by which also God created the world, the which name is Axineton; and by the Living God Who is One throughout the Ages, whose dwelling is in the Ineffable Light, Whose Name is Wisdom, and Whose Spirit is Life, before Whom goeth forth Fire and Flame ... Come ye, then, without delay, without noise and without rage, before us, without any deformity or hideousness, to execute all our will ... Come ye, come ye, Angels of Darkness; come hither before this Circle without fear, terror or deformity, to execute our commands, and be ye ready both to achieve and to complete all that we shall command ye.[12]

Besides these operations of high magic, which a modern occultist would be likely to interpret as the summoning and control of forces within the magician himself, the *Key* has processes for making a magic carpet and flying garters, discovering thieves, finding buried treasure, gaining love and esteem, and becoming invisible. It gives directions for making the necessary sacrifices to spirits. There are dauntingly elaborate instructions for choosing the right planetary day and hour for a magical operation; for the preliminary prayers, fasting and preparations through which the magician sets himself apart from everyday life, the better to enter an abnormal plane of experience and to protect himself against its perils; for making the 'pentacles' or talismans charged with magic power; for drawing the magic circle; for the manufacture of the magician's robes, symbols, perfumes and armoury of weapons – 'the knife, sword, sickle, poniard, dagger, lance, wand, staff, and other instruments of magical art'.

The 'grimoires', or grammars, of magic owe much to the Jewish mystical practice of meditating on the names and titles of God in the Old Testament, as clues to God's identity and gateways to the divine. The hidden meanings of these names were investigated and new names or aspects of God discovered, through mathematical and anagrammatical methods known collectively as *gematria*. Magicians shared the interest of mystics in the divine names, which to them were sources of power, and there was blurring at the edges between their mystical and magical uses.

In the Judaeo-Christian tradition the Hebrew language was the language with which God made the world. The twenty-two letters of the Hebrew alphabet could consequently be regarded as building-blocks of the universe and aspects of God himself, who in creating the world had made himself manifest. The Hebrew letters did double duty as numbers, which were viewed in the same light. It followed that whoever could achieve an understanding of the letters and numbers in their combinations and permutations would achieve an understanding, which for a magician meant mastery, of the universe and God. This is expounded in an obscure and visionary fashion in the *Sefer Yetsirah* or Book of Creation, which mingles Jewish, gnostic, Pythagorean and possibly Neoplatonist ideas and was written by an unknown author, probably in Babylonia, between AD 200 and 600.

The *Sefer Yetsirah* was influenced by Jewish Merkabah mysticism, which employed meditative techniques to induce visions in which the mystic seemed to leave his body and travel through the planetary spheres to the seventh heaven, where he beheld the awe-inspiring majesty of the Almighty, seated on his throne or chariot (*merkabah*). These experiences are described in the

Hekhaloth texts of the third century AD onwards. The visionary journey was perilous in the extreme, for the spheres – the *hekhaloth* or heavenly halls – were guarded by 'gate-keepers', which were hostile to the soul. (In similar gnostic systems the guardians of the spheres were called Archons.) To pass them in safety the mystic needed to know the correct 'seals' or talismanic names of power and had to recite long incantations. An account of the technique used to induce these visions, written about AD 1000, says that the mystic 'must fast a number of days and lay his head between his knees and whisper many hymns and songs whose texts are known from tradition'. The bodily posture has been described by Gershom Scholem as 'an attitude of deep self-oblivion which, to judge from certain ethnological parallels, is favorable to the induction of pre-hypnotic autosuggestion'.[13]

The goal was mystical but attaining it depended on magic, and in some cases the names and incantations were used as sources of power in themselves as well as rungs of the ladder of spiritual ascent. One distinctly magical procedure of Merkabah mysticism was 'the putting on of the name'. The mystic clothed himself in a garment into which the name of God had been woven, so investing himself with the divine attributes. Since it was dangerous, Merkabah mysticism was reserved for a spiritual elite. Candidates for entry had to possess high moral qualities, but they were also judged by physiognomy (character analysis by facial features) and palmistry. They had to have 'favourable' lines on their hands, and the *Hekhaloth* texts contain the oldest surviving documents on palmistry.

There was a similar mixture of mystical ideals and magical methods in the Cabala, a body of complex teachings elaborated by medieval Jewish authors on the basis of older Jewish traditions and gnostic and Neoplatonist speculations. The Cabalists emerged as a distinct group in southern France and Spain about 1200, and the *Zohar* or Book of Splendour, the most important medieval cabalist text, was written in Aramaic by Moses de Leon in Spain, soon after 1275.

Their belief in the hierarchical arrangement of the universe, of which man was the microcosm, provided the Cabalists with a ladder of mystical or magical ascent. Many of them used the divine names in meditation to induce visions of ascent, but they again tended to restrict this side of their teaching to an elite, partly for fear of Christian persecution. For example, the prolific writings of the great thirteenth-century visionary Abraham Abulafia, including twelve commentaries on the *Sefer Yetsirah*, were concealed. Abulafia's 'science of the combination of letters' was a method of contemplation of the letters of the Hebrew and other alphabets, through which the soul moved closer to God. He prescribed rules of bodily posture and breathing techniques, resembling those of Yoga. He also recommended meditation on the *sefiroth*, the ten major aspects of God and structural components of the universe, which the Cabalists linked with divine names, numbers and the planetary spheres (and which are used as names of power in the *Key of Solomon*).

Abulafia was as fiercely hostile to magic as he was to Christianity, but some of his successors regarded his methods as ways of attaining magical power. Paul Ricci, for instance, a Jew turned Christian who became Professor of Greek and Hebrew at Pavia University in 1521, said that through the Cabala, 'we attain more easily and beyond the use of nature to the glories of the Eternal Father *and our prerogatives in this world which resemble them*'.[14]

At the humbler level of folk magic, popular Jewish practices and superstitions resemble those found everywhere in Christian Europe: healing charms; image magic, especially for forcing thieves to restore stolen property and in affairs of love; the use of verses from the Bible as spells to cure disease, kill enemies, ward off hostile influences and bring good luck; divination by omens and portents, dreams, palmistry and physiognomy, by adding up the number-value of a person's name, and by lots – including tossing coins and throwing dice. Astrology was as popular among Jews as among Christians. Amulets and lucky charms were extensively used, like the coral necklaces hung round children's necks as protection against the evil eye and the crimson threads draped over horses' heads for the same purpose. The pentagram or Seal of Solomon and the hexagram or Shield of David were also popular protective symbols.

The prevalent Jewish attitude to magic in the Middle Ages was more tolerant than the Christian one, and this was one reason why the Jewish tradition proved so attractive to Christian occultists. Magic which worked through the divine names and the power of angels was perfectly permissible in principle, though it was considered highly dangerous in unskilled hands, and was condemned if it was intended for immoral purposes or smacked of idolatry. A Jewish writer in 1430, for example, classified as black magicians 'those who offer up their sperm to the spirits or demons with appropriate incantations'.[15] But even magic involving evil spirits, though officially forbidden, was regarded by many authors as legitimate if its motives were pure. If God had made it possible for man to control demons, who was to question the Almighty's dispositions? This attitude is partly responsible for the combination of prayers to God with invocations of demons in the grimoires.

The Devil never bulked as large in Judaism as in Christianity and the demons, though dangerous and frightening, had all been created by God himself and were part of the divine scheme of things. There was not the same deep horror of trafficking with them as in Christianity, in which they were dedicated enemies of the faith. Magic posed no threat to religion and society, and there were no persecutions of sorcerers and witches remotely comparable to the holocausts of witches in Christian Europe. On the other hand, the more relaxed Jewish attitude to magic and demons may have contributed to Christian persecution of the Jews, by reinforcing the belief that all Jews were demon-worshippers and sorcerers.

Accusations of black magic are frequently made against strangers and minorities who do not conform to accepted standards of belief and behaviour. This happened to the early Christians, and the cry attributed to the Jewish mob at the trial of Jesus – 'His blood be upon us and upon our children' – came mercilessly true in the Middle Ages. In Christian eyes the Jews were the children and servants of Satan, who had incited them to crucify Christ. They were suspected of poisoning wells and spreading epidemics, torturing wax images of Jesus, stabbing consecrated hosts, crucifying Christian children and using their blood in the Passover service (a Russian Jew was tried on this charge as late as 1913). Allegations of sorcery, not so much against individual Jews as *en masse*, were a frequent prelude to massacres.

The wicked Jew, shaggy, bearded, horned, filthy, stinking and skilled in evil magic – like Satan – was a stock figure of Christian folk belief. Attempts were made to force all Jews to wear horned hats as a mark of their diabolical allegiance. They were rumoured to worship the Evil One in the form of a cat or a toad in their synagogues, where they invoked his help in their malevolent designs. Many of the accusations made against them were also brought against Christian heretics and witches, and the terms 'synagogue' and 'sabbath' were taken over from Judaism and applied to the meetings of witches.

Alchemy, Astrology and Magic

The Middle Ages inherited alchemy from the ancient world by way of the Arabs. It was a mixture of religion, astrology and metal-working techniques. Through long and taxing operations in his workshop, with devout prayers to God for assistance, the alchemist tried to manufacture the Philosopher's Stone, the perfect gold. The Stone was believed to turn anything it touched into gold, cure all diseases and keep its owner perpetually young. Spiritually, it was the state of superhuman mastery and perfection which is the goal of high magic. Some alchemists, the despised 'puffers', were only interested in the practical business of trying to make gold. Others never went near a workshop and concentrated entirely on spiritual progress. The true art, however, seems to have combined both. The laboratory processes and the chemical changes occurring in the alchemist's materials were part and parcel of parallel spiritual changes taking place in the alchemist himself.

The early development of alchemy occurred in Hellenistic Egypt. Bolus of Mendes, about 200 BC, wrote a book on the making of gold, silver, precious stones and dyes, containing craftsmen's recipes. The emphasis was on changing the colour of a metal, yellowing it or whitening it to make it look like natural gold or silver. Changes of colour were taken to indicate real changes of substance and there were numerous varieties of 'gold' and 'silver' on the market. By about AD 300, in the writings of Zosimus of Panopolis in Egypt, the parallel between gold-making and spiritual progress had been drawn and alchemy had become an amalgam of metallurgy, visionary experience, Greek philosophy, high magic, astrology, pagan myths and mystery religions, gnosticism and Christianity, expressed in a rapturous, high-flown style full of mysterious symbols and cryptic allusions.

Early alchemical texts were put out under the names of Hermes Trismegistus, Isis, Osthanes, Cleopatra, Moses, Aaron, Mary the Jewess (Miriam, the sister of Moses), Pythagoras, Plato and other Greek philosophers and sages, and the Song of Solomon was interpreted as a veiled guide to alchemy. Each of the planets was believed to influence the development of its own metal in the ground, and the metals were arranged in a ladder of perfection, with lead (Saturn) at the foot, through tin (Jupiter), iron (Mars), copper (Venus), mercury (Mercury) and silver (the moon) to gold (the sun) at the top. Since the heavenly bodies were believed to influence human character as well, this was a factor in alchemy's alliance of metallurgical and psychological techniques. The ladder of metals was a stairway of spiritual ascent.

With the Arab conquest of Egypt and much of the eastern Mediterranean area in the seventh century, Greek texts were translated into Arabic and Arab experimenters took up alchemy. The most famous of them was Jabir ibn Hayyan, known in the West as Geber, a Sufi mystic who died about 815. He wrote numerous books, though not all the ones afterwards attributed to him, and adapted Pythagorean and Neoplatonist numerology to alchemical purposes. Books on alchemy, astrology, mathematics and medicine by Geber and other Arabs, including Moorish scholars in Spain, were translated into Latin from the twelfth century onwards and it was through them that alchemy, as distinct from ordinary metal-working, came into medieval Europe. The encyclopedias published in the thirteenth century included material on the art. Roger Bacon (died 1292), a learned Franciscan scientist who acquired an alarming popular reputation as a sorcerer, was particularly interested in alchemical medicine, the manufacture of curative and life-prolonging elixirs.

Alchemical writers continued to cloak their operations in a complex symbolic code and it is no accident that the word 'gibberish' is derived from Geber. Many employed both Christian and sexual symbolism, among them Arnald of Villanova (died 1311), a much-travelled Spanish doctor, alchemist, astrologer and suspected heretic. His difficulties with the ecclesiastical authorities eased for a time after he had successfully used an astrological talisman to treat Pope Boniface VIII for an attack of the stone. Arnald called alchemy the Philosopher's Rosary and likened the process to the Crucifixion followed by the Resurrection.

Some modern magicians believe that alchemical symbolism veiled the secrets of sexual magic, though it is doubtful whether this is true. The use of erotic symbolism by mystically-minded authors does not necessarily imply the use of any sexual technique, and alchemists employed erotic imagery because their art depended on a parallel between the 'life' of metals and human life. Any combination of two materials was called a copulation or marriage, just as the product was a birth and the rising of vapour when a material was heated was the spirit ascending from the corpse at death.

Ramon Lull (died 1315) was an eccentric Spanish polymath and missionary to Islam who was apparently not an alchemist, but many books on the subject were attributed to him. He was believed to have turned twenty-two tons of base metal into gold in the Tower of London as a contribution to the royal treasury during a visit to England. Lull was a pioneer of the art of memory, which arranged ideas in logical patterns so that they could be related, compared and remembered. He was influenced by the Jewish

practice of meditating on the twenty-two H
the figure of twenty-two tons of gold, presumab
diagrams with their circles and squares cont
putation as a magus.

Pope John XXII denounced all alchemists as swin
he died in 1334 he left so much money that it was be
have been an alchemist himself. The same rumour s
the immense wealth of the Order of Knights Templar, v
been suppressed a few years earlier. Nicolas Flamel, a Parisian
businessman, was also believed to have made alchemical gold and
when he died in 1417 his house was sacked by looters in search of it.
The story was that as a young man he bought a beautiful ancient
book of strange symbolic pictures. After years of vainly struggling
to make sense of the pictures, Flamel met a learned Jewish Cabalist
in Spain and with his help succeeded in deciphering the book and
making the Philosopher's Stone. As a result he acquired not only
riches but superhuman longevity, and he was reportedly seen
attending the opera in Paris in 1761.

Going back to the twelfth century, translations from Arab
authors, and in a few cases direct from Greek originals, were
equally important in a revival of sophisticated interest in astrology. Astrology had survived the fall of the Roman Empire but
its principal ancient sources were in Greek, which had then become
a lost language in the West. The leading Arab authority on the
subject was Albumazar (Abu Mashar of Baghdad, 805–85), who
believed that the world had been created with all the planets
together in the first degree of Aries and would end with a similar
conjunction in the last degree of Pisces. Ptolemy had discussed the
'aspects' or relative positions of the planets to each other, and the
Arabs developed the theory that conjunctions of Jupiter, Mars and
Saturn were portents of disaster, plague, famine and war. This
theory created considerable popular alarm at intervals in medieval
Europe. One of these conjunctions, in Aquarius in 1345, was
retrospectively identified as the celestial cause of the outbreak of
the Black Death in 1348.

The Church's attitude to astrology had all along veered between
hostility and acceptance. Any implication that destiny depended
on the planets rather than God could not be tolerated and there
was a settled conviction that the planetary deities, like all the
pagan gods, were evil demons. In 963, for example, Pope John XII
was accused of calling on the aid of Jupiter, Venus and 'other
demons' while gambling. On the other hand, astrology was so
entwined with all areas of life and thought that it was impossible to

it. For one thing, it was essential to medical practice, as
nmended by St Isidore of Seville (died 636), a respected
authority whose books transmitted many elements of Greek and
Roman culture to the Middle Ages. Herbs were still classified by
their planetary correspondences, which affected their gathering
and use. The signs of the zodiac were linked with different parts of
the body so that, for example, a surgeon would not operate on a
wounded knee when the moon was in Capricorn, which rules the
knees.

Many Christians firmly believed in astrology and regarded the
stars as signs through which the Almighty gave warning of his
intentions. And if the planets were powerful demons, it made sense
to keep a wary eye on them. St Thomas Aquinas in the thirteenth
century, following the same line of argument as St Augustine and
others before him, bridged the gap between Christianity and
astrology by saying that the stars governed the behaviour of most
human beings, who were slaves to their appetites. Astrologers
could therefore make accurate predictions about them, but not
about the minority of nobler souls who defied both their fleshly
inclinations and the heavens. 'The stars impel but do not compel'
has ever since remained the astrologer's maxim for reconciling the
irreconcilables of fate and free-will.

In the thirteenth and fourteenth centuries, and on into the
Renaissance period, astrologers were consulted by kings, noblemen, city governments and ecclesiastics, including some of the
popes, and there were chairs of astrology in Italian and Spanish
universities. Michael Scot (died 1235), a Scotsman who was court
astrologer to the Emperor Frederick II, wrote books on astrology,
alchemy, palmistry and physiognomy. He was popularly believed
to be a redoubtable wizard, who employed spirits to fetch him
delicious food by air from the French and Spanish royal kitchens.
He also sailed about in a demonic ship and rode through the sky on
a demonic horse. He is one of the sorcerers and diviners condemned
to eternal torment in Dante's *Inferno*. So is Guido Bonatti, author
of a well-known astrological textbook in the thirteenth century,
who made his living for a time by advising Count Guido de
Montefeltro on propitious moments for raiding his neighbours.
Bonatti himself was eventually killed by bandits, which seems
poetically just.

One of the problems about astrology, from the Church's point of
view, was that it was entangled with magic. It carried with it the
whole network of correspondences between the planets and
animals, plants, metals and other phenomena, including the angels

and demons, which had succeeded to the roles of the classical daemons. Aquinas ruled that it was legitimate, as in medicine, to use herbs or stones whose properties depended on their planetary affiliations. This 'natural magic', as it was called, was really science as understood at the time. But it was not legitimate to employ incantations or letters and symbols inscribed on amulets, which could only work through the activity of demons and implied a pact with the Devil. Amulets of this kind were in widespread use. Gems engraved with the symbols of Aries, Leo or Sagittarius, for example, were considered good for fevers, dropsy and paralysis, and were believed to make their owners talented, fluent and respected.

Writers like Roger Bacon, Avicenna, Peter of Abano, Arnald of Villanova and Cecco D'Ascoli believed that astrological 'images' of this kind were effective. They were also interested in the invocation of angels and spirits, classified by their planetary correspondences, for purposes of high magic. As in the grimoires, the correct rituals and incantations would compel the spirits to answer the magician's questions and supply him with occult knowledge and power. And an astrological image or talisman could be regarded as the container of a spirit which had been drawn down into it, so that it was a portable magical power-source. Ecclesiastical hackles inevitably rose at this unhealthy tampering with suspect forces. Bacon was often in hot water with his superiors, probably because of his interest in magic. Avicenna (Abu Ali ibn Sina, 980–1037) was an Arab philosopher, scientist and authority on medicine, also suspect as a magician. Peter of Abano, an Italian doctor who wrote on magic, prophecy and physiognomy, was twice tried by the Inquisition for practising magic. He was acquitted the first time and died during the second trial in 1316. His body was burned to ashes, which suggests what the verdict would have been had he lived.

Cecco D'Ascoli, who held the chair of astrology at Bologna University, was condemned by the Inquisition and he and his books were burned together at the stake in Florence in 1327. One of his offenses, apparently, was his insistence that Christ came into the world in accordance with the principles of astrology and that the course of the Saviour's earthly life was accurately foreshadowed in his horoscope, which Cecco had calculated. Cecco also believed that evil spirits could be controlled by ritual magic and astrological images. He supplied the names of powerful demons, which would give the magician reliable answers to questions if provided with a sacrifice of human blood and the flesh of a dead man or a cat, though he did point out that this 'Zoroastrian art' was dangerous and contrary to the Christian faith.

A magical textbook called *Picatrix* circulated widely in the Middle Ages in manuscript, but its reputation was so black that it was never printed. It is spiritually descended from the Hermetica and much of it is Graeco-Egyptian in origin. Written in the tenth century in Arabic, it was translated into Spanish in the thirteenth and subsequently into Latin. Peter of Abano was accused of having borrowed from it. It concentrates on the making of images in which the powers of planets, zodiac signs and decans are captured, and gives lists of planetary correspondences with animals, plants, stones, colours and perfumes. The images can be used for every purpose from alleviating toothache to attracting love, escaping from prison or achieving success in any field. There are also incantations invoking the planets. The one to Saturn hails the planet as the Supreme Master, the Cold, the Sterile, the Mournful, the Pernicious, the Sage and Solitary, the Impenetrable. 'Thou who hast cares greater than any other, who knowest neither pleasure nor joy; Thou, the old and cunning, master of all artifice, deceitful, wise and judicious; Thou who bringest prosperity or ruin, and makest men to be happy or unhappy. I conjure Thee, O Supreme Father, by Thy great benevolence and Thy generous beauty, to do for me what I ask. . . .'[16] The magician seems to be concentrating his imagination on the planet's nature and attributes, clothing himself with them as it were, so as to make himself the vehicle of its influence.

Other methods of divination trespassed on forbidden magical territory. One of them was the old art of scrying in a mirror or any reflecting surface, in which moving shapes and figures are seen. Christians and Jews in the Middle Ages used crystals, mirrors, fingernails, liquid wax, water or a mixture of soot and oil in the palm of the hand for scrying, often to identify thieves or discern the whereabouts of stolen property, and also to see into the future. But the figures seen were now officially classified as demons and scrying therefore became a way of summoning up spirits. In 1318 Pope John XXII accused several clerics at his court of scrying for this purpose. A few years later he issued the bull *Super illius specula* against malefactors who made a pact with Satan, offered sacrifices to demons and employed talismans, rings, mirrors and other devices as containers of spirits, whose power was used in magic. The Pope ordered all magical textbooks to be surrendered to the ecclesiastical authorities for burning. The growing fear of demonic magic was a major influence on the development of medieval beliefs about witchcraft.

Witchcraft and Sorcery

It is not easy to disentangle European witchcraft from other varieties of magic. A distinction is sometimes drawn by anthropologists working outside Europe between a witch, who possesses innate powers, and a sorcerer, who uses 'medicine' or equipment: herbs, potions, bits and pieces of animals, and so on. In Europe, however, both the witch and the sorcerer may have innate powers and both are likely to use 'medicine'. Nor is witchcraft in medieval and modern Europe definable simply as feminine magic. Men were also accused of it, though the typical witch of popular stereotypes is a woman and fear of the evilness of the female is an important factor in witchcraft beliefs.

The various words used for witches and witchcraft in European languages are vague and can cover almost any kind of magical activity. They are not normally applied to the intellectual high magician. In Elizabethan England a man who summoned up spirits to gain occult knowledge could be called a witch, but in general witchcraft is low magic and those accused of practising it were further down the intellectual scale. The most common medieval Latin terms for a witch were *striga*, 'screech-owl', meaning an evil night-flying creature, and *malefica*, 'evil-doer'. *Maleficium* originally meant any crime or harmful act, whether involving magic or not, but from the fourth century on it meant evil magic.

At popular levels, however, witchcraft was not invariably associated with evil. Three types of witch can be roughly distinguished. The first is the local 'wise woman' (or her rarer male equivalent, known in England as a 'cunning man'). She uses spells, including herbal remedies and scraps of Christian prayers, to cure disease and barrenness, smooth the path of love, and remove the effects of spells cast by a hostile witch. She also interprets omens and advises on courses of action, identifies thieves, locates stolen property and gives news of missing persons. Much of what she does is beneficial, but she can work destructive magic as well. She can put a curse on an enemy, supply poisons, infect people and cattle with mysterious ailments, injure crops, hinder love and prevent procreation. It is often believed that she comes from a long line of witches and inherited her innate powers from her mother or grandmother, who taught her the secret lore of her craft.

This witch has an accepted place in the community and has survived, here and there, down to the present day. Her witchcraft is believed in, by herself and others, because it 'works': partly by coincidence; partly because people unconsciously make it work; partly because some of her herbs and remedies may be genuinely effective; and partly because she may have clairvoyant and psychic powers developed to an unusually high degree. The same factors apply to the magic of a second type of witch.

The second type is the black witch, who is totally and unfailingly evil. This is the woman (or less often the man) who is believed to be filled with an appalling inward malevolence and spite, which she projects against her victims by ill-wishing, overlooking or for-speaking them, with an impulse, a glance or a word. She will also use spells, incantations and repulsive concoctions. The stereotype is the hideous, toothless crone, muttering curses while she stirs a nauseating brew in a cauldron; but a witch of this type is not always either old or ugly. Because she is evil and malevolent, she is a social reject, though in real life the rejection may come before the malevolence. In many cases people began to think themselves bewitched after they had given a neighbour justifiable cause for offence. An English Puritan minister, George Gifford, wrote in 1587: 'Some woman doth fall out bitterly with her neighbour: there followeth some great hurt, either that God hath permitted the devil to vex him: or otherwise. There is a suspicion conceived. Within a few years after she is in some jar with another. He is also plagued. This is noted of all. Great fame is spread of the matter. Mother W. is a witch.'[17]

Many accusations of witchcraft sprang from neighbourhood tensions in this way. One of the social roles of belief in witches was to reinforce accepted moral standards (though this could not have been much comfort to Mother W. and her kind). It was not wise to treat a neighbour unkindly, because one might have cause to regret it. Belief in witchcraft also supplied an explanation of otherwise inexplicable misfortune and some armour against it. There were magical methods of protection against witchcraft. When a victim was bewitched, there were ways of identifying the witch and breaking the spell, most drastically by lynching her or by demanding that the authorities try her and execute her, for her death would automatically dissolve her magic.

The black witch appeared to be human but she could readily change shape, especially at night when she would turn into a carnivorous creature – a bird of prey or a cat or a wolf – and sally out to kill babies in their cots, attack adults sexually and murderously, and bring them terrifying dreams. The 'screech-owls' mentioned by Ovid, which attacked children in the night, are an example and there were similar beliefs all over Europe, among both Christians and Jews. These witches were evil spirits, whose human form was only one of their many disguises. Lovers of darkness, they reversed all normal and decent values, and they were often thought to operate at night in packs.

These beliefs helped to create the third type of witch figure. This is the Satanist witch, who is again more often female than male. She is no longer an evil spirit herself but is closely allied with demons, through whom she works her magic. She is a worshipper of the Devil, and therefore a heretic, and meets with others of her kind at the 'synagogue' or 'sabbath', where unholy rites are celebrated. The Satanist witch is the enemy not merely of individual neighbours but of the whole society. She does not appear on the scene until very late and whether any witches of this kind ever existed is a disputed question.

Some of the folk beliefs which went into the making of the black witch and her descendant, the Satanist witch, may have been influenced by the feats attributed to shamans. The picture of hostile witchcraft in the Icelandic sagas was apparently coloured by the shamanism of the Lapps and other peoples of north-eastern Europe. Among the powers of witches in the sagas are the ability to change shape and to control spirits in animal form. There is no sign of any gathering of witches to revel together and plot evil, like the later witches' sabbath, but a witch while asleep or in trance can travel great distances, observe events, injure people and fight other witches. This travelling in trance or dream is called 'riding the *gand*', and the *gand*, it seems, was originally the shaman's guardian spirit in animal or other form.[18]

The fear of the night-flying witch has remained alive for centuries. The Church at first tried to discourage it. An ecclesiastical regulation called the Canon Episcopi, quoted by a German monk named Regino of Prüm about 906, says that there are wicked women who believe that they ride out on animals at dead of night with the pagan goddess Diana and a horde of other women, covering great distances. Many people believe in the night-ride, the Canon says, but it is really a dream or hallucination stimulated by the Devil to gain a hold on women's minds. A hundred years later another German ecclesiastic, Burchard of Worms, again condemned this belief and other related fantasies: that women, while apparently asleep in bed, flew up in the air and fought amongst themselves, or went on marauding expeditions and killed people and ate their flesh.

Although at this stage the night-ride is considered a delusion, it is a delusion induced by a real Satan to fasten his talons on human souls. Gradually, as the popular beliefs persisted and the Devil's power loomed ever greater, churchmen came to accept that witches did fly at night, through the magic of the Evil One, and that it was not merely a dream. Eventually it became a stock charge against Satanist witches that they flew to the sabbath on broomsticks or demonic animals.

The accusations of Satanism made against heretics were another source of the later witch stereotype. Heretics had been brought up in the true faith and had rejected it. It followed, or seemed to the Church to follow, that they had turned from the service of Christ to the worship of the Devil. They must therefore, like black witches, be dedicated to the total reversal of all civilized and Christian standards. From the twelfth and thirteenth centuries on, as one buzzing nest of heresy after another was smoked out, the Waldensians, the Cathars, the Luciferans and other heretical groups were accused of holding secret meetings by night with feasts and indiscriminate orgies in honour of Satan. He appeared to them as a cat, a toad, a goat or in human or semi-human form, and they kissed his hindquarters in obscene homage. They hated the Church, renounced Christ, spurned the cross, the Mass and all the sacraments, and desecrated hosts. To defy God and please the Enemy, they committed murders and injured faithful Christians in any way they could. Suspected devil-worshippers were forced by torture to confess to these accusations, and a pattern of Satanist behaviour was created, which was subsequently applied wholesale to witches.

Meanwhile, the developing fear of Satanism as a menace to the Church and society was stimulated by the sensational trial of the Templars. In 1307 French and English members of the Order of Knights Templar, famed for its military prowess in the Holy Land and its immense wealth, were tried on charges of worshipping the Devil in the form of a cat; worshipping an idol named Baphomet and anointing it with the fat of murdered children; copulating with demons which took the form of beautiful girls; denying God, Christ, the Virgin Mary and the saints; stamping, spitting or urinating on crucifixes; ritual homosexuality; and tampering with the Mass by omitting to consecrate the host.

Large numbers of Templars were tortured and brainwashed into confessing to the charges, though most of them afterwards denied that their admissions were true. The Grand Master of the order and the Preceptor of Normandy repudiated their confessions before they were burned alive in Paris in 1314. Over a hundred other Templars were sent to the stake in Paris. The prosecution, combined with a propaganda campaign against the order, was initiated by Philip IV of France, largely for political and financial motives: the order's confiscated riches went straight into his coffers. There is no reason to think that the accusations were true, but they made a profound impression and surrounded the Knights Templar with an aura of mysterious evil which has lasted ever since.

Politically inspired charges of sorcery were nothing new, but there was a rash of them in the early fourteenth century. In 1308 the Bishop of Troyes was accused of murdering Jeanne of Navarre, the wife of Philip IV, by magic. He was alleged to have consulted a Jewish sorcerer, a witch and finally a Dominican friar, who conjured up the Devil. The bishop was then supposed to have tried to kill the queen with a wax image, pierced with pins and thrown into a fire. He was also supposed to keep by him in a bottle a demon which spied on his servants. After several years the charges against him were dropped. In 1315 Enguerrand de Marigny, a powerful royal official, was accused of being implicated in a plot to murder Louis X of France with wax images. He was hanged and the images were exhibited on his scaffold.

In 1317 Pope John XXII, who persistently accused his opponents of heresy, sorcery and demon-worship, arrested Hugh Géraud, Bishop of Cahors. The bishop was accused of buying three wax images and a supply of poison from a Jewish sorcerer. The images were baptized with the names of the pope and two leading members of his court, and were wrapped in strips of parchment inscribed with spells against the intended victims. They were then concealed with the poison in loaves of bread, to be smuggled into the papal palace at Avignon. Hugh Géraud was burned at the stake and his ashes were thrown into the Rhône.

A case of ritual magic to recover stolen money was tried in Paris in 1323. The Abbot of Sarcelles was found guilty of employing a sorcerer to discover the thief. This the magician intended to do by summoning up the demon Berith, while standing in a magic circle made of the skin of a cat which had been fed on bread moistened with holy water and holy oil. The sorcerer was burned and the abbot was sentenced to prison for life.

In 1324 in Ireland there was the curious case of the Lady Alice Kyteler, which evidently arose out of acute family tensions. Lady Alice was an elderly and wealthy woman. Her step-children said she had bewitched and murdered three husbands in succession, so as to inherit their property to the children's disadvantage. Allegedly, her fourth husband became suspicious when he fell ill of a mysterious wasting disease. An investigation was undertaken by the Bishop of Ossory, who had recently denounced an anti-Christian sect which he said had appeared in the neighbourhood. Alice Kyteler fled to England, but her supposed accomplices were brutally interrogated. Some of them were burned and she was condemned in her absence as a heretic and magician. She had denied Christ and the Church, sacrificed animals to evil spirits which taught her how to work magic, and copulated with them. They included her familiar demon, named Robin, who appeared variously as a cat, a black dog and a black man. She and her accomplices held orgiastic meetings by night. They made magic powders and ointments by boiling worms, dead men's flesh and other noxious ingredients in a human skull, and adapted the Christian ritual of excommunication to put fatal curses on their enemies.

The odd thing about this case, which was the only one of its kind in Ireland until the seventeenth century, is that the Lady Alice is in many ways a Satanist witch years ahead of her time. The Bishop of Ossory seems to have piled charges of heresy, trafficking with demons and perversion of Christian rites onto what were originally accusations of low magic. He was probably influenced by the trial of the Templars, and by the recent French cases involving a similar mixture.

There is no sign of the witches' sabbath in other trials for *maleficium* and invocation of demons at this period. Norman Cohn has shown that the supposed confessions of Anne-Marie de Georgel and Catherine Delort of Toulouse in 1335, which were thought to provide the earliest accounts of the sabbath, are forgeries of much later date.[19] There was, however, a mounting fear of demons and magic associated with them. The fear was not shared by everyone. On the contrary, at a manor court in Yorkshire in 1337 a man complained that he had paid threepence-halfpenny for a demon, which one of his neighbours had agreed to supply, but the demon had never been delivered.

In the late 1360s Nicolas Eymeric, Inquisitor General of Aragon, wrote an inquisitor's guide in which he confirmed that the invocation of demons by magic implied a pact with them and was heretical. He himself had seized and burned numerous textbooks of ritual magic containing instructions for summoning up demons. He also said that scrying and other forms of divination relying on demons were heretical. He excluded palmistry from this stricture, but he regarded practising astrology as confirmatory evidence in cases of suspected demonic magic. In 1374 Pope Gregory XI told an inquisitor in France that most magic was worked with the assistance of demons and was therefore heretical and within the Inquisition's jurisdiction.

The effect of this attitude was to link witchcraft, as a variety of low magic, with the invocation of demons. There were trials in France in the 1390s, not involving the Inquisition, in which women originally accused of bewitching their victims were tortured into confessing that they had summoned evil spirits to help them. In a similar case in Geneva in 1401, a woman who specialized in identifying thieves was tortured until she admitted that she did it with the aid of the Devil.

About 1400 there were several trials of men and women from the Simmenthal, near Berne in Switzerland, not conducted by the Inquisition but by the civil authorities, and some were found guilty and burned. They were accused of causing storms, striking people with lightning, transferring crops from other farmers' fields to their own, causing sterility and madness, making love potions, seeing events occurring far away and predicting the future. They were also tortured into confessing that they belonged to an organized Satanist group. Candidates for initiation into the group had to renounce Christ in a church on a Sunday and do homage to the Devil, who appeared in human form as 'the Little Master'. They then drank a liquid made by cooking the bodies of murdered children in a cauldron. The group used ointments to turn themselves into animals, make themselves invisible and fly through the air to distant places by night.

These confessions were written up, about 1435, in the *Formicarius*, a book by a Dominican theologian named Johann Nider. Nider believed they were true, though he still regarded night-flying as a diabolically inspired delusion. He tells a story about a woman who rubbed herself with flying ointment and muttered the appropriate spells in the presence of several witnesses. She then fell into a disturbed sleep. When she woke up, she insisted that she had been out riding through the air with the Lady Diana and other women, but the witnesses testified that she had never left the room. Later recipes for the flying ointment include aconite and belladonna, which might cause delusions, and the conviction that witches could fly, as well as other details of their activities, rested partly on the beliefs of people who had experienced vivid dreams or hallucinations.

Between 1421 and 1440 the Inquisition held a series of trials in the Dauphiné district of south-eastern France. The suspects, most of whom were peasants, were tortured into confessing to the usual acts of harmful magic and to summoning evil spirits in animal or human form to help them. Many of these spirits seem to have been country boggarts and fairies, with homely names like Pierre or Jean, Griffart or Ginifert. But the suspects were also forced to confess that they belonged to an organized sect, which had existed for many years. They flew by night to meet at 'synagogues', riding on sticks smeared with ointment or on demonic horses. There they worshipped Satan, who appeared as a black cat or a man with shining eyes, wearing a crown and black clothes. They feasted, danced and copulated with each other, with their familiar spirits and sometimes with the Devil himself.

Many other details of the confessions afterwards became part of the stock pattern of witch behaviour. The witches made a formal pact with the Devil, paid him homage, gave him the obscene kiss and sacrificed children and black cats to him. They made magic potions from the children's bodies. The Devil ordered them never to make the sign of the cross, go to Mass or adore the consecrated host. He taught them how to work evil magic and they reported on the harm they had done since previous meetings. In some cases he made a mark on their bodies as a sign of their allegiance to him.

Similiar confessions were extracted under torture by the civil authorities in the district of Valais in Switzerland in 1428, where seven hundred people were said to belong to a Satanist sect. Their Master had promised them that they would triumph over Christianity. They renounced God, Christ and the Church, flew to meetings where they worshipped the Devil, and also flew about at night, entering houses and stealing children, whom they cooked and ate. Persecution continued in the Valais and spread into Savoy.

The emergence of the Satanist witch and the sabbath in the Alpine valleys seems to have been the result of renewed efforts to stamp out the Waldensians, who had retreated in large numbers into the French and Swiss Alps, where they continued to practise their faith. But the new stereotype soon appeared elsewhere. Based on the Church's old conviction that all beliefs and practices of which it disapproved were demonically inspired, it merged two anti-social figures into one. The Satanist perversions attributed to the heretic were combined with the night-flying, infanticide, cannibalism, demonic connections and harmful magic of the black witch. The effect was to make the black witch, who had long been blamed for poor harvests, mysterious diseases, cot-deaths and every kind of undeserved misfortune, into a member of an

organized conspiracy, directed by the Devi
structure of Christian society.

Belief in this organized conspiracy took a long time t
(and never did in some quarters) and meanwhile the ca
against evil magic of a more individual variety continued. In t
1430s and 1440s Pope Eugenius IV pressed the Inquisition to root
out magicians and diviners, who made pacts with Satan and
sacrificed to demons. In 1431 Joan of Arc was executed, primarily
for political reasons, as a heretic. Her mysterious influence over the
Dauphin, her claim to be guided by angelic voices and her successes
in battle against the English gave her a dangerous reputation for
supernatural powers, and her enemies denounced her as a black
witch in league with Satan. At Troyes in 1429 a Franciscan friar,
sent to parley with her, protected himself by sprinkling holy water
and making the sign of the cross. She smiled at him and assured
him she would not fly away.

In the early stages of Joan's trial some play was made with
vague allegations of witchcraft, involving dancing round the
Ladies' Tree or Fairies' Tree near her home at Domrémy. The tree
stood close to a healing spring and had no doubt been venerated
since pagan times. Much more damaging suspicions were roused by
Joan's angelic voices and visions, which could be put down to
demons. In the end the accusations of witchcraft were dropped and
she was condemned principally because she preferred her private
channels of communication with the divine to the Church's. She
was burned alive in Rouen and her ashes were thrown into the
river. She was then nineteen years old. Five hundred years later, in
1920, she was canonized.

In 1440 Gilles de Rais, a cultivated nobleman who had been one
of Joan's companions-in-arms, was executed at Nantes. A sadist
who preyed on children, he was accused of heresy, the sex murders
of numerous children, and the invocation of demons. His confession, made under threat of torture, contained details so
revolting that the crucifix in the courtroom was hastily veiled.
Though his enemies took full advantage of the sinister rumours
which had been circulating about him, the rumours themselves
seem to have been founded on fact. Desperate for money, he had
hired a succession of alchemists, who failed to make gold for him.
He also employed magicians, including Francesco Prelati, a
Florentine who claimed to be in constant touch with a demon
named Barron, though the sagacious spirit somehow never appeared when Gilles was present. Gilles signed pacts in his own
blood, which Prelati was told to offer to the demon in return for

out to no effect. He also offered,
t, eyes and blood of a child, but was
en rejected. Attempts were made to
b and other satraps of evil with magic
lles was mercifully strangled before his
escaped with a brief stay in prison.

he case of the Duchess of Gloucester made
as accused of attempting to murder Henry
age representing him. Her accomplices were
an astrologer and ritual magician, a priest
nd Margery Jourdemain, known as the Witch
of Eye. chess's defence was that she had consulted
Bolingbroke tain love potions because she wanted to bear her
husband a child. She was found guilty of treason and sent to
prison. Southwell's function had been to say Mass over 'certain
instruments' which Bolingbroke used in magic. He died in prison
and Margery Jourdemain was burned at Smithfield. Bolingbroke
was hung, drawn and quartered, after being put on public show
with his paraphernalia at Paul's Cross. He wore his wizard's robe,
held a sword and a sceptre, and sat in his magician's chair, which
had four swords attached to it. There were also astrological
'images', made of wax, silver and other metals.

These trials must have contributed to an uneasy impression that
evil magic was more prevalent than met the eye. At the same time
news of the sabbath was spreading. Martin Le Franc's poem *Le
Champion des Dames* (1440) refers to thousands of old hags flying
on sticks to the synagogue on Walpurgis Night. *Errores Gaz-
ariorum* (from *gazarius*, 'Cathar'), an anonymous tract written in
Savoy about 1450, describes the witches' synagogue with most of
the standard details of worshipping Satan, cannibalism, feasting,
dancing and orgies. Witches who flew on broomsticks were
discovered in Normandy in 1453 and a priest named Guillaume
Edeline confessed to worshipping the Devil at their meetings.
Writing in 1458, Nicolas Jacquier, who served as an inquisitor in
France and Bohemia, maintained that the Canon Episcopi was out
of date and that the witches' night-ride was a reality. The
Inquisition was hunting witches in Gascony and the Dauphiné at
this time and persecutions were continuing in Switzerland and
Savoy.

There was a sudden flare-up in 1459–60 at Arras, where witches
were called *vaudois* (from Waldensians). Thirty-four people were
arrested, twelve were burned and others were imprisoned. In a
progression subsequently all too familiar, a suspected witch was

tortured into naming confederates he had seen at the sabbath. These suspects were interrogated and forced to name more witches, and so it went on, until so much hostility and scepticism were aroused that the prosecutors reluctantly suspended their activities.

The emphasis at Arras was more on Satanism and the sabbath than on the harm which the suspects were supposed to have caused by magic. But plagues and disasters continued to arouse popular suspicions of black witchcraft, with or without the additional bogy of Devil-worship. During an epidemic at Marmande in 1453 several people suspected of causing it by magic were tortured and burned by a mob. In the same year a man was burned at Konstanz, on the Swiss-German border, for causing a hailstorm of exceptional violence. When the vineyards in Lorraine were seriously damaged by a late frost in 1456, the locals seized suspects and burned them. The authorities at Metz reported that some of them had confessed to attending the witches' sabbath. Nine women were burned in the same area in 1481 for damaging the crops with rain in June, and again in 1488 after a cold and stormy summer twenty-eight people were executed.

At Chamonix in Savoy in 1462 a woman found guilty of prostituting herself to men and demons at the synagogue and eating children's flesh was sentenced to sit naked on red-hot iron for three minutes before going to the stake. A man who had trampled on the host was to have the offending foot cut off before he was burned. A trial in 1480 at Calcinato, near Brescia in northern Italy, shows that the local wise woman was in danger of prosecution as well as the reputed black witch. Maria 'la Medica' admitted that the Devil, whom she called Lucibel, had enabled her to work healing magic. She confessed to worshipping him at meetings where God and Christ were formally denied and Mass was said in Lucibel's honour.

Many people in authority were still decidedly sceptical. Against them, in 1484, Pope Innocent VIII issued the bull *Summis desiderantes affectibus*, which put a seal of papal approval on witch hunting. The bull says that in various areas of Germany, including the districts of Mainz, Cologne, Trier, Salzburg and Bremen, numerous men and women have renounced the Christian faith and given themselves to demons. They use incantations and charms to kill human beings, cause disease, harm crops and cattle, hinder the procreation of children and commit all sorts of abominations at the instigation of the Enemy. Two Dominicans are authorized to proceed against this heretical depravity and the faithful are ordered to give them every assistance, on pain of incurring the wrath of Almighty God.

The two Dominicans were Jakob Sprenger (died 1495) and Heinrich Krämer (died 1505), also known as Institoris. Together they wrote the famous *Malleus Maleficarum*, or Hammer of Witches, published in 1486 and frequently reprinted in the sixteenth and seventeenth centuries. They had been busy smelling out witches in Germany and the Tyrol, but had encountered resistance from the local authorities, who denied that Satanist witchcraft existed in their areas. The papal bull does not mention the sabbath and there is scarcely anything about it in the *Malleus* either, which indicates that belief in it was still far from securely established.

The *Malleus* is a ponderous, pedantic work, which would be a strong candidate for a prize as the dullest of the world's influential books. Witch hunting on the grand scale did not begin for seventy years after its appearance, and by then it was considered authoritative, largely because of the backing which Innocent VIII had given its authors. In its own time it was written principally to combat scepticism, expatiate on the harm done by witches and lay down merciless rules for the interrogation and trial of suspects. It begins by quoting and then contradicting the view that 'there is not such a thing as magic, that it only exists in the imagination of those men who ascribe natural effects, the causes whereof are not known, to witchcraft and spells'. This strikingly modern opinion, the *Malleus* says, 'is contrary to the true faith, which teaches us that certain angels fell from heaven and are now devils, and we are bound to acknowledge that by their very nature they can do many wonderful things which we cannot do'.[20]

It is through these demons that witchcraft works. Witches make a pact with Satan, worship him and couple with him. They cherish a profound hatred of Christianity and the Church, and desecrate Christian ceremonies and symbols. The *Malleus* distinguishes between witchcraft and the magic of the grimoires: 'for witchcraft is not taught in books, nor is it practised by the learned, but by the altogether uneducated.'[21] Sorcery, scrying and the interpretation of dreams are condemned as open invocation of demons. Astrology, palmistry and the observation of omens depend on tacit invocation of demons. But witchcraft is a different and far worse crime, because its intentions are always evil and it rests on allegiance to Satan. The sorcerer and the diviner invoke the Devil's aid, but the witch surrenders herself to him utterly, body and soul.

In case this distinction might allow the wise woman to escape the net, care was taken to bring her into it. There are three kinds of witches: those who can injure but not cure; those who can do both; and those who through a mysterious arrangement with Satan can heal but not injure. For protection against bewitchment, the *Malleus* recommends the apparatus of Christian magic: piety and prayer; the sign of the cross; sprinkling with holy water; the use of herbs and salt which have been blessed by a priest; pilgrimage to a saint's shrine; and exorcism in cases of demonic possession.

Christians had long tended to blame all the world's wrongs on the Devil. Theologians emphasized the gigantic power of the Evil One, his infinite resourcefulness and his relentless hatred of the human race. William of Auvergne in the thirteenth century, for example, regarded the life of man as one long struggle against diabolical attack. 'In reading his description of the functions of the different classes of demons it would seem that almost all human ills were their work.'[22] Aquinas discussed the powers of demons and their ability to create apparently miraculous effects. At the same time demons were appearing more frequently in monstrous and terrifying forms in art. The lengths to which attribution of all ills to them could go is shown by a case at Bologna in 1468, when a man was found guilty of keeping a brothel staffed by demons in female form.

The beliefs current about the Waldensians, Cathars and other heretics suggested the existence of a human fifth column, dedicated to Satan's cause. The dualism of which the heretics were accused, the belief in a great power of evil who was the equal and opponent of God, though theologically improper, seemed to many Christians to explain how evil could exist in a world ruled by a God who was good. And the forces of evil seemed to be gaining ground. The Devil cast a deepening shadow in the fourteenth and fifteenth centuries, with wars and peasant revolts, famines and epidemics, including the Black Death (which some Christians attributed to the demonic magic of the Jews). The Church was under fierce attack from reformers. Medieval society was changing, the manorial system was breaking down, familiar institutions were in decline. 'Deprived of the old securities, people responded in panic that at that particular time found vent in terror of witchcraft.'[23]

The prosecutors at Arras sounded a note which was to be heard again in the centuries ahead. They were battling, they said, with a formidable conspiracy against Christian society. One third of all nominal Christians were secretly in league with the Evil One and unless these covert traitors were exposed and exterminated, wars and sedition would multiply and the whole social order would be destroyed, the young would rise against their elders and the poor would overthrow their masters.

Writers on witchcraft were already beginning to find its roots in the resentment of the oppressed. *La Vauderye de Lyonois*, a pamphlet of about 1460, says that people become witches in the hope of gaining wealth and sensual pleasure and of revenging themselves for their wrongs. Petrus Mamoris, writing about 1462, ascribed the spread of witchcraft in France to the devastation and suffering caused by the Hundred Years War. A few of the poor and downtrodden may have turned to the worship of Satan in all reality, once the possibility and methods of doing so had been brought to their attention by the trials of heretics and witches. But these trials were only the overture to the full horrors of the witch mania of the sixteenth and seventeenth centuries.

3
The Renaissance and Witch Mania

High magic reached its apogee in the Renaissance with the revival of Neoplatonism, the rediscovery of the Hermetica and the Christian adoption of the Cabala. These developments were part of the triumph of humanism, which dominated Italian culture by 1450 and then spread north of the Alps. Humanism implied a new conviction of the worth and potential stature of man, a conviction which was carried to its peak by the Renaissance magi – Ficino, Pico della Mirandola, Agrippa, Paracelsus, Dee, Bruno, and even the legendary Faust, the Mr Hyde to their Dr Jekyll. They restored the classical figure of the 'man of power' to his pedestal as a master of esoteric wisdom and a virtual god. 'There is this diversity between God and man', Pico said, 'that God contains in himself all things because he is their source, whereas man contains all things because he is their centre.' The corollary was that: 'There is no latent force in heaven or earth which the magician cannot release by proper inducements.'[1]

Medieval Christianity had idealized the monk, who renounced

the world and the flesh to devote himself humbly to the worship of God. The Renaissance turned to the ideal of 'the universal man', the man who values all aspects of his nature, who proudly attempts to experience and master all things. This was the old pagan ideal of high magic. The new breed of magus rebelled against the medieval brand of rationalism, believing that true wisdom is acquired by other means than reason, through imagination and inspiration. Paracelsus contrasted magic as a great secret wisdom with reason as a great public folly. A man, he said, is what he imagines himself to be: with the implication that, on the principle of imitative magic, the way to approach God is to think oneself divine.

This rejection of reason enabled Renaissance magic to contribute to the development of modern science and technology in the sixteenth and seventeenth centuries. The relationship between renascent magic and emerging science was double-edged. On one side, because their view of man demanded it, magicians clung to a picture of the universe which science came to deny. But on the other, a distrust of medieval attitudes, an interest in 'natural magic' or the exploitation of the mysterious properties of natural phenomena, and a driving belief in man's ability to be master of all he surveyed stimulated scientific and technological progress. The Renaissance magi, ironically enough, helped to create the new mechanical concept of the universe which by the end of the seventeenth century seemed to have made magic obsolete.

The Renaissance was not a sudden break in the continuity of history and humanists interested in magic were influenced by their medieval predecessors. But they also drew directly on the high magic of the classical pagan world, whose texts were now being rediscovered and made widely available as a result of the invention of printing in the fifteenth century. These texts enjoyed high prestige in an age passionately addicted to Greek and Roman civilization. In Plato and the Neoplatonists, the Pythagorean tradition, the Orphic hymns and the Hermetica, a profound secret wisdom was discerned, going back to earliest times, inspired by God long before the coming of Christ, known only to an elite and largely lost sight of during the dark and barbarous Middle Ages. The same wisdom could be discovered in the Cabala, in the hieroglyphs of ancient Egypt and beneath the surface of classical mythology, where it had been cloaked in fable to conceal it from the common herd.

This enticing conclusion was assisted by confusion about dates and influences. Pythagoras was thought to have drawn his teachings from the Cabala. Plato was dated after the Hermetica, by which he was supposed to have been influenced, and when a more accurate date for the Hermetica was established by Isaac Casaubon in 1614, writers like Robert Fludd and Athanasius Kircher ignored it. The Renaissance magi found the same doctrines in different traditions because their sources were generally late and did in fact contain important ideas in common. Their Platonism was largely Neoplatonism and their gnostic, Hermetic, Pythagorean and Orphic lore also came to them from the last centuries of antiquity.

The later pagan writers themselves had brought the old classical myths up to date by finding hidden meanings in them. Christian writers had followed suit and in the twelfth century John of Salisbury anticipated the Renaissance attitude by thinking pagan religion worthy of study, 'not out of any respect for false deities, but because under cover of words truths are hidden which may not be revealed to the vulgar'.[2] Most of the Renaissance magi had no intention of attacking Christianity. They believed that the secret wisdom of antiquity had anticipated Christian doctrine. But the sages whom they revered, the *prisci theologi* or 'pristine theologians', to whom the truth had been revealed before the coming of Christ, were also the *prisci magi* of classical tradition – Hermes Trismegistus, Zoroaster, Moses, Orpheus, Pythagoras – the founding fathers of high magic. The magicians consequently had an uneasy relationship with official Christianity. The ideal Renaissance magus, bestriding his world like a colossus, was hardly a promising candidate as an obedient son of Holy Church.

Many Renaissance works of art were essays in the hidden truth discerned behind both paganism and Christianity. For example, there was much interest in groups of three in pagan mythology, related to the God of Christianity, who is both Three and One, and to the Pythagorean theory of the number three as a pair of opposites with the unity that reconciles and transcends them. The myth that Mars and Venus, the opposites of war and love, had a daughter named Harmony was believed to inculcate this lesson, and Botticelli's *Mars and Venus* is an exercise on this theme. The classical image of the Three Graces and the story of the Judgment of Paris were treated in the same spirit.

Renaissance architecture was influenced by similar considerations. The only surviving classical work on the subject was the *De Architectura* of Vitruvius, which showed that a man's body with arms and legs extended fitted into both a circle and a square.

Since the circle could stand for eternity and God, and the square for solidity and the earth, the figure was understood as a demonstration of the theory of macrocosm and microcosm, that man is a miniature replica of the world and God. It was this theory which justified the magical view of man as potentially divine. Renaissance architects accordingly believed that buildings should be designed in relation to the proportions of the human body, as an image of the divine harmony of the universe. The circle, as a symbol of both God and man, came into architecture in the centralized church, with its focal point in the middle instead of at one end. The religio-magical design of the Gothic church, whose distant altar and soaring arches stood for aspiration and ascent to God in heaven, was replaced by the religio-magical symbolism of the centralized church with its crowning dome, intended to ensure the union of man at the centre with God in the infinite.

From Ficino to Bruno

Marsilio Ficino (1433–99) was a philosopher, priest, physician and classical scholar, brought up in the household of Cosimo de Medici in Florence. He was about to set to work on a translation of Plato when a Greek manuscript of the Hermetica arrived, brought from Macedonia by one of the Medici agents. The revered Plato was put aside in favour of this new and superior attraction and Ficino translated the Hermetica first. One of the texts, the *Asclepius*, had long been available in a Latin version and with Ficino's translation, which came out in 1471 and was frequently reprinted, the Hermetica became an influential fount of occult doctrine.

Hermes Trismegistus was already a well-known name in connection with alchemy, magic and astrological talismans, and the reverence of classical authors for the mysterious wisdom of ancient Egypt had already been transmitted to Renaissance humanists. Ficino believed that Hermes Trismegistus had devised the Egyptian hieroglyphs, which he and his circle regarded as containers of profound esoteric truths.

Ficino translated or paraphrased Plato, Plotinus and the Neoplatonist theurgists. He also translated the Orphica, a collection of hymns to various pagan deities, attributed to Orpheus but actually dating from the early centuries AD. He practised magical self-improvement by singing these hymns, accompanying himself on his 'Orphic lyre'. He believed that by singing the hymn to a particular planetary deity, while concentrating his thoughts and emotions on the planet, he could draw down into himself a flow of the planet's influence and power.

One of Ficino's pupils, Francesco da Diacetto, explained more clearly how this was done. To attract the influence of the sun, for instance, the Orphic hymn to the deity was sung when the sun was ascending in Leo or Aries, on a Sunday and in the hour of the sun. The magician surrounded himself with things corresponding to the sun. He wore a golden mantle and a crown of laurel, strewed sunflowers about him, burned myrrh and frankincense on an altar and anointed himself with saffron, balsam or honey made when the sun was in Leo. The technique induced a sense of superhuman power, which could be applied to curing disease or for any other purpose.[3]

In his medical textbook *Libri de Vita* (1489), Ficino recommended 'images' or talismans for tapping planetary energies. He was very conscious of the malign effect of Saturn on his own life (it was powerfully placed in his horoscope, in Aquarius in the ascendant, with the baleful Mars in the same sign), and he thought that scholars and students frequently suffered from Saturn's melancholy influence. It could be countered by attracting cheerful and strengthening emanations from the sun and certain planets – Jupiter, Venus and Mercury. A suitable image of the sun would show a throned king with a crow. An image for acquiring happiness and physical vigour would show a young Venus holding apples and flowers.

This type of magic was not new and Ficino acknowledged his debt to Peter of Abano. Some of his images almost certainly came from the ill-famed *Picatrix*, which he prudently did not acknowledge. He probably drew on the Neoplatonist concept of the astral or etheric body, the soul's spiritual envelope, which was formed by influences from each planet in turn as the soul descended through the heavenly spheres to enter a physical body on earth. The astral body supplied a set of consonances between man and the heavens through which starry forces could be manipulated.

The art of constructing astrological images had reached its peak in Botticelli's famous *Primavera*, which was probably intended to be a talisman of Venus, a magical device for capturing in the mind the harmony, beauty and love associated with the goddess and planet. Ficino recommended his images hesitantly. The *Malleus Maleficarum* had come out only three years before and there had been plenty of attacks on astrological and ritual magic. Ficino insisted that his magic was entirely of the good 'natural' kind, depending on the links between the stars and factors inside and outside the magician. Suspect 'spiritual' or 'demonic' magic relied on supernatural intelligences but, as many of these spirits were also connected with the planets and the signs of the zodiac, the two were not so readily distinguishable in practice.

Ficino's prodigiously brilliant pupil Giovanni Pico della Mirandola (1463–94) created the synthesis which has been the foundation of high magic ever since, by blending the Cabala with the gnostic-hermetic-Neoplatonist tradition. The Cabala had in fact been influenced by gnosticism and Neoplatonism, and the Hermetica by Jewish mystical speculations, and the two systems are genuinely complementary. Pico could read Hebrew and Aramaic, was on friendly terms with Jewish scholars and seems to have known Abulafia's work. He believed that the Cabala, which he dated back to Moses, foreshadowed and confirmed the truth of Christian doctrine, but Christian cabalism brought into the Renaissance synthesis another source of spiritual or demonic magic. It used the names of angels and demons, and indeed of God himself, to exert power. Pico's own goal was the mystical one of self-annihilation in God, but it is not surprising that he was viewed with misgiving at Rome and was imprisoned for a time.

Pico found in both the Cabala and the hermetic-Neoplatonist tradition the technique of escaping from the body in meditative trances, in which the soul explored higher realms and ascended ultimately to the divine. Ficino had commended the pagan Bacchic revel as a way of escaping from normal human limitations into an ecstasy in which the soul was 'miraculously transformed into the beloved god himself'. Ficino and Pico, whatever their own practices may have been, provided a theoretical justification for sexual magic as an ecstatic reconciliation of opposites in which a higher state of being is attained. They regarded desire as a current of energy which was responsible for the cohesion of the entire universe (as in Orphic mythology). Since man was a microcosm of the universe and God, erotic love could be a method of absorption into, or magical mastery of, the world and the divine.[4]

Pico's adaptation of the Cabala to Christianity was further developed by Johann Reuchlin (1455–1522), a learned German academic. He wrote *De Arte Cabalistica* (1517), in which he related the Cabala to Pythagorean numerology and explained that the letters of the Hebrew alphabet were linked with the angels and could be used to control them. Reuchlin in turn influenced Trithemius and Agrippa.

Johann Tritheim or Trithemius (1462–1516), the abbot of a

Benedictine monastery in Germany, acquired a mile
reputation for vast erudition and occult arts. He was inter
alchemy and magic, and the Cabala stimulated his fascina
with codes and ciphers. His book on this subject, *Steganographia*,
was not printed till 1606 but circulated previously in manuscript.
It contains quantities of abstruse numerological and astrological
calculations connected with angels and gives instructions for using
images of them to summon them, to gain knowledge and also to
send messages by angelically transmitted telepathy.

Heinrich Cornelius, who promoted himself to noble rank as
Agrippa von Nettesheim, was the author of *De Occulta Philosophia*
(1533), whose wide scope, comparative clarity, poetic qualities and
exalted claims made it one of the most influential books on magic
ever written. It was largely through the *Occult Philosophy* that the
magic of Agrippa's predecessors descended to subsequent gen-
erations. Agrippa was well aware of the psychological aspects of
magic. Human emotions fit into the system of correspondences
and exert power through its channels. Passionate hatred attracts
the energy of Mars, for example, and passionate desire the current
of Venus. The passions not only affect the magician himself but can
be directed outwards to influence other people and the environment. Magic depends heavily on the confident assertion of will,
since belief in magic causes it to work. 'Therefore he that works in
Magick must be of a constant belief, be credulous, and not at all
doubt of obtaining the effect. For as a firm and strong belief doth
work wonderful things, although it be in false works, so distrust
and doubting doth dissipate and break the virtue of the mind of
the worker. . . .'[5]

Agrippa goes on to deal with the whole range of magic in his day,
drawing on the Cabala, the Hermetica and the *Picatrix*, and
covering numerology and divination as well as natural magic and
the control of angels and demons by ritual magic. One of his
chapters is headed, 'How good spirits may be called up by us, and
how evil spirits may be overcome by us.' He also refers to the
ability of the astral or etheric body, as 'the chariot of the soul', to
leave the physical body like a light escaped from a lantern, to
comprehend all space and time, to explore mysterious regions and
rise through the spheres and the spiritual hierarchies to the
Archetype, or God. Some medieval Christian mystics had recommended 'astral travel' of this kind and Jewish cabalists had
experienced what modern occultists describe as the separation of
the astral body from the physical body: 'suddenly I saw the shape
of myself standing before me and myself disengaged from me'.[6]

89

..., Agrippa distinguishes between good magic,
...agic, and the evil variety, but his mainspring is
...ather than mystical. He is concerned with the
...reme power by the magus who has dominated
...wered the heavens and mounted above the angels to
...chetype itself, of which being then made a cooperator
...o all things. ...' Man can achieve this because his true
...elf is divine. 'Whoever therefore shall know himself, shall
... ...ll things in himself; especially he shall know God, according
to whose Image he was made. ...'[7]

His English translator believed that Agrippa had attained the
supreme heights, 'being himself a Philosopher, a Demon, an Hero,
a god and all things'. Most of his life is shrouded in mystery. Born
at Cologne in 1486, he lived by his wits as a court astrologer. doctor
and lawyer, financial adviser and government agent. Lectures
which he delivered on the Cabala and the Hermetica caused
trouble with the ecclesiastical authorities. He travelled restlessly
about Europe, founding secret societies. Before he died in 1535, at
Grenoble in Switzerland, he had already acquired a reputation as a
black magician and stories afterwards multiplied about his
dealings with demons. An evil spirit was said to go everywhere
with him in the form of his pet black dog.

One of Agrippa's contemporaries, with a blacker reputation
still, was Faust. Who exactly the original Faust was is extremely
unclear. Apparently he was a charlatan who travelled about
Germany, claiming to be a great magician, astrologer and alchemist, and impressing persons of doubtful sobriety in pothouses.
Tales began to spread about his wonderful feats and, all publicity
being good publicity, his reputation swelled after his death (about
1540), when he was denounced by various Protestant ministers,
who said he had sold his soul to the Devil in return for magical
power. Lurid stories circulated about Faust's death, when the
Devil claimed his bargain. The Prince of Darkness came for Faust
one night at midnight, when the whole house shook, and in the
morning the magician was found strangled, with his head twisted
right round to the back. Or according to a more gruesome tale, in
the hour after midnight a fearsome wind howled round the house
and Faust was heard shrieking, 'Help! Murder!', but no one dared
to go to him. In the morning his mangled body was found in the
yard, near the dung-heap. His room was drenched with blood,
brains and teeth, and his eyes were stuck to one wall.

When a book about Faust was published in Germany in 1587, it
sold out immediately and was reprinted in four pirated editions

before the end of the year. Further editions and translations into many European languages followed in profusion. The Faust legend has inspired two plays of genius, Marlowe's *Faust* and Goethe's *Faust*, a novel by Thomas Mann and numerous other works. An early element of the tradition, which was particularly responsible for drawing serious writers to it, was that Faust's reason for signing his soul away to the Devil was not only a desire for pleasure and power, but for knowledge. In the spirit of high magic, he wanted to know everything that there is to know. He consequently challenged the prerogatives of God, who alone knows all things: and it was for trying to rival God that the Devil, Faust's master, had been hurled from his high seat in heaven long ago and condemned to eternal damnation. It was this attempt to become God which was the centre of the romantic attraction of both Faust and Satan as heroic figures, standing for man's defiant longing for supreme mastery.

After Agrippa's death a *Fourth Book* was added to the three books of his *Occult Philosophy*. It provides instructions for the ritual conjuration of evil spirits and explains how to make a book of them, with an image of each demon, his name and 'character' or signature and his functions and rank in the infernal hierarchy. Each demon must then be summoned and compelled to swear an oath of obedience to the magician. Psychologically, this procedure seems to amount to forming a clear mental picture of the world of demons, to reduce it to order and to subdue it. The *Fourth Book* also describes the appearance of the spirits of each planet, apparently so that the magician can take their characteristic forms into his mind as an aid to summoning and dominating them there.

Many other magical textbooks were in circulation in the sixteenth and seventeenth centuries, though in most cases they were not printed till the eighteenth century or later, if at all. The most interesting is the *Lemegeton* or *Lesser Key of Solomon*, which contains an impressive arsenal of incantations for summoning and controlling the seventy-two principal demons, whose names, appearance, rank, functions and 'characters' are listed. The demon Baal, for instance, who commands sixty-six legions of lesser spirits, 'appears in divers shapes, sometimes like a cat, sometimes like a toad and sometimes like a man, and sometimes all these forms at once; he speaks very hoarsely'. The demon Agares appears as a man riding a crocodile and carrying a goshawk on his wrist, and Paimon shows himself as 'a man sitting on a dromedary with a crown most glorious on his head; there goeth before him an host of spirits like men with trumpets and well sounding cymbals and all other sorts of musical instruments'. These spirits are primarily teaching demons, who supply knowledge of all arts and sciences and all the secrets of the universe, though they are also powerful in operations of low magic. The *Lemegeton* also provides a dauntingly exhaustive catalogue of spirits of the hours of day and night, the signs of the zodiac and the four directions.

The *Grimorium Verum*, purportedly published by Alibeck the Egyptian at Memphis in 1517, and the *Grand Grimoire* are based on the *Key of Solomon*, with considerable variations. The *Grand Grimoire* (also known as *The Red Dragon*) incorporates 'the Powerful Clavicle of Solomon and of Black Magic, and the Infernal Devices of the Great Agrippa for the Discovery of all Hidden Treasures and the Subjugation of every Denomination of Spirits'. The *Arbatel of Magic*, supposedly published at Basle in 1575, is not connected with the *Key* and is mainly concerned with the seven great Olympic Spirits of the planets, who must be invoked in the correct planetary day and hour with a prayer asking God to send the spirit to the magician. The *Heptameron* or *Magical Elements*, attributed to Peter of Abano but in reality a supplement to the *Fourth Book*, supplies methods of invoking the spirits of the air and the days of the week.

The textbook with the most sinister reputation of all is the *Constitution of Honorius* or *Grimoire of Honorius*. Its false attribution to Pope Honorius III gave it a spurious air of authority and allowed it to open with a fake papal bull. The grimoire owes its evil repute to its use of Christian processes and prayers. It can be employed only by a magician who is a priest and its method of calling up demons requires repeated sayings of Mass.

These rituals and their humbler relatives, copied out with greater or less accuracy and passed quietly from hand to hand, were used by people anxious to put themselves in touch with angels, demons, fairies and ghosts. They circulated in large numbers and many have survived in manuscript. Material on the less dangerous subject of divination meanwhile flooded openly onto the popular market in cheap printed books and pamphlets. The dream textbook of Artemidorus was published in Venice in the early sixteenth century. Translated into English in 1518 as *The Judgment of Dreams*, it went through twenty editions by 1722. Guides to palmistry, physiognomy, moleosophy (divination by the location of moles on the body) and other varieties of fortune-telling appeared in quantity. Cheap handbooks of this kind were often part of the equipment of wise women and cunning men.

The fifteenth century saw the production in Italy of the earliest

Tarot cards which have survived. Their origin and purpose are still in doubt, but they seem to have been meant to convey esoteric teaching and they are certainly laced with astrological symbolism. Astrology remained an integral part of medicine and agriculture, and the well-to-do had their children's horoscopes drawn up. Astrologers also issued general forecasts for each coming year. Conrad of Heingarter's predictions for 1476, addressed to Louis XI of France, make the safe announcement that many women will quarrel with their husbands, and forecast rising prices of grain, lead, camels and elephants in the spring because of adverse influences from Saturn. Regiomontanus (Johann Müller, 1436–76), the brilliant German mathematician and pioneer of trigonometry who improved the astrological system of house-division in the horoscope, issued tables of favourable times for 'new undertakings, bleeding and pharmacy, sowing, planting and cultivation of vines, or even for entering one's bath or having one's hair cut'.[8]

Printing put predictive astrology of this kind within reach of everyone who could read, in the form of almanacs, which combined a calendar and diary with general forecasts. When it was realized that all the planets would be together in the watery sign of Pisces in 1524, a second Noah's Flood was expected. A man in Toulouse built himself an Ark, 20,000 people left London in panic, and the Elector of Brandenburg took refuge on top of a high hill. It did prove to be an unusually wet year.

Pico della Mirandola objected to all astrological predictions on the ground that they reduced human beings to spineless dependence on the stars, but his premature death, which occurred precisely at the hour and day predicted by the astrologers, impressed his contemporaries in the opposite sense. Jerome Cardan (1501–76), an Italian mathematician of genius and the founder of probability theory, was a practising astrologer and on a visit to England drew up the horoscope of Edward VI. He also wrote on dreams, moleosophy and metoposcopy (divination by the lines on the brow, related to the planets). Copernicus, the founder of modern astronomy, who was influenced by Ficino and the Hermetica, put forward the heliocentric theory in 1543, but it did not become generally accepted in educated circles for another hundred years. Tycho Brahe and Kepler both accepted astrology. 'Thus the Renaissance saw no contradiction between astrology and science; rather, the dominion of the heavenly bodies over all earthly things was viewed by some as the natural law par excellence, the law which assures the regularity of phenomena.'[9]

The principal figure in alchemy in the sixteenth century was the wild and extraordinary Bombast von Hohenheim (1493–1541), who called himself Paracelsus. Born in German Switzerland, he was taught medicine and alchemy by his father and as a young man worked in the mines and metallurgical workshops of Sigismund Fugger, himself an enthusiast for alchemy, in the Tyrol. Subsequently Paracelsus wandered erratically through Germany, France, the Low Countries, England, Scandinavia and Italy, full of drink and bravado. He lectured to crowds of cheering students, met and impressed the great, practised as a doctor and infuriated the local medical men with his unorthodox methods and his blistering abuse of their old-fashioned ways. He was rumoured to have discovered the Philosopher's Stone but his real alchemical achievement was as a pioneer of the use of minerals in medicine. He was influenced by the hermetic-cabalist synthesis and wrote obscure books on occultism. He was rarely sober and reading him is like groping through a pitch-dark room lit by occasional flashes of blazing lightning.

In 1547 Catherine de Medici, who was an enthusiastic patron of astrologers and magicians, became Queen of France. Her most famous protégé was Nostradamus (Michel de Nostredame, 1503–66). He was born in Provence of a Jewish family which turned Roman Catholic when he was a boy, and was influenced by the Cabala and by Iamblichus's book on the Egyptian Mysteries. A doctor and astrologer, from 1550 he published an annual almanac of predictions. By scrying in a bowl of water standing on a tripod, as recommended by Iamblichus, he saw visions of events far in the future, which he wrote down in obscurely alluring symbolic verses, couched in a mixture of French, Provençal, Italian, Greek and Latin. For example: 'In the third month, at sunrise, the Boar and the Leopard meet on the battlefield. The fatigued Leopard looks up to heaven and sees an eagle playing around the sun.' This has been interpreted as an allusion to the battle of Waterloo.[10]

Nostradamus published his first set of prophecies in 1555 and the complete collection came out in 1568. They created a sensation, editions were printed all over Europe and forged Nostradamus predictions were put out for propaganda purposes (a tradition renewed during the Second World War). The prophecies appeared at a time of extreme tension between Catholics and Protestants – the Massacre of St Bartholomew occurred in 1572 – coinciding with the onset of the worst period of witch hunting in Europe. Their veiled form makes them applicable to a large number of situations and the persistent interest in them has always mounted at times of crisis, when people have turned to them in search of security in an uncertain world.

The most notable English magician of the period was John Dee, who may have been the model for Prospero in Shakespeare's *Tempest*. A distinguished mathematician, he was born near London in 1527. He early acquired an uneasy reputation as a sorcerer and was imprisoned for a time on a charge of attempting to murder Queen Mary by enchantment, apparently because he had cast her horoscope for her heir, Princess Elizabeth, to discover when the queen would die. When she did die, he was employed to fix an astrologically favourable day for Elizabeth's coronation. Dee was influenced by Trithemius and Agrippa, whose *Occult Philosophy* he used as a textbook, and wrote an abstruse work on cabalistic, alchemical, astrological and numerological magic, *Monas Hieroglyphica* (1564).

Dee became passionately interested in scrying and, being insufficiently psychic himself, employed professional clairvoyants. His principal collaborator, from 1582, was Edward Kelley, 'a terrible zombie-like figure,' as Edith Sitwell picturesquely described him, 'a medium inhabited by an evil spirit'. Kelley's ears had been cropped for forgery and he was reputed to have dug up a corpse for necromantic purposes. Dee and Kelley made alchemical experiments and held long conversations with angels through their crystals and polished stones. They summoned the angels with 'calls' in the mysterious Enochian language, whose origin is unknown. (It is a genuine language, not gibberish.) The angels appeared, to Kelley, in and outside the crystal and he put Dee's questions to them and relayed the answers. Dee's interest in his angels was both scientific and religious. He wanted them to teach him the secrets of nature and God, which he had failed to find in books and in discussion with learned men.

In 1583 Dee and Kelley and their wives went abroad and tried to interest the King of Poland and the Emperor Rudolf II in their angelic communications and in Kelley's supposed ability to make alchemical gold. While they were away, a mob took vengeance on the notorious wizard Dee by wrecking his laboratory and library, and the English government invited him to come home and make gold for the defence of England against Spain. Dee and Kelley continued their partnership despite quarrels and scenes, which grew worse after Kelley announced that the angels wanted them to share their wives, to which Dee reluctantly consented. No other tangible satisfactions came of their travels and Kelley was killed in 1595, trying to escape from prison in Prague. Dee had returned home in 1589 and died in poverty at Mortlake nineteen years later.

The contrast between high and low magic, and the extent of overlapping between them, comes out in the career of Dee's contemporary Simon Forman (1552–1611). Forman was a successful cunning man in London, a self-taught doctor, astrologer and professional magician. He kept careful records of his activities, including his flourishing sex-life and his dreams, which he took seriously as portents of the future. He was constantly in hot water with the Royal College of Physicians, which doubted whether his knowledge of astrology was adequate, but he himself was genuinely convinced of the validity of his arts. Clients from every social level consulted him for cures, for astrological advice in matters of love and marriage, to find out if anyone was scheming against them, and to trace things lost, stolen or strayed, including missing pets. Sailors' wives enquired about the safety of their husbands at sea. People who thought they were bewitched or felt themselves impelled by evil spirits to commit suicide or murder came to him for help. One clergyman wanted to know if he would be appointed Bishop of London. Businessmen required astrological guidance. In 1602, for instance, an eminent City merchant asked, whether there be any north-west Passage to Cathay and whether the ships now intended to send shall find it; whether best to adventure his goods in them or no'.[11]

Forman made his own herbal medicines and sold talismans and erotic figurines to induce love. The Countess of Essex bought potions and figurines from him to entice Robert Carr, King James I's favourite, into her amatory net, and several other aristocratic ladies consulted him for similar purposes. But he also published a book on longitude, tried to make the Philosopher's Stone, summoned up angels and spirits, which he 'heard and sensed' but did not see, and wrote books on medicine, magic, the Cabala, astrology and alchemy, which were not published. He was a low magician with high interests and aspirations, whereas Dee was a high magician forced in old age to scratch a living by casting horoscopes. Forman's casebooks show how strong a demand there was among all classes for advice about matters ranging from a headache or the loss of a pet canary to serious marital, financial, medical and psychological problems. Magicians, wise women, astrologers and fortune-tellers tackled the work now undertaken by social workers, marriage counsellors and psychiatrists: and perhaps with more success, because there was greater confidence in

1 ABOVE Prehistoric hunting magic: the 'dancing sorcerer' from the Trois Frères cave, probably representing a tribal shaman or magician.

2 BELOW Mummification in Egypt involved magic to secure a happy afterlife for the dead: the mummy of Pharaoh Rameses II.

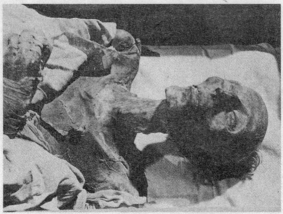

3 So-called 'gnostic gems', often used against disease: at the top right is the *ankh*, the Egyptian symbol of life, now again in vogue.

4 Amulets are used as portable magical power-sources: the Abracadabra charm was believed to cure fever by gradually shrinking it away to vanishing point.

5 Astrology began in Mesopotamia: astrological symbols on a boundary stone of the 12th century BC.

6 ABOVE The magic mandrake, pulled up by a dog, which was killed by its screech.

7 RIGHT The inspired prophetess who dictated the Sibylline Books; by Michelangelo.

Belief in the magic of
Christ and the Church
was an important
factor in the spread of
Christianity. The
gospels stress the effects
of Jesus's feats of
healing and exorcism in
drawing attention to
him and his teaching.
Later, Christian
specialists in casting
out demons from the
sick and the insane
were appointed, and
had many successes.

8 RIGHT An exorcism,
from the Winchester
Bible, 12th century
AD: a demon is
expelled from the
patient and flies out of
his mouth.

9 BELOW Jesus healing
the blind man from
Jericho; from an early
Greek bible.

10 *St Wolfgang and the Devil*, by Michael Pacher (1483): one of the principal functions of the Church, in medieval popular belief, was to provide magical protection against evil, misfortune and stratagems of the Devil. Satan and his demons were depicted in grotesque, unnatural forms to emphasize their threat to civilized, Christian values. The second face, on the buttocks, is a mark of the Devil's lordship of matter and dirt.

Sacrifices are religio-magical ceremonies in which an offering to the god binds him to the worshippers.

11 LEFT Drawn when interest in the Druids was reviving, this picture illustrates Julius Caesar's account of the Celts: 'Some tribes have colossal images of the gods made of wickerwork, the limbs of which they fill with living men; they are then set on fire and the victims burnt to death.' From Aylett Sammes, *Britannia Antiqua Illustrata* (1676).

12 BELOW This man was hanged or strangled and thrown into a peatbog in Denmark, probably as a sacrifice to a fertility goddess.

Language is an instrument of power in magic, believed from very early times to give man control of natural and supernatural forces.

13 RIGHT Rune stone: the runes, the letters used in pre-Christian northern Europe, were thought to give magical effect to whatever was stated in them.

14 BELOW The magic circle and triangle of Solomon, with pentagrams, from a late medieval magical textbook, the *Lemegeton*. Names and titles of God are used to tap divine energy. The magician stands inside the circle, in which his power is concentrated and which protects him from harm, and summons evil spirits to appear within the triangle.

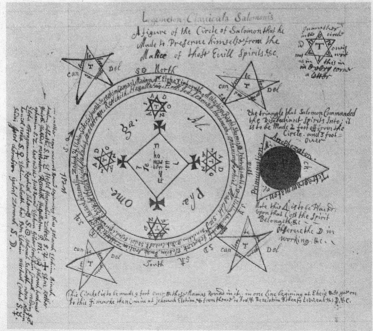

15 RIGHT Zodiac man: each part of the human body was linked with a zodiac sign, and these links were used in medical practice.

16 BELOW Alchemy's mysterious code of symbols mingled mysticism, magic, astrology and metal-working. Here the alchemist's material rises from the waters of rebirth to gain new spiritual life; from *Splendor Solis*, 16th century AD.

In the 16th and 17th centuries magic and science were not yet separate areas of exploration.

17 ABOVE Title page of Robert Fludd's book on man as a miniature replica of the universe.

18 RIGHT Gold disc used by John Dee, a distinguished mathematician who tried to learn the secrets of nature from angels.

FACING PAGE:

21 In 1634 a priest named Urbain Grandier was burned alive for bewitching the nuns of a convent at Loudun in France. He was accused of signing a pact with the Devil. The pact and a formal acknowledgement, written backwards and signed by Satan and other leading demons (*above left*), were produced in court.

22 ABOVE RIGHT Witch hunting in England was on a comparatively small scale. Matthew Hopkins, the self-styled Witch Finder General, was responsible for the largest mass execution of witches in England, when nineteen were hanged at Chelmsford in 1645. He is shown with witches and their pet demons or 'familiar spirits'.

23 BELOW Witches and demons at the sabbath, from Guazzo's *Compendium Maleficarum*. The sabbath was the gathering at which Satanist witches were believed to meet for feasting, dancing and orgiastic sex, and to worship their god, the Devil.

MALLEVS
MALEFICARVM,
MALEFICAS ET EARVM
hæresim framceâ conterens ,

EX VARIIS AVCTORIBVS COMPILATVS,
& in quatuor Tomos iustè distributus ,

QVORVM DVO PRIORES VANAS DÆMONVM versutias , prastigiosas eorum delusiones , superstitiosas Strigimagarum cæremonias , horrendas etiam cum illis congressus ; exactam denique tam pestifera sectæ disquisitionem , & punitionem complectuntur. Tertius praxim Exorcistarum ad Dæmonum , & Strigimagarum maleficia de Christi fidelibus pellenda; Quartus verò Artem Doctrinalem , Benedictionalem , & Exorcismalem continent.

TOMVS PRIMVS.
Indice Auctorum , capitum , rerúmque non defuit.

Editio nouissima , infinitis penè mendis expurgata ; cuique accessit Fuga Dæmonum & Complementum artis exorcisticæ.

Vir siue mulier,in quibus Pythonicus, vel diuinationis fuerit spiritus, morte moriatur ; Leuitici cap. 10.

LVGDVNI,
Sumptibus CLAVDII BOVRGEAT, sub signo Mercurij Galli.

M. DC. LXIX.
CVM PRIVILEGIO REGIS.

Witches were feared for their malevolence and their uncanny powers. The Church's belief that they were servants of Satan in a conspiracy against order and civilization led to fierce persecutions of supposed witches in the 16th and 17th centuries.

19 ABOVE A witch with her cat, a Breton wood carving.

20 RIGHT Title page of the *Malleus Maleficarum* or 'Hammer of Witches' (1669 edition), written by two Dominicans in the 15th century to combat scepticism about witchcraft and lay down merciless rules for the interrogation of suspects.

Magic was in the doldrums for most of the 18th century, but one symptom of a coming revival was the growing interest in the Rosicrucian manifestos of the previous century, which had set out a programme for the reconciliation of science and religion, largely through the medium of alchemy. Small Rosicrucian groups proliferated on the fringes of Freemasonry, with their own secrets, symbols, elaborate rituals and hierarchies of initiates. At the end of the century Mesmer's discovery of 'animal magnetism' (hypnosis) was a powerful influence on the development of modern magic.

24 RIGHT German Rosicrucian alchemical diagram of factors and forces in the universe related to the body of 'the celestial and earthly Eve, the Mother of all Living', linked with the Sophia, or Heavenly Wisdom, of the ancient gnostic sects; from *Geheime Figuren der Rosenkreuzer* (1785–8).

25 BELOW 'Mesmer's Tub, a Faithful Representation of the Operations of Animal Magnetism': Mesmer's patients sat round a tub filled with water and iron filings.

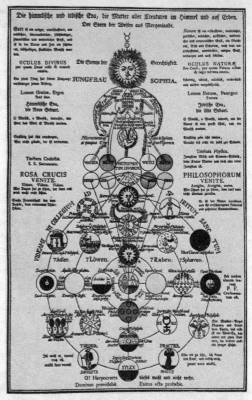

26 ABOVE LEFT Fortune-telling from moles on the face.

27 ABOVE RIGHT Poster by Albinet for the third Rosicrucian Salon in Paris, 1894. The Master of the Templars is shown with Joseph of Arimathea, Grand Master of the Grail.

28 LEFT Portraits of demons by Francis Barrett, who said he drew them from life.

29 BELOW Tantrism has influenced modern magic: the Sri Yantra, a Tantric symbol.

30 Aleister Crowley, self-styled Great Beast 666 and Baphomet, intellectually the most formidable
magician of his time. He restated the theory of magic from a modern psychological point of view.

31 The Order of the Golden Dawn, founded in 1888, functioned as an occult university. Led by MacGregor Mathers, its members included W. B. Yeats (*left*), Aleister Crowley and A. E. Waite.

32 BELOW Austin Osman Spare, artist, magician and recluse, was a pupil of Aleister Crowley. He painted weirdly powerful pictures of witches and semi-human intelligences.

33 Portrait of an atavism, by Austin Osman Spare. Spare worked out his own
methods of what he called 'atavistic resurgence', the summoning up into
consciousness of strange, powerful and terrifying creatures from the most
ancient and primitive layers of the mind. This is one example of a more
widespread recent interest in altered states of consciousness, in the exploration
of 'inner space' and in magic as a method of self-discovery and self-
development.

their arts.

The practice of magic could be lethally dangerous, however, as the contemporary persecutions of witches demonstrated. Strict Protestants, in England and on the Continent, denounced magic with a hostility all the fiercer because they associated it with popery. Roman Catholics returned the compliment with interest. The unfortunate Dee was suspect at court in Bloody Mary's time as a magician and probable Protestant. When the religious tables were turned under Elizabeth, he became popularly suspect as a magician and probable Papist.

The whole magical protective apparatus of the Church, which had been the ordinary Christian's bastion of defence against evil and misfortune, was attacked by Protestants as an engine of ungodly mumbo-jumbo. Ludwig Lavater, for example, a Protestant minister in Zürich, published *De Spectris* (1569), in which he repudiated the 'superstitious' use of holy water, the sign of the cross, the relics of saints, the host and exorcism. Johann Georg Gödelmann, a Protestant professor at Rostock and author of *De Magis* (1591), lumped together the Cabala and the Catholic ritual of exorcism as methods of enchantment and (like Peter of Abano earlier) described the Mass itself as a piece of magic. The more extreme Protestants said that the Mass was no better than sorcery. They also traced many folk customs and ceremonies which had made their way into the Christian calendar back to their pagan origins and condemned them accordingly.

On the Catholic side, Martin del Rio wrote *Disquisitionum Magicarum* (1599), defending the practices attacked by Protestants and claiming that the prevalence of sorcery and witchcraft was an inevitable consequence of the spread of Protestantism, to which they bore the same relationship as the shadow to the body. Both del Rio and the Protestants drew the genealogy of magic from Zoroaster and the other *prisci magi* and denounced it.

It seems to have been largely in reaction against the religious hostilities of his time that Giordano Bruno, magician, philosopher and poet, rejected Christianity altogether. Ficino, Pico, Agrippa, Paracelsus and Dee were Christians, sincerely or nominally. Bruno proclaimed that Judaism and Christianity had corrupted the true religion, the religion of ancient Egypt, by which he meant the mysticism and magic of the Hermetica. He hoped for the abolition of Christianity, the restoration of the Egyptian religion and a radical reform of society. Born at Nola, near Naples, in 1548, Bruno like his fellow magi was constantly on the move from one country to another. Brilliant, eloquent and irascible, he is another candidate as a possible model for Prospero.

Bruno accepted Copernican astronomy and went further by conceiving that the universe is infinite and our solar system but one of innumerable worlds. This realization shattered the classical and medieval picture of the universe, but Bruno did not reject the theory of macrocosm and microcosm. On the contrary, he magnified the greatness of man as an image of the infinite. Like his predecessors, he recommended the use of real or mental pictures of planets and stars to acquire divine powers, but with his repudiation of Christianity went a rejection of its angels, and he made no bones about stating that the supernatural intelligences which his magic mastered were demons. An ex-Dominican, he contrived to join and be excommunicated by both the Lutherans and the Calvinists. He finally returned to Italy, where he was seized by the Inquisition and was burned alive in Rome as a heretic in 1600.[12]

The Rosicrucians and the Burning Court

The seventeenth century saw the scientific revolution which eventually sent both religion and magic into decline. In the same period witch hunting reached its peak of ferocity and gradually died away, and alchemy attained the summit of its influence. Magic and science were not yet totally separate areas of exploration. John Napier, for instance, the inventor of logarithms, was a student of alchemy. Van Helmont, the chemist, witnessed the transmutation of base metals to gold and was impressed. William Harvey, who discovered the circulation of the blood, regarded it as a microcosm of the flow of forces in the universe at large. Isaac Newton himself believed that his system had been revealed by God to the *prisci theologi*, was deeply interested in alchemy and spent a remarkable amount of his time and energy working out elaborate prophetical calculations from Daniel and Revelation.

Kings, governments and noblemen pursued the quest for alchemical gold with hungry enthusiasm. The Emperor Rudolf II (1552–1612), who held court at Prague, immersed himself in magic, the Cabala and alchemy, and was rumoured to have discovered the Stone. Adventurers swarmed over Europe manufacturing gold to the wonder and greed of numerous beholders, and medals and coins were struck from the 'gold' which they produced. Christian IV of Denmark struck several medals of this kind in the

1640s. A medallion of silver transformed into gold for the Emperor Leopold I in 1677 was examined in 1888 and found to have a specific gravity between that of gold and silver. Charles II rashly constructed an alchemical laboratory underneath his bedchamber in Whitehall.

Mystical alchemy continued to appeal to Catholics and Protestants. Benedictus Figulus wrote an alchemical version of the Mass. An obscure German Protestant, Heinrich Khunrath, wrote a treatise on Christian cabalistic alchemy, *Amphitheatrum Sapientiae Aeternae*, published not long after his death in 1601. Khunrath believed in the Philosopher's Stone both as a substance which turned metals into gold and cured disease, and as the state of Christian spiritual perfection. Alchemy came from the same background as the Hermetica and blended readily into the Renaissance magical synthesis. Several of the sixteenth-century magi had been interested in it from this point of view and the Rosicrucian manifestos of the early seventeenth century put forward a hermetic-cabalist-alchemical programme.

The three original Rosicrucian documents, all anonymous and published in Germany, aroused widespread interest and excitement. The *Fama Fraternitatis* (1614) and the *Confessio Fraternitatis R.C.* (1615), printed at Cassel, announced the existence of a secret brotherhood of magi and invited readers worthy of admittance to join it, though without telling them how to do so. This brotherhood was said to have been founded by Christian Rosenkreutz, born in Germany in 1378 and brought up in a monastery. He travelled to Damascus, Egypt and Fez in Morocco, gathering on the way a rich store of knowledge from great masters of arcane wisdom (the prestige of the Arabs in this field was evidently still considerable). Returning to Germany, Rosenkreutz was joined by three brethren from his former monastery, identified only by their initials, G.V., I.A. and I.O., who formed the Brotherhood of the Rosy Cross. They wrote down the magical secrets which they learned from Rosenkreutz and healed the sick, who came to them in great numbers.

Five more brethren were later accepted into the Fraternity, all of whose members were pledged to chastity. Rosenkreutz himself died at the age of 106 in 1484 and was buried in a seven-sided vault, illuminated from within by a supernatural light and containing a circular altar, a collection of books, including some by Paracelsus (who had not been born yet), magic mirrors, bells, perpetual lamps and 'wonderful artificial songs'. The remaining brethren handed their knowledge on in secret to a few carefully chosen successors, some of whom opened the tomb of Rosenkreutz 120 years after his death, in 1604, and found his body perfectly preserved.

The third Rosicrucian book, the *Chymische Hochzeit*, or 'Chemical Wedding', was published at Strasbourg in 1616. It is a symbolic account of the alchemical mysteries in the form of the story of Christian Rosenkreutz's perilous journey to a royal wedding in an enchanted castle. It was written by Johann Valentin Andreae (1577–1638), a Lutheran theologian and mystic of Württemberg, who may or may not have written the *Fama* and *Confessio* as well.

The manifestos date the Rosicrucian philosophy back to Adam, Moses and Solomon. and give it the allure of eastern wisdom. The Brotherhood claim to know the secret of practical alchemy, or gold-making, but to be more interested in its spiritual applications. The *Fama* hopes for 'a universal and general reformation of the whole wide world'. This is to be achieved through the union of Protestant Christianity with magic, alchemy, the Cabala and advances in medical, mathematical and scientific knowledge, and requires the collaboration of wise men of all disciplines. The programme was an attractive one at a time of violent ideological antagonisms and it was evidently these antagonisms which inspired it.

Many people, including the youthful Descartes, and Leibniz later on, were drawn to the Rosicrucian ideal and searched for the Brotherhood. They failed to find it, almost certainly because it did not exist. The Brotherhood was a fiction, though one with a serious purpose. The story of Christian Rosenkreutz has been taken as literal truth by modern Rosicrucian groups. But whoever inspired it probably intended it as a myth that would promote and give authority to 'the universal and general reformation' in which religious and intellectual differences would be peacefully resolved. The resolution was to come largely through the medium of alchemy, with its twin practical and mystical aspects, as a bridge between the scientific and the spiritual. Alchemy could also bridge the gulf between Catholic and Protestant, since it was an individual not a denominational path to God. Frances Yates has argued that the manifestos express hopes centred on the Protestant Elector Palatine as 'the politico-religious leader destined to solve the problems of the age'.[13]

The problems of the age were not solved, the tensions were too strong, and Germany plunged almost immediately into a bitter religious conflict, the Thirty Years War of 1618–48. It was not until much later that the fictitious Brotherhood was brought to life by its admirers. But meanwhile Michael Maier, Robert Fludd and others wrote books in sympathy with Rosicrucianism and some writers claimed to be Rosicrucian initiates themselves. Michael Maier (1566–1622) was a Lutheran, born in Holstein, a Paracelsist doctor who was court physician to Rudolf II and subsequently to the Landgrave of Hesse. He wrote *Atlanta Fugiens* (1618) and other books on spiritual alchemy. He believed in the existence of the Rosicrucian Brotherhood and traced its spiritual ancestry back to fraternities of Ethiopian sages, Persian Magi and Indian Brahmins, which suggests a concealed reference to Apollonius of Tyana.

Maier visited England and may have met Robert Fludd (1574–1637), another Paracelsist physician, practising in London. Fludd wrote *Utriusque Cosmi Historia* (1617), a cabalist-alchemical account of the macrocosm and the microcosm, with liberal quotations from the Hermetica and Agrippa, and much recondite Pythagoreanism. Francis Bacon (1561–1626), although he denied the theory of man as the microcosm, which was the foundation of the whole Renaissance occult synthesis, was interested in Rosicrucian ideas, sufficiently so for the modern groups to have claimed him as a leading initiate, or even as the founder of the Brotherhood.

The Rosicrucians were fiercely attacked in other quarters, sometimes on scientific grounds and sometimes as a heretical group under the patronage of the Devil. There was a hubbub in Paris in 1623, when certain high Rosicrucian adepts were reported to be present in the city 'visibly and invisibly'. An anonymous pamphlet denouncing these 'Invisible Ones' said they had made a pact with Satan. They offered him sacrifices at 'great sabbaths' where they forswore Christianity and trampled on the host in return for magical power. A French Jesuit accused the Brotherhood of being a secret society of sorcerers, and Descartes had to defend himself from suspicion as a Rosicrucian by pointing out that he was visible.

Johann Valentin Andreae and his circle were interested in the Utopian plans of Tommaso Campanella (died 1639), another ex-Dominican magician, who spent many years in prison in Naples after the failure of a revolt which he had led against Spanish rule. He had hoped to establish the ideal hermetic City of the Sun, where astrological magic would be used as an umbrella of protection against disasters. In 1628 he was employed in Rome by Pope Urban VIII, who feared an imminent eclipse which he thought might be the signal for his death. Campanella and the pope sealed off a room, installed two lamps to stand for the sun and moon, and five torches for the planets, assembled jewels, plants, perfumes and colours corresponding to the benevolent planets Jupiter and Venus, and played 'Jovial and Venereal' music. They were trying to create their own little favourable sky in the sealed room, to guard the pope against the eclipse outside. They should have been pleased with their efforts, as Urban VIII did not die until 1644. In the meantime Campanella had recommended his City of the Sun to Cardinal Richelieu, but without success.

A more influential hermetic enthusiast in the long run was Athanasius Kircher (1602–80), a German Jesuit and mathematician, who invented the magic lantern and experimented with a primitive microscope. He wrote an enormous work on the Egyptian hieroglyphs, *Oedipus Aegyptiacus* (1652). Kircher was particularly interested in the myth of Isis and Osiris, in which he thought the Egyptian priests had concealed a true knowledge of God. He related the hieroglyphs to the Cabala and attempted to bring material from Mexico and Japan, which had now been opened up by Jesuit missionaries, into the occult synthesis. He was also interested, with Paracelsus and Fludd, in 'magnetic' healing, which later turned into hypnosis. He helped to transmit to the modern occult revival a romantic fascination with Egyptian wisdom and the belief that the same teachings are hidden behind ancient traditions all over the world.[14]

Interest of this same kind had already begun to build up in the Druids. The principal classical texts about them were now available in translation, some of which credited them with Pythagorean doctrines and linked them enticingly with the Magi, the priests of ancient Egypt and the Brahmins. The figure of the recently discovered American Indian as 'the noble savage' helped to stimulate an admiring regard for Celtic and Germanic antiquity in general, and for Druids in particular as repositories of ancestral wisdom. In his *Polyolbion* (1622), Michael Drayton pictured them as 'sacred Bards' and philosophers, 'like whom great Nature's depths no man yet ever knew'.[15] John Aubrey, writing in 1649, took a much more hard-headed view of the Druids, but he associated them with the great prehistoric stone circles of Stonehenge and Avebury, which he thought had been their temples, and so provided fuel for a romantic fire which has blazed ever since.

In 1652 Thomas Vaughan, a mystic and martyr to alchemy – he died from inhaling mercury fumes – published an English translation (not his own) of the Rosicrucian *Fama* and *Confessio*, under his pseudonym of Eugenius Philalethes. In the preface he brought out into the open Maier's dangerous hint at the Brotherhood's spiritual descent from Apollonius of Tyana: dangerous because an interest in Apollonius was considered anti-Christian. The modern Rosicrucians claim Vaughan as an initiate, along with Sir Kenelm Digby (1603–65) and Elias Ashmole (1617–92). Digby was a cultivated Catholic gentleman who had an alchemical laboratory in his house in Covent Garden. He acquired from a much-travelled Carmelite a 'powder of sympathy', which healed wounds at a distance. It was applied not to the wound but to a cloth stained with blood from it. Digby's 'weapon ointment' worked in a similar way, being smeared on the weapon that had made the wound. In either case, the wound itself was cleaned, bandaged and left alone, which no doubt accounts for the success of the treatment.

Elias Ashmole was a founder-member of the Royal Society, a famous antiquarian and collector of curiosities, an authority on heraldry and the history of the Order of the Garter, and an ardent student of botany, astrology and alchemy. In 1653, he noted in his diary, a friend revealed to him 'the True Matter of the Philosopher's Stone', though he does not say what the secret was. Ashmole admired Dee and the Rosicrucian manifestos. In the preface to his collection of English alchemical texts, *Theatrum Chemicum Britannicum* (1652), he quoted a passage from the *Fama* mingling spiritual aspiration with gold-making and the subjugation of evil spirits: 'And certainly he to whom the whole course of Nature lies open rejoiceth not so much that he can make gold and silver or the devils be made subject to him as that he sees the heavens open, the angels of God ascending and descending, and that his own name is fairly written in the Book of Life.'[16]

Ashmole's diary shows that in 1646 he was initiated as a Mason (and it is possible, though far from certain, that Robert Fludd was connected with a Masonic lodge in London in the 1620s). The early history of Freemasonry is obscure. It probably developed from the late medieval masons' guilds, in lodges which turned away from 'operative' Masonry, or the actual practice of the stonemason's art, to 'speculative' or philosophical Masonry. This process apparently began in Scotland and England in the seventeenth century, but much earlier the masons had claimed an ancient pedigree. In English documents of about 1400 the history of the craft is traced from before the Flood to the construction of the Tower of Babel and the building of Solomon's Temple. In one of them it is said to have been founded in Egypt by Thoth-Hermes, who is eccentrically identified with Euclid. There was therefore already a certain hermetic, Solomonic and potentially cabalistic tinge to operative Masonry, with an attractive air of hidden wisdom, reinforced by the secret grips, passwords and initiation rites which were common in all craftsmen's guilds. The ancient magical mystique of craftsmen has been reborn in modern Freemasonry and it may be that the Rosicrucian elements in Masonry, which were certainly present in the eighteenth century, first came into it in the seventeenth with 'speculative' recruits like Ashmole.

Ashmole was a friend and patron of William Lilly, the leading astrologer and political prophet of the day. Lilly emerged from obscure poverty in Leicestershire, where he was born in 1602, went to London and married a well-to-do widow. His marriage gave him leisure to study astrology, which he learned from books and from a drunken and disreputable Welsh clergyman named Evans, whose daughter scryed for angels in a crystal and who was versed in the conjuration of spirits. In his entertaining autobiography, Lilly tells the story of how Evans agreed to summon up a spirit for Sir Kenelm Digby and a friend of his. While all three were in the magic circle, invoking busily, Evans was suddenly transported out of the room to a field in Battersea, where he was found fast asleep the next morning. Sir Kenelm and friend professed themselves much puzzled by this mysterious occurrence.

Lilly's autobiography and casebooks show that an astrologer's clientele and their problems remained much the same as in Simon Forman's day. He was rather nervous of spirits: they created a sudden alarming storm round his ears when he was divining for buried treasure in Westminster Abbey cloisters with a hazel wand or 'Mosaical rod'. But he had a plentiful acquaintanceship of crystal-gazers and experimenters earnestly occupied in summoning up the Queen of the Fairies and other 'Angelical Creatures'. The incompetent Mr Gladwell of Suffolk 'formerly had Sight and Conference with *Uriel* and *Raphael*, but lost them both through Carelessness'. He offered Lilly a substantial sum to help him recover them, but Lilly declined. On the other hand, a scryer named Sarah Skelhorn told Lilly that her angels had followed her about for so long that she was thoroughly bored with them.

Lilly issued almanacs under the pseudonym of Merlinus Anglicus and published an introduction to astrology, *Christian Astrology* (1647). He took Parliament's side in the astrological and prophetic pamphlet-warfare which accompanied the battles of the Civil War. The tensions of the time created, as in Nostradamus's case, an urgent need for reassurance of what the future held. Cavalier and Roundhead prophets sniped at each other on paper, and Lilly's predictions of success seem to have had a genuine influence in promoting confidence and helping to keep Parliament's soldiers and supporters in good heart. He survived the Stuart Restoration without undue difficulty and died in 1681, comfortably off, a churchwarden and respected citizen, mourned by a distinguished circle of friends.

The Cabala was now becoming more accessible through translations into Latin. The *Sefer Yetsirah* had been translated by Guillaume Postel (1510–81), a highly eccentric French mathematician, Cabalist and mystic, and was published in 1552. In the following century Christian Knorr von Rosenroth (1636–89), a German Protestant mystic and poet, provided translations from the *Zohar* in the two volumes of his *Kabbala Denudata* (1677 and 1684). He also included selections from the great sixteenth-century Palestinian Cabalist, Isaac Luria, and extracts from a work on cabalistic alchemy, the *Esch ha-Mezaref*, which according to legend was the mysterious book owned by Nicolas Flamel.

Much more sinister dealings with the supernatural were going on in France, where between 1673 and 1680 at least fifty priests were executed on charges of using the Mass and the sacraments in murderous or amatory sorcery, and others were imprisoned. Father Davot was convicted of saying Mass over the naked body of a woman and also of using the Mass in magic by placing under the altar-cloth papers bearing the names of those it was hoped either to kill or to seduce. Father Lemeignan was imprisoned for life, accused of murdering two children and hacking them to pieces during the celebration of Mass. Father Tournet was found guilty of saying Mass on the body of a girl he had made pregnant, with the intention that she would miscarry: she died of fright. Father Cotton had baptized a child in holy oil and strangled him as a sacrifice to the Devil. Father Gérard was convicted of using a girl's body as his altar and copulating with her during the Mass.

Many of the offending priests were arrested as a result of the activities of a special court, set up by Louis XIV in 1679 to deal with cases of poisoning in which some of the nobility were implicated. The court sat in secret and there was no appeal from its verdict. Meeting in a room draped in black and lit by candles, it was called the *Chambre Ardente* or Burning Court. Its investigations, headed by the police chief of Paris, Nicolas de la Reynie, rapidly extended from poisoning into the neighbouring territory of sorcery. Confessions were extracted by torture, but there seems to have been a substantial element of truth underlying the evidence.

De la Reynie discovered that various ladies of quality had consulted fortune-tellers, who frequently doubled as abortionists and suppliers of poisons, love potions and wax images. His enquiries centered round a widow named Catherine Deshayes, known as La Voisin, who told fortunes by palmistry, physiognomy, card-reading and crystal-gazing, and who had achieved a certain flashy celebrity. It turned out that she also arranged abortions and disposed of unwanted babies, sold aphrodisiacs, beauty preparations, medicines and poisons, and provided magical ceremonies for some of her clients. When the police searched her house in the Rue Beauregard, they found grimoires, priestly vestments and black candles. In the grounds was a pavilion fitted up as a chapel. The walls were hung in black and behind the altar was a black curtain with a white cross on it. A mattress rested on the altar, covered by a black cloth, and on top of this were black candles. There was also a furnace in which the bodies of babies and aborted embryos had been incinerated.

La Voisin was burned alive in February 1680. In October Louis XIV suspended the sittings of the court, probably because his mistress, Madame de Montespan, had been implicated. The police investigation continued, however, in secret. The beautiful Françoise Athenais, Marquise de Montespan, born in 1641, had first consulted La Voisin in 1667. She wanted to supplant the king's current favourite, the Duchesse de la Vallière, and hoped eventually to become queen. La Voisin arranged for a priest, the Abbé Mariette, to say three Masses in which prayers were offered for the Marquise's success in these ambitions. On the last occasion two doves, birds of passion sacred to Venus, were sacrificed. Madame de Montespan became the mistress of Louis XIV in that same year.

She did not feel secure in the royal affections. More Masses were said and aphrodisiac charms, compounded of powdered moles, bat's blood and Spanish fly, were blessed by the priest, to be slipped into the king's food. In 1673, when there was a serious danger that Madame de Montespan might be supplanted in her turn, stronger measures were taken. La Voisin called in the elderly Abbé Guibourg, a bloated and sinister cleric who horrified even the hardened de la Reynie. Guibourg said three Masses over the Marquise's naked body, subjecting the host to various sexual manipulations. A child's throat was cut, some of its blood was drained into the chalice, and two powerful demons, Astaroth and

Asmodeus, were invoked to accept the sacrifice and ensure that the king remained faithful to Madame de Montespan and would make her his queen. She took the host and some of the blood away, to be fed surreptitiously to the king.

Three years later, Guibourg was called in again and further amatory Masses were celebrated. In 1679, driven desperate by the king's passion for a rival, Madame de Montespan resorted to death magic. Guibourg said Mass for the dead in the name of the king, chanting murderous incantations against him. The rite also required a confection of semen, menstrual blood, bat's blood and flour. It failed to take effect.

The Burning Court wound up its proceedings in 1682. Guibourg was imprisoned in the castle of Besançon, where he remained chained to the wall of his cell until his death in 1686. No public accusation was ever made against Madame de Montespan and the king, anxious to avoid scandal, treated her with distant courtesy till she retired from court in 1691. She devoted herself to piety and good works, and died in 1707.

The Witch Mania

In the last years of the fifteenth century and the first quarter of the sixteenth there were savage persecutions of witches in the Alpine valleys of northern Italy. Seventy men and women were burned at Brescia in 1510, and 300 at Como in 1514. In 1523 it was reported that a hundred witches a year were being burned in Como. This war on witches ended about 1525, when the local people would no longer tolerate it. Another was being waged sporadically among the Basques in the Pyrenees, and there were extensive witch hunts in Navarre in 1527 and 1538. There were also outbreaks of persecution in the Tyrol, Lombardy and the district round Rome, in Alsace and at various places in Germany.

In 1520 an Italian lawyer, Gianfrancesco Ponzinibio, published a book denying that the witches' night-ride and the sabbath were real and condemning the practice of torturing suspects into confessing and implicating other people. There were several other writers sceptical of Satanist witchcraft at this period, but the authors of most of the gradually swelling number of books on the subject believed in the entire Satanist stereotype. One of them was Bartolomeo Spina, a Dominican theologian and papal official, who wrote *Quaestio de Strigibus* (1523), attacking Ponzinibio. He mentions the walnut tree at Benevento, which was famous as a gathering place of witches, and it is clear from what he says that popular beliefs about witches in Italy were still far closer to the old model of black witchcraft than to the newer Satanist one.

In 1517 Johann Geiler von Kaysersberg published *Die Emeis*, the first book on witchcraft in German. He took up an earlier suggestion that witches sometimes went to the sabbath in the flesh and sometimes stayed at home and enjoyed it in hallucinations induced by Satan, and this later became the accepted view. He also announced that the Devil saved witches from feeling any pain when they were burned to death. He objected to the state of the law in the Holy Roman Empire at that time, which distinguished between healing magic and harmful magic, and punished only the latter. Geiler said that all magic was contrary to the law of God.

About 1525, Paolo Grillandi, a lawyer who had acted as a judge at witch trials near Rome, wrote *Tractatus de Sortilegiis*, which was frequently quoted by later writers. He was profoundly impressed by one woman, who told him, voluntarily and without torture, that she had been a witch for fourteen years and had killed men, injured cattle and damaged crops. Demons carried her to the sabbath, where the Devil was worshipped and the witches feasted, danced backwards and celebrated an orgy with evil spirits in human form. This appears to be one of many cases in which people in disturbed states of mind fastened their fantasies onto the stereotype which had been created and believed themselves to be Satanist witches. Voluntary confessions of this kind had an important effect in convincing intelligent observers that Satanist witchcraft was a reality. The fact that witches so often confessed to the same things also reinforced the credibility of the stereotype, though it seems clear now that it was the result of responses to leading questions and was a consequence of growing general agreement about what witches did.

There was a lull in witch hunting from 1525 to 1560, during a generally peaceful and prosperous period, though there were sporadic outbreaks here and there. The tide of systematic persecution on a grand scale began to flow in the 1560s and mounted in scope and ferocity in the seventeenth century. The reason for this was the rise to power of Protestantism and the Roman Catholic reaction to it. Each side was convinced that its opponents were inspired by the Devil, and while the Prince of Darkness himself was safe from torture and execution, his supposed human agents were not. It was not simply a matter of Protestants and Catholics persecuting each other as witches, though they sometimes did, but of a situation in which each group believed itself to be opposed by a Satanic conspiracy. This belief induced fear and resentment which readily fastened onto any suspicion of evil witchcraft aroused by serious misfortune. The Satanist witch was a scapegoat for aggressive hostility rooted in the failure of each religious party to make everyone else conform to it.

Thus to envision the witch persecution solely as a variety of frenzy or hysteria is to miss the point, though it certainly became that on the level of popular action. The persecution is rather to be compared to the action taken in modern America against supposed Communists or in modern Russia against supposed social fascists: organized, self-righteous repression, rational within the narrow bounds of what current orthodoxy considers rational, of elements believed to be representative of the ultimate Enemy.[17]

Protestant and Catholic persecutors were at one in seeing the Enemy at work in the world on a hitherto unprecedented scale and, despite their mutual hostility, commended each other's books on witchcraft. Both sides believed that Satan's activities threatened the whole fabric of civilization and that they were being carried on under license from God. Why the Almighty should allow the Evil One to sap and tunnel at society in this way was a disturbing mystery, usually put down to 'the increasing wickedness of mankind'.

Luther believed that he was locked in personal battle with Satan, who inspired the resistance to his ideas, and he had no sympathy for Satan's allies. He used to recall how his mother had been forced to be kind to a witch in the neighbourhood, for fear of offending her. 'I should have no compassion on these wretches', he said, 'I would burn all of them.'[18] Calvin was equally convinced of the Devil's massive and malevolent opposition to his own brand of truth and found ample authority in the Old Testament for the ruthless extirpation of witches. In 1545 at Geneva, the headquarters of Calvinism, thirty-four people were executed for causing by witchcraft a plague which had struck the city three years before. Zwingli in Zürich was not interested in witchcraft, but some of his successors were. Erastus, the leading Zwinglian theologian in Germany in the sixteenth century, thought that all witches and practitioners of demonic magic should be exterminated.

A witch hunt in Göttingen in Lutheran Brunswick, in 1561, was conducted with such ferocity that, according to a contemporary writer, scarcely any old woman was safe from the stake. Trials continued in Brunswick and in 1590, when witches from all around were taken to Wolfenbüttel for burning, there were so many stakes that the place of execution looked like a small wood. There were trials in Brandenburg and Württemberg in the 1560s and 1570s, and 48 witches were burned in Württemberg in 1582. The Protestant authorities in Hesse, on the other hand, were sceptical and discouraged accusations of witchcraft. In Bavaria 63 witches were burned in 1562–3. In Saxony a new law code of 1572 prescribed execution by burning for all suspects convicted of making pacts with demons, regardless of whether they were believed to have harmed anyone, and this example was followed elsewhere. At Quedlinburg in Saxony 133 witches were burned in one day in 1589.

Roman Catholics were equally merciless. There were numerous burnings in the 1580s in Trier, where campaigns to stamp out Protestantism and banish Jews were followed by persecution of witches. A succession of poor harvests and the ravages of Protestant troops in the countryside were ascribed to the machinations of Satan and his human allies. In 1586 unusually cold weather lasted till June and 120 people were executed for prolonging the winter by witchcraft. Dietrich Flade, the Vice-Governor of Trier, began to have doubts about the justice of the crusade and was promptly burned as a witch himself.

The revival of witch hunting had impelled Johan Weyer (1515–88) to publish his book *De Praestigiis Daemonum* (1563). He thought that belief in witchcraft had been stimulated by the Devil in his hatred of mankind and he appealed to the authorities to stop assisting Satan by promoting the belief. Witches, he said, did not really do any damage but wished people harm and then, if harm occurred, assumed that they had caused it. (The same point about magic and wishful thinking had been made hundreds of years before by Philostratus in his biography of Apollonius of Tyana). Old women were accused by their neighbours, through malice or mistaken suspicion, and were tortured until they would confess to anything put to them, however absurd and untrue. Weyer distinguished between witches, who were poor, ignorant and desperate, and magicians who summoned up demons with incantations and rituals, to gain knowledge and power.

Weyer wrote a revised version of his book, *De Lamiis*, in 1577. A Protestant, born in Brabant, he was a pupil of Agrippa and studied medicine in Paris. He became court physician to the Duke of Cleves in the Netherlands and was influential in discouraging the persecution of witches there until he was forced out by pressure from the Duke of Alba, the Catholic governor of the Netherlands.

The effect of Weyer's books was the opposite of what he intended since they roused believers in witchcraft to enter the lists against him. He was swiftly contradicted by Lambert Daneau, a French Calvinist, whose *Les Sorciers* was published at Geneva in 1564. Daneau thought that witches were a danger to the human race and should be rigorously hunted out and punished. *Les Sorciers* was the first textbook on witchcraft to be published in England, where it came out in 1575 as *A Dialogue of Witches*.

Witches were burned at Poitiers, Bordeaux, Le Mans, Toulouse, Avignon and elsewhere in France in the 1560s, '70s and '80s. There were numerous executions in Alsace from 1575 on and in Luxemburg from 1580. A savage persecution erupted in Lorraine from 1580 to 1595.

In 1580 the celebrated philosopher, economist and lawyer Jean Bodin (1529–96) published his *Démonomanie des Sorciers*, which was frequently reprinted. Bodin had been impressed by a confession made without torture by a witch who said she had been initiated into the Devil's service as a girl of twelve by her mother, who had subsequently been burned. He maintained that people who denied the reality of witchcraft were almost invariably witches themselves and propagated their pernicious scepticism at Satan's bidding. As Bodin was widely regarded as the most brilliant intellect of his day, his book was a powerful addition to the witch-hunter's arsenal. It was written to help judges in dealing with cases of suspected witchcraft and recommended the most brutal methods of interrogation, including the torture of children to force them to give evidence against their parents. Bodin thought burning in a slow fire was too good for witches, as it took them only half an hour or an hour to die. He said that people were frightened to give evidence against them and it would be wise to adopt the Scottish custom of putting a box in each church, in which anonymous accusations could be deposited surreptitiously. As it was, hardly one witch in a thousand was being punished and if judges made the mistake of conforming to the letter of the law, it would be scarcely one in a hundred thousand.

Peter Binsfeld (died 1603), a Catholic bishop who took a prominent part in the atrocities at Trier, published *Tractatus de Confessionibus Maleficorum* in 1589, remarking that the world was hurtling headlong to greater wickedness and therefore God had permitted the Enemy to persecute the human race with greater force than ever before. His book was cited for a hundred years afterwards by Catholics and Protestants busy with their own persecuting. An even more authoritative witch-hunter's manual came out in 1595, the *Demonolatreiae* of Nicolas Remy (1530–1612), a lawyer who claimed to have condemned 900 witches to the stake in ten years during the holocaust in Lorraine. Remy's eldest son had died a few days after refusing to give money to a beggar woman and the grieving father prosecuted her as a witch. His book supplies full details of the worship of the Devil at the sabbath and the feasting, dancing and orgies, the powers of demons and their sexual relationships with witches, and the harmful magic worked by the demons through their human minions.

Remy's book and Martin del Rio's *Disquisitionum Magicarum* (1599) largely replaced the *Malleus* as standard guides to the discovery and extirpation of witches. Martin del Rio (1551–1608) was a prodigiously learned Spanish Jesuit, born in Antwerp. His book deals with magic, witchcraft and divination, and provides instructions for judges in witchcraft cases. An eminent lawyer, Henri Boguet (died 1619), published *Discours des Sorciers* in 1602. It was based on his experiences as a judge in Burgundy, which convinced him that: 'There are witches by the thousand everywhere, multiplying upon the earth even as worms in a garden . . . I would that they might all be burned at once in a single fire.'[19] Another authoritative textbook, *Compendium Maleficarum* by Francesco Maria Guazzo, an Italian friar, came out in 1608.

The cruelty and credulity of the witch-hunting manuals can only be appreciated by reading them, which is a disagreeable experience. They all insist that the Devil's power, under license from God, is almost limitless and that multitudes of depraved wretches have enlisted under his banner to revel in debauchery and filth and to bring down Christian society in ruins. The number of witches is daily increasing and they must be smelled out and ruthlessly exterminated. Anyone who doubts the reality of the peril is a traitor to humanity and probably a witch himself.

Ridiculous stories of impossible feats performed by demons and witches are gravely told and retold by each author in turn. Boguet discusses the question of witches moving crops from one farmer's field to another's and decides that what really happens is that the Devil transposes the two fields, crops and all. Del Rio and Guazzo solemnly relate the story of the soldier who shot an arrow into a black cloud and down tumbled a fat, naked and drunken female of mature years, wounded in the thigh. Remy, who had read his classical authors and swallowed them whole, says that demons can erect mountains in the twinkling of an eye, cause rivers to run backwards, solidify fountains, put the stars out and bring the sky falling round men's ears. It is difficult but essential to remember that these authors were not ignorant barbarians but men of intelligence, education and culture, convinced of a threat to everything they valued in life.

By this time it was commonly believed that witches used consecrated hosts, holy water and holy oil in evil magic and celebrated perverted forms of the Mass to dishonour Christ and exalt the Devil. There were stories of renegade priests in black copes consecrating slices of turnip in place of hosts, of black hosts and black chalices containing water or urine, of the Devil himself saying Mass at the sabbath and elevating the host by impaling it on one of his horns. Whether there was any truth in these rumours or not, the belief that the Mass had innate magical force was carried by some priests to remarkable lengths. Paolo Grillandi refers to the use of the Mass, the host, holy water and blessed candles in love magic and the saying of Mass for the dead against the living with intent to kill. Johan Weyer describes a German priest saying Mass on the belly of a young nun to cure her of bewitchment. It was this type of magic which culminated in the Montespan affair.

Meanwhile the fires were blazing hungrily in Germany, on the French–German borders and in Switzerland and the Low Countries. Boguet is believed to have executed as many as 600 witches in Burgundy. Between 1591 and 1610 over 500 were burned in the Vaud district of western Switzerland. There were numerous trials in the German and Italian Tyrol and in Alsace. In the Netherlands a decree of 1592 announced that although a great many women had been burned, many more remained to be dealt with. In some villages fourteen or fifteen witches had been executed after conviction by the water ordeal. This was 'swimming a witch', by tying her hand and foot and throwing her into a pond. If she floated she was guilty and if she sank she was innocent, because witches were well-known to be preternaturally light. In Holland people prudently had themselves weighed by a public official and if they did not weigh less than the standard for their size and appearance they were issued with a certificate, as a protection against accusations.

From 1589 in Bavaria, where Lutheran preachers had been encouraging witch hunts, the Catholic reconquest of the country intensified the persecution. A woman at Freising incautiously remarked after a hailstorm that there was worse weather in the offing. She was arrested and tortured until she confessed that she was a witch and implicated eleven other women, who in turn were forced to name others. In 1592 one of the judges wrote to the authorities at Freising asking for the prosecutions to be halted: 'If all those denounced were treated as the others more than half the women of the district would be brought under suspicion and have to be tortured, which would be the destruction of the land. He had not prisons to hold the accused or money to pay the torturers and executioners.' The prosecutions did stop, 'to the great relief of the population, which had besieged the Freising authorities with petitions to put an end to it'.[20]

Victims were often strangled before burning, but this final mercy was not always granted. In Munich in 1600, when eleven people were executed, six of them were torn with red-hot pincers on their way to the stake, one woman had her breasts cut off, five men were broken on the wheel and one was impaled, before they were all burned alive.

Duke Maximilian I of Bavaria believed that his wife's barrenness was caused by witchcraft and he repeatedly incited his judges to destroy Satan's allies. He was urged on by his Jesuit chaplain, Jerome Drexel. At Eichstätt 122 people were executed between 1603 and 1627, in which year the Bishop of Eichstätt, pained that unworthy suspicions of his motives had somehow arisen, announced that he would no longer appropriate the property of all those condemned.

In 1609 a lawyer and civil servant named Pierre de Lancre (1553–1631) was sent to investigate reports of witchcraft among the Basques in the French Pyrenees. De Lancre was another civilized and charming witch hunter and, if possible, even more credulous than the rest. He soon decided that most of the population were witches. Their extreme poverty, he said, made them ready recruits for the Devil's service and the majority of the priests in the area were dedicated Satanists. He busily burned almost a hundred suspects but, fortunately, his commission ran out before the end of the year. He wrote a book based on his experiences, *Tableau de l'Inconstance des Mauvais Anges* (1613), and published two more books on sorcery and witchcraft in 1622 and 1627.

While de Lancre was at work, the authorities across the border from him in Navarre took alarm at the prevalence of witches and demanded that the Inquisition take action. It did, but only seven witches were burned, in 1610. A comparatively sceptical Spanish writer, Pedro of Valencia, investigated the case and came to the conclusion that, shorn of the fantastic details to which suspects were forced to confess, the witches' meetings were real. But the Devil had nothing to do with them, or no more than with other human misdeeds. 'The evidence of all my senses leads me to feel that the meetings have been between men and women who have come together for the same reasons that they have always come together; to commit sins of the flesh.' Another careful investigator, however, Alonso de Salazar, eventually concluded that 'none of the acts which have been attested in this case really or physically occurred at all'.[21]

Witch hunting was stimulated by cases of apparent demonic possession, which were frequently put down to the malice of witches. Boguet began his book with an account of a little girl of eight, into whom a witch sent five demons, so that the child was 'struck helpless in all her limbs' and 'had to go about on all fours; also she kept twisting her mouth about in a very strange manner'. The most spectacular cases of this sort occurred in convents where nuns were stricken with mass hysteria. After an outbreak of hysterical mania at a small convent at Aix-en-Provence, a priest named Louis Gaufridi was arrested and tortured until he admitted bewitching the nuns, signing a pact with the Devil in his own blood and presiding over cannibal revels at the witches' sabbath, where he celebrated the Black Mass. He was sent to the stake in 1611. There was another famous case at Loudun, where Father Urbain Grandier was burned alive in 1634. Produced at his trial, and still surviving, were the pact he had signed with the Devil and an acknowledgement written backwards and signed by Satan and five other demons. There were similar cases at Louviers in 1642 and at Paderborn in Germany in 1656.

The witch mania reached its peak in Germany in the 1620s and '30s, in Bamberg and Würzburg, Mainz, Cologne, Brunswick, Nassau, Baden, Brandenburg, Bavaria, Trier and Württemberg, at the same time as the graph of religious hatred climbed to its highest point in the Thirty Years War. The same period saw fierce persecutions again on the borders in Burgundy, Lorraine and Alsace – where 5,000 are said to have perished between 1615 and 1635 – and in Normandy between 1600 and 1645, with many witches burned in Rouen. What may have been the most savage outbreak of all occurred in Bamberg from 1624 to 1630. The Vice-Chancellor was executed because he was sceptical and many leading citizens of the town were burned alive. One of them was the Burgomaster Johannes Junius, who smuggled out of prison a pitiful letter to his daughter, lamenting that under excruciating torture he had finally given way, admitted his guilt and named as witches neighbours whom he knew to be as innocent as he was himself.

The Prince-Bishop of Würzburg was as fanatical a witch hunter as his cousin of Bamberg and both were urged on by their Jesuit advisers. Hundreds were executed in Würzburg and, as elsewhere, the more who were arrested and tortured, the larger the numbers implicated became. In 1629 one of the bishop's officials wrote to a friend: 'It is beyond doubt that, at a place called the Fraw Rengberg, the Devil in person with 8,000 of his followers, held an assembly and celebrated Mass before them all, administering to his congregation (that is, the witches) rinds and parings of turnips in place of the Holy Sacrament of the Altar. I shudder to write about these foul, most horrible and hideous blasphemies.'[22]

Friedrich von Spee, the Jesuit author of *Cautio Criminalis* (1631), acted as confessor to accused witches in Würzburg and the experience turned him prematurely white. He believed that although genuine witches existed, all the suspects he knew had been wrongfully condemned. He denounced the extraction of confessions by torture and pointed out that accusations occurred because storms, epidemics and other misfortunes were popularly attributed to witchcraft, while others were based on an envious feeling that anyone who seemed favoured by fortune must be a worker of magic. The book infuriated witch hunters, but it was translated into German, Dutch, French and Polish and may have had influenced the decline of witch persecution after about 1640.

By comparison with the Continent, witch hunting in England was on a modest scale. Less than a thousand victims were executed, by hanging not burning, against 100,000 or more in Germany. Although suspects were bullied, beaten and hurt, the use of torture to obtain confessions of witchcraft was illegal in England. Probably as a result, the picture which emerges from the confessions is closer to the stereotype of black witchcraft than to the Satanist variety. Witchcraft in England was far more a cottage industry than an organized conspiracy of diabolists and little is heard of the sabbath and its ceremonies.

Witch hunts began in the 1560s and continued in fits and starts until 1682, when three women were hanged at Exeter. The last person to be tried and convicted of witchcraft in England was Jane Wenham, a wise woman of Hertfordshire in 1712, and she was reprieved.

There was, in fact, no clearly defined periodic wave of witch-mania sweeping throughout the country, but rather a succession of sporadic outbursts. The underlying current of superstition, always present, manifested itself unpleasantly whenever and wherever fanaticism was unusually rampant, the influence of one man often being sufficient to raise the excess of zeal to the danger point.[23]

One such man was Matthew Hopkins, the self-styled 'Witch-Finder General', who was responsible for the largest mass execution of witches in England, when nineteen were hanged at Chelmsford, Essex, in 1645. Hopkins was a Puritan lawyer who smelled out witches with great cruelty for pay, but his activities in the eastern counties lasted for only a year, by which time he had gone too far and stirred up so much local opposition that he could not continue.

The persecution in England seems to have been sparked off by Protestant–Catholic tensions which created alarm about magic in general. In 1562 the Countess of Lennox and four others were condemned for treason because they had consulted 'wizards' to find out how long Queen Elizabeth would live. In the following year Sir Anthony Fortescue and others were indicted for casting the queen's horoscope for the same purpose. The Protestant hold on England was precarious, depending heavily on the survival of Elizabeth herself, and the consequent anxiety focussed on magic, 'popish superstition' and witchcraft. After Elizabeth's accession in 1558, extremist Protestants who had taken refuge in Switzerland and Germany returned home and quickly began railing against witches and sorcerers, who they said had multiplied exceedingly during the recent Roman Catholic years under Bloody Mary. The first notable witch trial occurred at Chelmsford in 1566. But in the main the Church of England declined to stir itself into an excitable lather over witchcraft and magic.

The situation was very different in Scotland, where it is estimated that 4,400 witches were executed between 1590 and 1680. The Kirk and the Protestant lords were fierce against witchcraft, torture was legal and the sabbath reappears in the confessions. John Knox himself preached against a condemned witch at St Andrews in 1572, before she was burned at the stake. The best-known case is that of the North Berwick witches in 1590–2. Among other things they were accused of worshipping the Devil in a church at night, flying in sieves, raising storms and attempting to murder King James by melting a wax image of him in a fire. The king himself interrogated them and one witch, Agnes Sampson, was able to whisper in his ear the words he and his wife had spoken privately to each other on their wedding night, which naturally impressed him.

Isobel Gowdie of Auldearne made a series of long and fantastic confessions, voluntarily and without torture, in 1662. She believed that she could turn herself into a cat or a hare, had frequently flown through the air on a wisp of straw or a toy horse to worship the Devil at the sabbath with dancing and orgies, and had visited fairyland. It is not known whether she was executed. The last major trial in Scotland was in Renfrewshire in 1697, when twenty-four people were indicted and seven were burned.

Witchcraft beliefs were taken to North America by immigrants and there were apparently eleven hangings for witchcraft in Connecticut between 1647 and 1662, with another case at Boston in 1688. But the only major outbreak was the famous one at Salem Village, Massachusetts, in 1692, following a hard winter and an epidemic of smallpox. It was believed that a group of witches had allied themselves with Satan to destroy the Church of God and set up the kingdom of the Devil. The contagiously hysterical behaviour of various children and adolescent girls who threw fits was put down to witchcraft. A former minister of Salem Village, George Burroughs, was hanged as a witch. Eighteen others were hanged, one was pressed to death for refusing to plead, and two died in prison. A reaction set in almost at once, with a feeling that the accused had been condemned on inadequate evidence. In 1696 the jurors at the trials four years before signed a Confession of Error, saying that they had been misled by the Devil.

Were there ever any real Satanist witches, as distinct from wise women and people trying to practise black witchcraft? All told, the victims of the witch persecutions may have numbered anything from 250,000 to a million. The great majority of them were almost certainly innocent but were tortured and brainwashed into admitting guilt. There were others, like Isobel Gowdie, who were mentally disturbed, believed themselves to be Satanists and readily confessed to flying and assorted fantasies. Probably, there were also a few who really did worship the Devil and who came as close to being Satanist witches as was humanly possible. The example of the modern witchcraft movement (see chapter four) shows how a fictitious stereotype can appeal to people who then proceed to bring it to life, and the same thing is likely to have happened hundreds of years ago. The righteous were horrified by the Satanist witch figure, but a few of the unrighteous may well have been sufficiently attracted to meet in small scattered groups for feasting, dancing and unfettered sex and to honour the Devil in the person of his earthly representative, their leader.

The Satanist stereotype itself made it easier to be a witch, because there was no longer any need to have innate powers or a knowledgeable grandmother. And Satan had been built up into a figure of colossal power, attractive to those intensely dissatisfied with their lot in God's world and Christian society. Witchcraft flourished, Bodin thought, because people hoped to gain by it what they could not obtain by conventional means. Remy said of Satan: 'For such as are given over to their lusts and to love he wins by offering them the hope of gaining their desires: or if they are bowed under the load of daily poverty, he allures them by some large and ample promise of riches: or he tempts them by showing them the means of avenging themselves when they have been angered by some injury or hurt received.' Boguet said: 'For he takes men when they are alone and in despair or misery because of hunger or some disaster which has befallen them.' The unfairness of life, which helped to create belief in Satanist witchcraft, probably also created Satanist witches. In our own time the same motives have led people to join Satanist groups of whose real existence there is no doubt at all.[24]

It has been forcefully argued that in England the Protestant reformers destroyed ordinary people's defences against witchcraft. The sign of the cross, holy water and other symbols and rites of the Church were dismissed as superstitious and ineffective mumbo-jumbo. The populace was consequently left with no defence except to insist that witchcraft was dealt with by the courts: hence the unprecedented witch trials of the sixteenth and seventeenth centuries in England.[25] But it is not clear how this argument is to be applied to the Continent, where witch hunting began much earlier and there was persecution in Roman Catholic areas as well as in Protestant ones.

All witch hunts were carried on with popular approval, and when they outran it they stopped. But popular fear of witches was much the same everywhere and yet large areas of Europe were not affected or were only slightly affected by the witch mania: southern Italy and Sicily, Spain and Portugal, Ireland, Scandinavia. The crucial factor was apparently not popular demand but the attitude of authority in different areas. There was no witch craze in eastern Europe under the Greek Orthodox Church. The Inquisition in Spain took a cautious and sceptical attitude to accusations of witchcraft. Even in districts most affected by Protestant–Catholic tension, the attitude of authority was decisive. In 1602 the Prince-Abbot of Fulda, in central Germany, who had been ousted by Protestants, re-established himself in his principality and set about the local witches. Balthasar Ross, the self-styled 'Witch Master of Fulda' who was paid by the head, claimed to have sent more than 700 suspects to execution by 1606. But in that year a new Prince-Abbot succeeded, the trials stopped and Ross was sent to jail. In Cologne the city council successfully resisted pressure for persecution until 1629, when it was overruled by the Archbishop of Cologne. The local authorities at Nuremberg in witch-ridden Bavaria kept the persecution out of their city altogether, and there are other examples.

When the witch mania began to decline, it was because authority turned against it, not because of any sudden alteration in popular attitudes. Lynching of witches continued after trying them had stopped. The decline may have been caused initially by a reaction against the excessive horrors of the previous decades, which had driven home the fact that once a witch hunt began there was no logical end to it. In 1650 Queen Christina of Sweden ordered all witch prosecution in Swedish-occupied areas of Germany to cease. 'It is a remarkably enlightened document. The Queen states that the spread of witch-trials is of dangerous consequence, past experience showing that the longer they are allowed to continue, the deeper men are involved "in an inextricable labyrinth".'[26]

There had always been sceptics, as the witch hunters bitterly complained, but in the 1650s they at last began to exert a strong and growing influence. Doubts about the validity of evidence given under torture eventually brought torture itself into disrepute. The witch craze was a long time dying and there were sporadic outbursts of persecution for the rest of the seventeenth century and on into the eighteenth. At Neisse in Silesia a capacious oven was built for the convenient roasting of witches. Forty-two people died in it in 1651 and by 1660 it is estimated to have claimed a thousand victims, including children as well as adults. There were witch hunts in Geneva in 1652, in Saxony in 1666 and 1676, in Sweden in the 1670s, in Salzburg from 1677 to 1681, in Styria and Mecklenburg in the late seventeenth century, in Bavaria in 1715–22 and 1728–34. The last legal execution was at Glarus in Switzerland in 1782.

Hand in hand with the decline of witch hunting went a decline of belief in the Devil. Not that everyone stopped believing in the Prince of Darkness, far from it. But the scientific revolution of the seventeenth century and the philosophy of Descartes made it increasingly difficult for intellectuals to accept the possibility of constant interferences with the order of nature by Satan and his subordinate fiends. The *Malleus* had maintained that when harmful events occurred, they might be caused by demons, acting alone or in concert with witches and sorcerers; or they might be caused by angels on orders from God; or they might happen in the ordinary course of nature. This view catered to the old tendency to blame evil spirits and evil magic for events which would now be put down to natural causes. But in the seventeenth century a new picture of the universe became established, in which nature was a machine that ran by itself. An honorific place in the system was reserved for God, who had designed the machine and set it running in the first place, but neither he nor the Devil any longer intervened in the world, to help or to harm. This mechanical concept of the universe spread slowly from educated circles to less educated ones. There was no room in it for the interventions of spirits and demons or for magicians and witches who worked supernatural marvels with their aid.

4
The Modern Revival

The new scientific view of the world demolished the theory of macrocosm and microcosm, and the whole edifice of magic which had been built on it. The universe was no longer constructed on the model of a man, alive all through, pulsing with currents of divine energy, responsive to human will and desire. Man could not now climb the ladder of his own nature to scale the heights of power. He did not contain the heavens in himself, so that he was influenced by the stars and could dominate them in turn. The links of sympathy and correspondence which the magician sought to employ were consigned to the rubbish heap of discarded theories. The spirits and demons he hoped to master no longer had a place in the scheme of things which made them worth mastering, and indeed it became questionable whether they existed at all. Predicting the future changed into a scientific instead of a religious, magical or psychic exercise.

The universe was now a dead piece of machinery, its cogs and wheels turning in accordance with immutable laws which left no scope for magical manipulation and little for effective religion. People began to look instead to improved technology for control of the environment. A certain respect remained for religion, though it proved hollow, but magic ceased to command respect or cause much alarm in intellectual circles. It was dismissed with contempt as irrational and ridiculous. At popular levels, improved agricultural and medical techniques weakened – without entirely destroying – the hold of magic, witchcraft, herb-lore and astrology on the most important areas of most people's lives. The rationalism of the Enlightenment cut the arteries of folk customs and ceremonies, which began to die out. These trends were far more pronounced in Protestant quarters than in Roman Catholic ones, where the old religion and the old traditions fared better. The reaction, when it came, was correspondingly stronger in Protestant than in Catholic spheres of influence.

The Eighteenth Century

For most of the eighteenth century magic was in the doldrums. The great Renaissance magi were replaced by such ludicrous figures as Cagliostro and the Count of St-Germain. Many of the grimoires were first printed in the eighteenth century, which shows that there was still a demand for them but also that they were no longer considered too dangerous for public consumption. Alchemy retained more of its appeal as a bridge between the scientific and the spiritual, and the Philosopher's Stone had not lost its old power to excite. Goethe interested himself in alchemy and astrology as a young man, and there was a sensation in England in 1782, when a Fellow of the Royal Society, James Price, turned mercury into gold in the presence of distinguished observers. But the feat turned out to have been fraudulent and the unfortunate Price committed suicide.

Most well-to-do families ceased to consult astrologers, though there was still a Hapsburg court astrologer in Vienna when the ill-fated Marie Antoinette was born in 1755, and her horoscope threw the court into justified gloom. But in France and Germany astrology sank almost completely out of sight. In England it was kept alive in a rudimentary form in the almanacs. The most popular of them was *Vox Stellarum*, which was put out under the name of the astrologer Francis Moore long after his death in 1715. It sold over 100,000 copies in 1768 and subsequently became the well-known *Old Moore's Almanac*, which is still published. But less than half a dozen new astrological textbooks were published between 1700 and 1780.[1]

The Witchcraft Act of 1736 showed how official opinion in Britain had changed by repealing earlier statutes and prosecuting, not witches and sorcerers, who were no longer believed to exist, but people who falsely held themselves out to be witches, magicians or diviners: those who 'pretend to exercise or use any kind of Witchcraft, Sorcery, Enchantment, or Conjuration, or undertake to tell Fortunes. . . .'[2] Popular suspicion of witchcraft remained alive but was rarely sanctioned by authority and villagers who took vengeance on witches were now themselves in danger from the courts.

There was a marked change of attitude to demonic possession, which was now much more often explained in non-demonic terms: by those in authority at least, if not always at popular levels. In 1752 the Archbishop of Cologne complained of amateur exorcists, who charged patients money to cure diseases which they pretended were demonic and caused by hostile magic. The Bishop of Ypres complained about the same thing in 1768. St Alphonsus Liguori, the Neapolitan theologian, maintained that there might be rare instances of genuine demonic possession, but that the great majority of cases had nothing to do with demons. On the other hand, as late as 1830, when a woman in Germany with all the symptoms of a split personality was sent to the local doctor, he assumed that she had been invaded by an evil spirit.

The dread of demons and witches that had haunted the sixteenth and seventeenth centuries was replaced in the eighteenth by an exaggerated terror of secret societies. Undercover groups became the focus of the same fear of an organized conspiracy against society and civilization, responsible for all seriously damaging events. In the new climate of opinion, however, the secret societies were not normally accused of worshipping the Devil or causing harm by magic. Their secrecy was suspected to be a cloak for debauchery and crime, but it was their natural, not their supernatural influence that was principally distrusted.

The proliferation of these societies sounded the first distant trumpet calls of the reaction which was to develop against rationalism and materialism and the new science and technology. The centre of the whole movement was speculative Freemasonry, which spread rapidly after 1717, when the first Grand Lodge of England was formed in London and the first Grand Master elected. The great majority of Masons, then and since, could not by any stretch of the imagination be called magicians. Most of them were always content with the honourable morality, charitableness, good citizenship and sociable comradeship, backed by a vague and tolerant deism, which their rules enjoined. Most never ventured beyond the three stock degrees, or stages of initiation as Entered Apprentice, Fellow Craft and Master Mason. But the growth of Masonry does demonstrate the need for a supernatural mystique in a world which rationalism was robbing of it. The Churches were no longer felt to meet this need, and there was a corresponding necessity to find a new and not specifically Christian foundation for personal morality.

It is significant that eighteenth-century Masonry emphasized the secrecy of the Craft and its alleged descent from the mysterious wisdom of the ancient world, relayed through the Knights Templar and the Rosicrucians. The mythical and occult antiquity of the Craft, though now recognized as fable by Masonic historians, was evidently needed as a rock of authority once Christian spiritual authority had been undermined.

Masonry swiftly invaded the Continent and America. In its obscurer corners and on its stranger fringes it attracted members eagerly interested in the occult. William Stukeley, the spiritual father of the modern Druid movement, became a Mason because he hoped that the Craft's secrets concealed 'the remains of the mysteries of the ancients'. Born in 1687, Stukeley was a clergyman, physician and archaeologist, a Fellow of the Royal Society and a founder of the Royal Society of Antiquaries. He was also a member of the Egyptian Society, founded in 1741 to promote the antique wisdom of the Nile. He investigated Stonehenge and Avebury, and published books on the two sites as 'temples of the British Druids' in the 1740s. He laid out a Druid shrine round an old apple tree in his garden in Lincolnshire and his friends, with affectionate amusement, called him 'the Arch-Druid of this age'. He died in 1765.

Stukeley was dismayed by the atheism of his time and, in the Renaissance spirit, hoped to re-establish the authority of Christianity by tracing its essence back to the ancient world and the earliest times. In a book published in 1736 he carried his efforts to the remarkable length of identifying the Roman Bacchus with God the Father. In Druidism he found 'the aboriginal patriarchal religion', the pure and ancient knowledge of God which the Druids, he thought, had brought with them from among the Hebrews when they left Palestine for Britain about the time of Abraham.

On the Continent, Masonry was denounced by the Vatican and by some absolutist governments as subversive, which made it even more attractive to the occultly inclined. The first papal bull against it was issued by Clement XII in 1738. From the 1740s on, especially in Germany and France, numerous 'side' or extra degrees were devised in Masonic and pseudo-Masonic lodges, with their own secrets, signs, symbols, passwords, regalia, romantic titles, elaborate and mysterious rituals and enticing hierarchies of initiates. The hermetic-cabalistic-alchemical synthesis of the seventeenth century revived in fringe Masonry.

In Germany in 1710 *The Perfect and True Preparation of the Philosopher's Stone by the Brotherhood of the Golden and Rosy Cross* had been published by Sigmund Richter, under the pseudonym of Sincerus Renatus. According to Richter, the great Rosicrucian adepts had emigrated to India some years before (an interesting anticipation of Madame Blavatsky's theories), but the Brotherhood still existed secretly in Europe. Its sixty-two members were ruled by an Imperator, who was required to change his name and place of residence at least once every ten years to preserve his anonymity.

Whether Richter was writing about a real secret society or an imaginary one is not known. However, in France in the 1750s a system of Masonic side degrees including a Rose Croix grade was devised, supposedly by Jacobite Scots exiled in Paris. Known as the Ancient and Accepted Rite, it was exported to America in the 1760s and is now also naturalized in Britain. There are thirty-three degrees, one for each year of Christ's life on earth. The eighteenth is Knight of the Pelican and Eagle, Sovereign Prince Rose Croix of Heredom (possibly from Greek *hieros domos*, 'holy house'). The initiation ritual is based on the Crucifixion and has justifiably been regarded with particularly dark suspicion by Christian opponents of Masonry.

With the advance of science and the retreat of Christianity, the original Rosicrucian programme for a reconciliation of the two, to be carried out by an elite of the wise and leading to a regeneration of religion and society, retained its appeal. Anyone in sympathy with it could consider himself one of the wise and a true Rosicrucian in spirit. He could then construct some tenuous historical link between himself and the supposed original Brotherhood as a warrant of authority. By the early nineteenth century many serious writers on Masonry believed in the Rosicrucian origin of the Craft itself.

Self-styled Rosicrucians tended to be especially interested in magical self-development, alchemy and healing, and communication with spirits, all within the framework of an individualistic, mystico-magical brand of Christianity. Presumably taking a cue from Sigmund Richter, an Order of the Golden and Rosy Cross was set up in Germany in the 1750s. In 1767 this organization gave birth to a fringe Masonic group, the Sublime, Most Ancient, Genuine and Honourable Society of the Golden and Rosy Cross, Abiding in the Providence of God. Its structure of nine degrees was afterwards adopted by other occult groups: Zelator, Theoreticus, Practicus, Philosophus, Adeptus Minor, Adeptus Major, Adeptus Exemptus, Magister Templi, and finally and most exalted of all, Magus. With several other contemporary societies, it left another enduring legacy by claiming to be directed by mysterious 'unknown Superiors', the descendants of the earlier Rosicrucian 'Invisible Ones'.

The Golden and Rosy Cross traced its secret doctrine back to Adam, from whom it had been passed on through Noah, Isaac, Moses and Aaron, Joshua, David, Solomon, Hiram Abiff, the chief architect of the Temple in orthodox Masonic legend, and Hermes Trismegistus. In the sixth century AD Seven Wise Masters had reformed the teachings, and conventional Masonry now constituted a preparation for initiation into them. Frederick William II, King of Prussia from 1786 to 1797, joined the Golden and Rosy Cross after recovering from an illness with the aid of a secret elixir known to the order. His two principal advisers, Baron de Bischoffswerder and J. C. Wöllner, also belonged to it, so that for eleven years a Rosicrucian trinity presided over the country's affairs. The effect was to put an end to 'enlightened' state policies in Prussia.[3]

The importance of Solomon's Temple in Masonic mythology contributed to a fascination with the medieval Knights Templar as possessors of profound oriental wisdom who had been persecuted by both Church and State. Templar side degrees and fringe groups proliferated, especially in Germany, where the reaction against the Enlightenment was in part a rebellion against French cultural domination. It was said that Jacques de Molay, the Templar Grand Master executed by the French king in 1314, had passed on the order's secrets, including the secret of alchemy, to a few carefully chosen knights, from whom they had been handed down secretly from generation to generation until they reappeared in Masonry.

In 1755 the Baron von Hund founded a new Masonic rite in Germany, the Strict Observance. He maintained that it was directly descended from the Templars and was governed by unknown Superiors. He formed an alliance with a Protestant minister, Johann August Starck, who claimed to represent another line of Templar descent in St Petersburg. Both men were interested in alchemy. Together they created the United Lodges, with the Duke of Brunswick as Grand Master, which spread into France, Sweden, Russia, Hungary and Italy.

Meanwhile in France in the 1760s an obscure Roman Catholic magician named Martinez de Pasqually (1727–79) formed lodges of his Ordre des Chevalier-Maçons, Elus Cohens de l'Universe (Order of Knights-Masons, Chosen Priests of the Universe). This organization also claimed to be guided by unknown Superiors and had nine degrees, the highest of which was Master Réau Croix. Martinez was influenced by gnosticism, the Christian Cabala, the Hermetica, Agrippa and the writings of Emanuel Swedenborg (1688–1772), the Swedish philosopher, scientist and clairvoyant who explored the spirit world in visions. Martinez returned to the old concepts of the universe as a living divine organism and man's ascent through the spheres, and resurrected the gnostic idea of the 'true self' or 'higher self', which was divine. The first major stage in his system was attained through a magical ritual in which the initiate evoked and united himself with his 'guardian angel', which was his own higher self. The Elus Cohens performed other ceremonies in which spiritual beings were summoned up, with the eventual cabalistic aim of the 'reintegration' of man and the universe, the restoration of the splintered primordial unity, the lost wholeness of God.

Martinez never completed his major work, the *Traité de la Réintégration*, but his ideas were publicized by his principal disciple, Louis Claude de St-Martin (1743–1803), author of *Tableau Naturel des Rapports* (1782), on the correspondences between God, man and the universe. Though the Order of Elus Cohens disintegrated after the founder's death, various Martinist organizations loosely dedicated to Martinez's system flourished subsequently.

Groups formed and reformed and shifted their allegiances with a kaleidoscopic reassembling of the same basic ideas in varying patterns. Jean Baptiste Willermoz, for example, a high-minded Mason and a draper in Lyons, was initiated into the Elus Cohens in 1767. He had earlier founded his own Order of the Knights of the Black Eagle and the Rosy Cross, which studied alchemy. In 1774 he joined von Hund's Strict Observance and established its Lyons lodge. From this lodge four years later emerged Willermoz's Order of the Holy City, which combined the Templar legend with Martinism and freed him from German control.

Another ingredient in the magical melting-pot was the perennial glamour of Egyptian wisdom. Mozart was a Mason and *The Magic Flute* (1791) is set in ancient Egypt and identifies the mysteries of Masonry with those of Isis and Osiris as the pathway to salvation. By this time the Sicilian adventurer Giuseppe Balsamo, who called himself Count Cagliostro, had founded his Egyptian Rite of Masonry, with himself at its head as Grand Copht and his beautiful wife presiding over the women's lodges as the Queen of Sheba. Born at Palermo in 1743, Cagliostro travelled about Europe in high society and great state. He was credited with miraculous healing powers. He claimed to know the alchemical technique of making gold, how to prolong sexual potency, how to dominate spirits and how to extend human life to a span of 5,557 years (it is probably not by chance that $5+5+5+7 = 22$, the number of letters in the Hebrew alphabet). He employed children to scry for him in a mirror or a carafe of water and, as a precursor of Spiritualism, held seances at which the spirits of the dead were summoned and manifested themselves as vague shapes in darkened rooms.

Statues of Isis, Anubis and Apis, the Egyptian sacred bull, stood in Cagliostro's seance room in Paris. The servants were dressed as Egyptian slaves and the walls were covered with Egyptian hieroglyphs. The hieroglyphs had not yet been deciphered, and would not be till the 1820s. They were still believed to be charged with esoteric and compelling wisdom. Cagliostro was eventually expelled from France and went to Italy, where he was arrested as a heretic and sorcerer by the Inquisition in 1789. He died in prison in 1795.

As a young man, Cagliostro met an even more famous Italian adventurer, Giacomo Casanova (1725–98), who used his own adaptations of cabalistic and astrological magic to siphon money out of credulous pockets. One of his victims was the elderly, wealthy and quite remarkably eccentric Marquise d'Urfé, who owned an alchemical laboratory and an extensive occult library. Madame d'Urfé wished to be reborn as a man. On Casanova's advice she wrote to Selenis, the spirit of the moon, for instructions, posting the letter by burning it in an alabaster cup. Ten minutes later a reply from Selenis, written in silver ink on green paper, appeared magically floating on Madame's bath-water. Casanova and Madame were together in the bath for the occasion. After various mishaps, including the dereliction of a spirit from the beyond in human form, who was found to have syphilis – it was hastily explained that he had been infected by a malevolent female gnome – Casanova and one of his mistresses performed a ceremony of sexual magic with Madame d'Urfé. The purpose was to impregnate her with a baby son, into whom her personality would be transferred. But no pregnancy resulted, and the great lover made himself scarce.[4]

About this time, 1763, Casanova met another celebrated charlatan, the Count of St-Germain, who was supposed to have discovered the 'water of rejuvenation' and the Philosopher's Stone, which he used to make gold and the jewels with which his person was liberally garnished. Said to be more than 2,000 years old, he was believed to be either the Wandering Jew or the offspring of an Arabian princess by a salamander. At one time he was in high favour with Louis xv and Madame de Pompadour. He liked to reminisce about the wedding feast at Cana, where he had been one of the guests when Jesus turned water into wine. He died in Germany in 1784, but modern Rosicrucian groups, who claim him for one of their own, deny that he died at all and identify him as the immortal adept earlier known as Francis Bacon.

The careers of Cagliostro and St-Germain show that a revival of interest in the occult was gathering strength (and the vogue for Gothic horror-stories is another indication of it). A more important figure for the subsequent history of magic established himself in Paris in 1778. Franz Anton Mesmer (1734–1815) studied medicine in Vienna. He joined the Golden and Rosy Cross, and later founded his own Order of Universal Harmony. Mesmer was interested in magnetic therapy. He thought that the planets influenced human beings through 'the fluid of animal magnetism', a universal medium in which all bodies were immersed. This medium was required because the older explanation of starry influence on man, the theory of macrocosm and microcosm, was no longer scientifically tenable. Mesmer was influenced by Paracelsus, who had suggested that the mysterious power of the magnet was a force emanating from the stars and possessed by all living things. Paracelsus and his followers used magnets in treating patients. As a result of his experiments, however, Mesmer dropped the magnets. He found that animal magnetism could be directly controlled by the human will and healthfully transmitted to patients by touch and gesture.

Forced out of Vienna by orthodox physicians who accused him of practising magic, Mesmer set up a clinic in Paris. His numerous successful cures, achieved in a highly theatrical atmosphere and depending on the suggestibility of his patients, caused a sensation. What he had actually discovered was hypnosis.

Mesmer was a powerful influence on the development of

Spiritualism, Christian Science and the New Thought movement. His significance for magic was that he appeared to have demonstrated the existence of a universal medium or force responsive to the human mind, which could employ it to affect the behaviour of others. For magicians this was a welcome gift and Eliphas Lévi, the leading French magus of the nineteenth century, turned Mesmer's magnetic fluid into one of the bastions of modern magical theory.

Mesmerism aroused great interest and awe for years in Europe and the United States. One of Mesmer's impressed contemporaries was Johann Kaspar Lavater (1741–1801), Calvinist pastor of St Peter's, Zürich. According to Eliphas Lévi, Lavater summoned up spirits in 'a circle which cultivated catalepsy by the help of a harmonica' and experimented with automatic writing, produced by a medium ostensibly under the control of a spirit.[5] He is better known for his passionate belief in physiognomy. Goethe helped him with his *Physiognomische Fragmente* (1775–8), which had a tremendous vogue, and character analysis from physical features was all the rage for a time. So was the new and allied art of phrenology, or character reading from 'bumps' on the head, developed by a German doctor, Franz Joseph Gall (1758–1828). His lectures on phrenology in Vienna were popular from 1796 to 1802, when the Austrian government banned them as a danger to religion. Many phrenological societies were formed elsewhere in Europe – Queen Victoria had the royal children's heads examined by a phrenologist; and in the United States travelling showmen and hucksters who dealt in patent medicines and cure-alls often dabbled in mesmerism and phrenology as well.

Phrenology appeared to be and was meant to be scientific, but interest in more old-fashioned methods of fortune-telling was reviving at all social levels. Marie Anne Lenormand (1772–1843), a fashionable Parisian clairvoyant and card-reader, was consulted by Napoleon's consort, the Empress Josephine, and welcomed to her salon Madame de Staël, the painter David and other prominent figures of the day. A fresh flow of popular books on palmistry, cartomancy, numerology, moleosophy and dreams began to come off the presses. The first dream textbook published in America was *The New Book of Knowledge*, which came out at Boston in 1767. *The Universal Interpreter of Dreams and Visions* (Baltimore, 1795) provided a dictionary of dream meanings. The stream broadened in the nineteenth century and a dream book issued in Glasgow, about 1850, ended with an apologetic observation which proved singularly ill-founded: 'The foregoing pages are published principally to show the superstitions which engrossed the minds of the population of Scotland in a past age, and which are happily disappearing before the progress of an enlightened civilization.'[6]

One other significant development in the late eighteenth century was Court de Gébelin's identification of the Tarot pack as a reservoir of ancient Egyptian wisdom. The Tarot cards had been in existence since the fifteenth century and were used for card games and telling fortunes, but there is no definite evidence that anyone earlier had attached a deep esoteric meaning to them. Antoine Court de Gébelin (1725–84) was a Protestant pastor and a Mason, and one of Mesmer's satisfied patients. In 1781, in the eighth volume of his massive work *Le Monde Primitif*, he announced that the 'trumps' of the Tarot pack were symbolic pictures of the structure of the world. They contained the secret teachings of the Egyptian priests, who had deliberately disguised their arcane knowledge in the form of a mere game and so had enabled it to survive the triumph of Christianity and the collapse of paganism. This theory was entirely mistaken but, like Mesmer's animal magnetism, it was a major influence on magic in the nineteenth century.

The Rising Tide

Since 1800 a rising tide of interest in the occult has brought the high magic of the Renaissance back to life. Modern magicians share many of the attitudes of the Renaissance magi. They too exalt the worth and potential stature of man as a virtual god. They too believe in a profound wisdom of great antiquity, lying beneath the surface of different traditions and concealed from the common herd. They have blended it from much the same materials: the Cabala, gnosticism, the Hermetica, alchemy, Neoplatonism, Pythagoreanism and the classical mystery religions, with additions from Indian sources. Much of this blend filtered from the seventeenth century to the nineteenth through the fringe Masonic, Rosicrucian and Martinist groups, but magicians also went back directly to the grimoires and to Agrippa, Paracelsus, Dee and their contemporaries. As time went by, there was a fresh return to some of the classical and medieval sources, which became easier of access through translations and commentaries. In England, for example, C. D. Ginsburg's classic work on the Cabala came out in 1863 and G. R. S. Mead published translations of gnostic texts and the Hermetica in the early 1900s. Egyptology and other developing scholarly disciplines were plundered by magicians, who picked out what fitted into their synthesis and ignored what did not.

An early example of a return to Renaissance inspiration appeared in 1801, when an obscure English magician named Francis Barrett published *The Magus, or Celestial Intelligencer*, a pedestrian work enlivened by the portraits of demons which its author drew for it. Described as 'a complete system of occult philosophy', it deals with 'the sciences of natural magic', alchemy and hermetism, astrological and talismanic magic, magnetism, the Cabala and ceremonial magic. The book is a melange of material from the grimoires, Agrippa, Paracelsus and Kircher, with bows in the direction of Mesmer and the Rosicrucians. It includes instructions for making astrological 'images' and for summoning up spirits. Barrett taught magic in London and had an influence on later British magicians.

Barrett was a believer in astrology and interest in it was now reviving in Britain, though it remained a poor relation of phrenology until the second half of the century. Astrology was sufficiently popular by 1824 for Parliament to attack it in the Vagrancy Act, which prohibited fortune-telling and the casting of horoscopes. Several astrologers fell resentfully under the Act's lash. But ironically, in the same year there emerged Robert Cross Smith (1795–1832), 'the founder of modern popular astrological journalism'.[7] He was appointed editor of a short-lived weekly, *The Straggling Astrologer*, which pretended to carry Mademoiselle Lenormand's imprimatur. Material from it, with additions, was published as *The Astrologer of the Nineteenth Century* (1825), a cross between an occult textbook and a Gothic horror-novel. Smith, who used the pseudonym Raphael, went on to produce *The Prophetic Messenger*, an almanac with astrological predictions for every day of the year, which eventually turned into *Raphael's Almanac*. Smith was also interested in alchemy and ritual magic. His death was kept quiet and a long succession of 'Raphaels' stepped unobtrusively into his shoes.

Smith was a friend of Richard James Morrison (1795–1874), a retired naval officer who became a professional astrologer and published *Zadkiel's Almanac*, which survived until 1931. 'The evil Mars is now in Aquarius', Zadkiel proclaimed for April, 1831. 'On the 7th he joins Herschel [Uranus] in the 18th degree of that sign. The last time he passed Herschel in Aquarius was in April, 1830, when *King George the Fourth* was *seized with a fatal illness*! Affliction will again affect the *royal brow*.'[8] Morrison wrote several textbooks, including an introduction to astrology which was based on William Lilly's *Christian Astrology*. He was also devoted to scrying, using a child as a medium and a crystal ball consecrated to the Archangel Michael, which he believed brought him into touch with the spirits of the dead and other supernatural intelligences.

Smith and Morrison laid the foundations of a new popular or 'low' astrology, accessible to the masses and disowned by more discriminating students of the subject. Their almanacs, unlike the earlier ones, concentrated on astrology, catering to and fostering an interest in it. Like other occultists of the period, however, they tried earnestly to register their art as a 'science', though this was peculiarly difficult in Morrison's case as he rejected Copernicus and regarded the earth as the stationary hub of the solar system. The nineteenth-century notion of 'occult science' was in part an attempt to recover magic's lost prestige. But it was also a restatement of the old Rosicrucian demand for a new synthesis and a reaction to the contemptuous refusal of most scientists to allow any possible validity to experiences which challenged their own orthodoxy. Some aspects of reality worth serious study – including hypnosis, clairvoyance, telepathy and other psychic abilities, and dreams – were consequently tarred with the occult brush to their detriment.

Meanwhile there had been action on the Druid front. The Welsh poet Iolo Morganwg (Edward Williams, 1747–1826), hailed by Robert Southey as 'Iolo, old Iolo, he who knows', was convinced that the bardic traditions of his native Glamorgan had preserved the esoteric lore of the Druids. He devised a ritual called the Gorsedd of Bards, involving the ceremonious sheathing of a naked sword amid a magic circle of stones. With a small group of fellow-Welshmen he performed this Druidical rite on Primrose Hill in London in 1792. In 1819 he succeeded in infiltrating the Eisteddfodd, the Welsh festival of arts, and the Gorsedd has remained part of its ceremonial ever since. Later in the century a diminutive Druid Order emerged from the obscure fringes of Masonry under the command of an irascible Irish Protestant lawyer and Member of Parliament, E. V. H. Kenealy (1819–80). This group was the ancestor of the present Druid factions.

The most influential single figure in the modern revival of high magic was born in Paris in 1810. Alphonse Louis Constant, better known as Eliphas Lévi, was the son of a poor shoemaker. A withdrawn and intelligent boy, he was trained for the Catholic priesthood in a seminary whose headmaster believed that animal magnetism was a force wielded by the Devil. The pupil was more attracted than alarmed. He was eventually ordained as a deacon, but he fell in love with a girl and decided that he had no vocation. He scratched a living as a teacher and left-wing political journalist, serving three brief terms in prison for his opinions, but his interest in magic increasingly preoccupied him.

Lévi read Swedenborg, Jacob Boehme and St-Martin, studied Knorr von Rosenroth's *Kabbala Denudata* and acquired a reverence for Paracelsus and Guillaume Postel. He also sat at the feet of an extraordinary Polish sage named Wronski, from whom he imbibed a Polish and Russian strain of cabalistic Martinism and Masonry, itself influenced by the cabalist religious revival movement in Polish Jewry in the eighteenth century.[9] Josef Maria Hoëne-Wronski (1776–1853) was an impoverished mathematician, astronomer and inventor, regarded by his disciples as a genius and by others as a lunatic. He believed in the divine potential of man, had discovered 'the Absolute', or ultimate truth, and expected a reform of human knowledge and society in the light of it. Lévi thought that Wronski had achieved the longed-for reconciliation of rationalism with religion and admired him immensely.

In 1856 Lévi published his masterpiece, *Le Dogme et Rituel de la Haute Magie*. Wildly romantic, full of rhapsodical purple passages and spiced with eerie Gothic horrors, its penetrating insight and its evocative power impressed and excited the next generation of magicians. Lévi's later books include an unreliable history of magic, but his only other work of importance is *La Clé des Grandes Mystères* (not published till 1897). For the rest of his life – he died in 1875 – Lévi lived by his pen and by giving lessons in occultism. The wife of the British Consul in Paris studied 'holy Science' with him and described him as a man who had attained 'a state of profound peace'.[10]

Lévi was much more a theoretician than a practitioner, though on a visit to London in 1854 he attempted to summon up the spirit of Apollonius of Tyana by ritual magic. A shrouded figure appeared, which frightened him, but he did not believe it was Apollonius. On a second excursion to England, in 1861, he stayed with Bulwer Lytton (1803–73), the novelist and politician, author of *The Last Days of Pompeii*. Lytton wrote occult novels, including *Zanoni* (1842) and *A Strange Story* (1862), and studied magic, mesmerism, astrology and scrying. He attended R. J. Morrison's scrying sessions and is believed to have organized an occult group which Lévi joined.

Lévi coupled Mesmer's theories with the notion of the astral body by identifying animal magnetism as the 'astral light', a universal medium in some ways analogous to the all-pervading 'ether' of nineteenth-century physics. This enabled him to restate the old tradition that the ultimate reality is a unity compounded of opposites. Like a magnet, the astral light has opposite poles. It carries good and evil, it transmits light and propagates darkness. It responds to the human will and the astral body is formed of it. It is the astral light, he says in *The Key of the Mysteries*, which is 'the fluidic and living gold' of alchemy and to control it is to master all things. 'To direct the magnetic forces is then to destroy or create forms; to produce to all appearance, or to destroy bodies; it is to exercise the almighty powers of Nature.'

Influenced by Mesmer's belief that animal magnetism could be mentally controlled, and perhaps also by Agrippa, Lévi claimed limitless power for the trained magician's will. 'To affirm and will what ought to be is to create; to affirm and will what ought not to be is to destroy.'[11] All the procedures and trappings of ritual magic, for him, were devices through which the magician concentrated and directed his will. They were part of the network of correspondences, which Lévi brought back into magical theory in a modified, psychological form. The correspondences were links between the universe and the human soul, which contained in miniature all factors existing in the world outside it.

Lévi shared the contemporary fascination with ancient Egypt and accepted the Egyptian origin of the Tarot. However, he thought that the Tarot cards in circulation were of Jewish devising and he was the first writer to fit the Tarot systematically into the Cabala. He connected the twenty-two trump cards with the Hebrew letters as aspects of God and the universe. Occultists have taken the link between the Tarot and the Cabala for granted ever since, though there is no independent evidence of the connection.

Much of the impetus behind the occult revival is revealed in Lévi's remark: 'It remained for the eighteenth century to deride both Christians and magic, while infatuated with the homilies of Rousseau and the illusions of Cagliostro.'[12] He himself was an enthusiast for the synthesis implied in 'occult science'. He reconciled his Catholicism with magic, as the tradition of the *prisci magi*, by believing that the doctrines of Rome, though worthy of reverence, formed only the outer shell of the true religion. The inward secret heart of Christianity had always been concealed from the vulgar mob. It was contained in the Cabala and had been revealed by Jesus to the author of the Book of Revelation, which significantly has twenty-two chapters. The concept of an 'esoteric Christianity' was much in the air in Lévi's time and afterwards.

Lévi attributed table-turning and the other phenomena of Spiritualism to his 'universal magnetic agent', the astral light. The modern Spiritualist movement dates from 1848, when an epidemic of mysterious knocks and rappings broke out at the home of the Fox family in Hydesville, New York State. The young Fox daughters, Maggie and Kate, seemed to be able to communicate with the spirit believed to be making the noises – the ghost of a man who had been murdered in the house and buried in the cellar. Similar rappings, occurring wherever the sisters went and diagnosed as coded messages from the dead, caused a furore. The Fox girls and others who claimed to have mediumistic powers began to give public displays and charge fees for sittings. The movement soon spread from America to Europe.

The excitement which Spiritualism aroused shows the strength of the latent reaction which had built up against prevailing intellectual trends. Spiritualism appeared to demonstrate the reality of the human soul and its survival of bodily death, and so met a demand for a faith to fill the vacuum which sceptical rationalism had created. It drew on Paracelsus, Swedenborg, Mesmer and the idea of esoteric Christianity for support, and also on oriental religions and the shamanistic traditions of American Indians. Most Spiritualists were not magicians, but magicians were attracted to Spiritualism and dabbled in it, usually finding it wanting because its passive, accepting attitude to the spirit world failed to satisfy their appetite for power.

There were other signs of the contemporary need for a leaven of spiritual hope to quicken the secularist dough in the revival of medieval religio-magical customs. One was the growth of Lourdes as a centre of pilgrimage after St Bernadette had seen visions of the Virgin Mary there in 1858. Catholics began to flock to Lourdes in quest of healing and spiritual grace on a scale not seen since the Middle Ages. Another was the growth of interest in folklore and the renaissance of folk festivals. Many flourishing folk ceremonies of supposedly immemorial antiquity are nineteenth-century revivals and some are nineteenth-century inventions. A spectacular example of the latter is the immensely impressive fire festival called Up-Helly-Aa, held in January at Lerwick in the Shetland Islands. Patterned on a Viking ship-burial, it was introduced in 1889 to foster Shetlands–Norse nationalism and Christian Socialist ideals. It has grown into a genuine folk institution, which effectively expresses aspirations for freedom and independence.

The wise woman and the cunning man survived in some country places into the nineteenth century and beyond, though they were a dying breed. Fear of witches now exploded into drastic action only on rare occasions. In France in 1885 a woman was burned alive as a witch by her daughter and son-in-law. In 1894 a woman was tortured to death in Ireland, at Clonmel, County Tipperary. At York, Pennsylvania, in 1929 a man named John H. Blymyer was sentenced to life imprisonment for the murder of Nelson Rehmyer, who was notorious in the area as an evil magician. Rehmyer was killed in a struggle to obtain a lock of his hair, which was to be buried as part of a charm against him.

Among more sophisticated occultists the Rosicrucian ideal remained a powerful magnet. The first Rosicrucian order in America was founded by Paschal Beverly Randolph (1825-71), a mulatto who styled himself Supreme Grand Master of Eulis, Pythianae and Rosicrucia, Hierarch of the Triple Order. One of his satellites, F. B. Dowd, published a magazine called *The Gnostic* on the West Coast in the 1880s. Randolph travelled in Europe and is said to have met Eliphas Lévi and Bulwer Lytton. He was interested in the consciousness-expanding properties of ether and hashish. He was also interested in the magical uses of sex. He kept his views on this subject extremely dark, but passed them on in secret to a small group of French disciples in the Hermetic Brotherhood of the Light. Randolph was no fool and it was presumably his interest in sex that was responsible for the otherwise unaccountable awe in which he held Hargrave Jennings.

Hargrave Jennings (1817-90) was a minor official at the Italian Opera in London. He wrote *The Rosicrucians, Their Rites and Mysteries*, which came out in 1870 and has been frequently reprinted. It is a comic muddle of fake antiquarianism, romantic Druidry, the Grail legends, gnosticism, the Cabala, the mysteries of Mithras and lunatic philology. The scholarly study of philology had been founded by Jacob Grimm and others early in the nineteenth century and was now being turned to weird and wonderful purposes by undiscriminating enthusiasts. Jennings was obsessed with sex, believed that worship of the sex organs was the root of all religions and saw genital emblems nodding and winking at him wherever he looked. He had read Richard Payne Knight's pioneering book on *The Worship of Priapus* (1786), which had helped to convince him that the Rosicrucian rites and mysteries were of a sexual character.

Jennings influenced a fringe Masonic group, the Societas Rosicruciana in Anglia, familiarly known as the Soc. Ros., which was founded in London in 1866 with Bulwer Lytton as honorary Grand Patron. Members included Frederick Hockley (1809-85), a scryer and collector of magical texts, who had been trained by a pupil of Francis Barrett; William Stainton Moses (1839–92), the celebrated Spiritualist leader and medium; and Kenneth Mackenzie (1833–86), a pupil of Hockley and a devoted admirer of Eliphas Lévi. The Soc. Ros. took its system of grades from the Golden and Rosy Cross and was interested in the Hermetica, the Cabala, Spiritualism, unorthodox medicine and the development of clairvoyant powers. It spawned a branch in Scotland, which in turn chartered Rosicrucian groups in Philadelphia and New York in 1879–80. In 1908 a Soc. Ros. in America was formed by a journalist, Sylvester C. Gould, editor of an American *Notes and Queries*.

A more important event had occurred with the foundation of the Theosophical Society in New York in 1875, the *annus mirabilis* of the occult revival, which also saw the death of Eliphas Lévi and the births of Aleister Crowley and C. G. Jung. The Theosophical Society was dominated by the personality and gifts of Helena Petrovna Blavatsky (1831–91), born in Russia and a former Spiritualist medium. Her apparently magical ability to produce unearthly knocks and rappings and to materialize letters and other objects out of thin air, created a sensation. W. B. Yeats described her as 'a great passionate nature, a sort of female Dr Johnson'. She told Yeats that she and George Sand had dabbled in magic together, and he quotes W. E. Henley saying of her: 'Of course she gets up fraudulent miracles, but a person of genius has to do something; Sarah Bernhardt sleeps in her coffin.'[13]

The goal of the Theosophical Society was, in effect, to fulfil the seventeenth-century Rosicrucian programme by building a bridge between science and religion, through the investigation of powers latent in man. The Masters of Theosophical theory, the superhuman adepts who guide humanity's destiny from their headquarters in Tibet, owe much to the 'Invisibles' and 'unknown Superiors' of Rosicrucian tradition, and the Society was another expression of the yearning for a new synthesis which would create an oasis for the human spirit in the arid deserts of scientific rationalism and atheism. It was also intended to reconcile the eastern and western occult traditions, and Madame Blavatsky and her lieutenants became deeply absorbed in Hinduism and Buddhism. Here again, occultism fed on a growth of scholarly interest in eastern thought, which had produced a spate of translations of oriental religious texts. A broader popular interest was also springing up in Indian religions as being uncorrupted by the western spiritual malaise.

In the history of magic, as distinct from the wider area of occultism, the Theosophical Society's importance lies in the stimulus which it gave to magicians, many of whom joined it and left it again. They were encouraged by the publicity the Society gained and its impact on influential circles, but Eliphas Lévi had a more direct and lasting effect on their own systems.

In France, the Marquis Stanislas de Guaita (1860–98), a poet and admirer of Baudelaire, took up magic with passionate devotion after reading Lévi. He studied the *Sefer Yetsirah*, which Lévi had praised as 'a ladder of truth', and wrote books on the Tarot. He shortened his life by experimenting with morphine, cocaine and hashish, which he commended because it assisted the magician to leave his physical body and explore mysterious realms of consciousness in his astral body. Presumably this stimulated the rumour that he could dematerialize his body and project himself through space. He was also said to own a familiar spirit, which was kept locked in a cupboard when its services were not required.

Guaita's secretary and enthusiastic disciple was a Swiss practitioner of 'curative magnetism' named Oswald Wirth, a Mason and Theosophist. The two men became interested in the dubious practices of Joseph Antoine Boullan (1824–93), a defrocked priest, exorcist and sex-magician. Boullan was head of the Church of the Carmel, a small sect in Lyons, and claimed to be a reincarnation of John the Baptist. He taught a doctrine of spiritual regeneration through 'unions of life' or ritual copulations, and prescribed sexual union with archangels and other supernatural beings – either conjured up in the operator's imagination or represented by another member of the sect – as a method of climbing the ladder of the spiritual hierarchies. Posing as disciples, Guaita and Wirth discovered what was going on in Lyons, which they said amounted to wholesale promiscuity. In 1887 they told Boullan that they had judged him and condemned him. Boullan took this to mean, perhaps rightly, that they intended to kill him by magic. He defended himself with vigour and the air between Lyons and Paris throbbed with the fearsome anathemas, conjurations and incantations which he propelled against the foe.

Boullan was assisted by his housekeeper, Julie Thibault, Priestess of the Carmel and the Apostolic Woman, who spied out the stratagems of the enemy by clairvoyance. On one occasion she reported that they were saying a Black Mass against him and putting his portrait into a coffin, to murder him by imitative magic. He retaliated with a tremendous ceremony called the Sacrifice of Glory of Melchizidek, summoning the angels of heaven to strike down the hierophants of Satan. Boullan also employed consecrated hosts in his magic. His side of the battle was reported by his friend J. K. Huysmans, the novelist. 'Boullan jumps about like a tiger-cat, clutching one of his hosts and invoking the aid of St Michael and the eternal justiciaries of eternal justice: then standing at his altar he cries out "Strike down Péladan, s.d.P., s.d.P." And Maman Thibault, her hands folded on her belly, announces "it is done".' Péladan was one of Guaita's group.[14]

Huysmans believed that he himself had become a target of Guaita's magic. He felt menaced by invisible forces and was struck by unearthly cold draughts of air, which he called 'fluidic fisticuffs'. His cat seemed to be suffering from the same symptoms. He protected himself, and the cat, by drawing a magic circle on the floor, standing in it and reciting incantations. When Boullan died, in 1893, Huysmans was convinced that he had been murdered by sorcery.

Guaita had met Josephin Péladan (1858–1915) in 1884. Péladan was a strange, exuberant, wildly bearded novelist and a devout if eccentric Catholic. He was much in love with ancient Chaldean magic and bestowed on himself the titles of Sar ('king' in Assyrian) and Roman Catholic Legate. In 1888 Guaita and Péladan founded the Kabbalistic Order of the Rosy Cross. Its grades were achieved by passing examinations and it was directed by a council of twelve, six of whom were 'secret Chiefs'. The six visible chiefs included Paul Adam, the novelist, and Gérard Encausse, a young doctor who wrote on occultism under the name Papus.

Péladan, who was an impossible colleague, broke away in 1890 and formed his own Order of the Catholic Rosy Cross, the Temple and the Grail, intended for Catholics, artists and women. Erik Satie wrote musical accompaniments to the order's rituals and Péladan founded a Rosicrucian theatre, which presented plays on esoteric themes and two lost dramas of Aeschylus which he claimed to have discovered. From 1892 he organized a series of Rosicrucian art shows, dedicated to restoring 'the cult of the Ideal', at which Gustave Moreau, Puvis de Chavannes, Félicien Rops and Georges Rouault exhibited. Both artistic and fashionable circles in *fin-de-siècle* Paris were permeated by enthusiasm for the supernatural and the success of the Rosicrucian Salons was unaffected by a solemn pronouncement from Guaita in 1893, denouncing Péladan as an apostate and schismatic Rosicrucian.[15]

Papus or Gérard Encausse (1865–1916) was similarly successful with his popular books on occultism, including *Traité Elémentaire de Science Occulte* (1888) and *Traité Methodique de Science Occulte*

(1891). He also translated the *Sefer Yetsirah* into French and in 1889 published the first handbook to the Tarot, *Le Tarot des Bohémiens*. It was illustrated with a set of trumps designed by Oswald Wirth under Guaita's influence, intended to restore their ancient Egyptian and cabalistic symbolism. The Tarot was now regarded as a container of supreme hermetic wisdom and a key to ultimate reality. As a young man, Papus was briefly a member of the Theosophical Society, but he was far more impressed by Eliphas Lévi's books. In 1891 he took over the leadership of a small Martinist group and energetically increased its membership. He visited Russia in the 1900s and became a friend of Tsar Nicholas II and the Tsarina Alexandra. The Tsarina later fell under the spell of Grigori Rasputin, the holy man, clairvoyant and healer, who was regarded as the court's evil genius and was murdered in 1916. His influence at court stemmed from his ability to stop the bleeding of the haemophiliac heir to the throne, the Tsarevich Alexis, apparently through semi-hypnotic suggestion.

In England, a branch of the Theosophical Society had been formed in 1883 and Madame Blavatsky herself settled in London in 1887. Madame and her followers believed in the influence of the stars and gave a powerful impetus to astrology. Alan Leo (William Frederick Allen, 1860–1917), the most successful British astrologer since William Lilly, joined the Society in 1890 and under its influence promoted astrology, not only as a way of predicting events but as an ancient symbolic system, related to the true nature of the universe and man. He thereby watered the seeds of sophisticated interest in it, but he was also an efficient businessman and the pioneer of the mass-produced horoscope. Like Aleister Crowley later, he detested his upbringing among the Plymouth Brethren. He worked as a commercial traveller, studied astrology in his spare time, married a professional palmist and phrenologist, and in 1898 set up in business as an astrologer. By 1903 he was employing nine assistants, such was the demand for horoscopes and advice. He owned the magazine *Modern Astrology* and wrote popular textbooks under the general title of *Astrology for All*.

The liveliest and most influential of modern magical groups had meanwhile appeared and flourished for a few years before disintegrating. The Hermetic Order of the Golden Dawn was founded in London in 1888. It was ostensibly a branch of a Rosicrucian order in Germany, though the German order did not really exist and the documents on which the connection rested were forged. The leaders of the Golden Dawn all came from the Soc. Ros.

in Anglia. William Robert Woodman (1828–91) was Supreme Magus of the Soc. Ros., a doctor, a Mason and an enthusiast for the Cabala. William Wynn Westcott (1848–1925) was a doctor, a coroner in London, a Mason and a member of the Theosophical Society. He published an English version of the *Sefer Yetsirah* and a book on the occult powers of numbers, and succeeded Woodman as Supreme Magus of the Soc. Ros. He was the prime mover in the founding of the Golden Dawn, but before long was overshadowed by the far more formidable talents and personality of his protégé, MacGregor Mathers.

Samuel Liddell Mathers was born in London in 1854, the son of a merchant's clerk. A Mason, a Celtic romantic and a passionate Jacobite, he adopted the name MacGregor and the title of Comte de Glenstrae as marks of his supposed descent from the Scots clan. He was also an armchair strategist, a would-be Napoleon and a determined autocrat, accustomed in moments of adversity to repeat solemnly, 'There is no part of me that is not of the gods.' Aleister Crowley, his pupil, said that, 'He had that habit of authority which inspires confidence because it never doubts itself'; and to W. B. Yeats, another pupil, with his 'gaunt resolute face' he was 'a figure of romance'.[16]

Mathers spent almost half a lifetime in the British Museum and the Arsenal library in Paris, delving into magical and alchemical texts. In 1887 he published material from Knorr von Rosenroth as *The Kabbalah Unveiled*. His edition of the *Key of Solomon* came out in 1889 and he translated several other grimoires. He was on friendly terms with Madame Blavatsky and is believed to have taught magic to Anna Kingsford (1846–88), a proponent of esoteric Christianity, who founded the Hermetic Society in 1884 for the study of the hermetic and cabalistic tradition. She used magic in attempts to murder scientists engaged in vivisectionist experiments. She claimed she had killed two of them and made Pasteur extremely ill.

Mathers was principally responsible for the Golden Dawn's greatest achievement, the construction of a coherent magical system embracing the Cabala, the Tarot, alchemy, astrology, numerology, divination, Masonic symbolism, visionary experience and ritual magic. The strands of the western magical tradition were knitted together into a logical and consistent whole. This was a remarkable intellectual feat and it accounts for the Golden Dawn's dominant influence on subsequent occult groups. Mathers wrote the order's rituals and much of its teaching material, and worked out a detailed system of correspondences between external factors and the human psyche as 'the magical mirror of the universe'. Eliphas Lévi's system of magic was taken over, with some alterations, and the spiritual ancestry of the Golden Dawn was traced back through Lévi to the Rosicrucian Brotherhood, and from there by way of the Cabala to ancient Egypt, which still cast its romantic spell. The order's 'temples' or branches were named after Egyptian deities. Its rituals contained material from the Graeco–Egyptian magical papyri and the lure of Egyptian myth and mystery was a persuasive element of its appeal.[17]

Another was the Golden Dawn's emphasis on the psychological factors in magic as a technique of self-development, now stated more clearly and forcefully than in the Renaissance period. Imagination was added to will-power as an essential weapon of successful working. The gods and spirits of earlier traditions were regarded as forces partly or wholly within the magician himself. The order's purpose was to teach 'the principles of occult Science and the Magic of Hermes' with the aim of achieving supreme perfection and power, an objective implied in the word Hermetic in its title. Its most impressive ritual was conducted in a replica of Christian Rosenkreutz's funeral vault and re-enacted the Crucifixion. The initiate was bound on the Cross of Suffering and swore an oath: 'I will, from this day forward, apply myself to the Great Work – which is, to purify and exalt my Spiritual Nature so that with the Divine Aid I may at length attain to be more than human, and thus gradually raise and unite myself to my higher and Divine Genius, and that in this event I will not abuse the great power entrusted to me.'[18]

Mathers wrote a ritual for 'the Invocation of the Higher Genius', based on a Graeco–Egyptian papyrus, in which the magician summoned up his 'divine genius' or true self as 'the Terrible and Invisible God'. He identified himself with it and declared his domination of it and, through it, of all forces in the universe: 'Come thou forth and follow me and make all spirits subject unto me so that every spirit of the firmament and of the Ether, upon the Earth and under the Earth, on dry land and in the Water, of whirling Air and rushing Fire, and every spell and scourge of God the Vast One may be obedient unto me.'[19]

The Golden Dawn functioned as an occult university, teaching its magical curriculum to members who climbed the ladder of its degrees by passing examinations. The system of degrees was taken from the Soc. Ros., with a tenth grade of Ipsissimus ('most himself') added at the top to make ten degrees corresponding to the ten *sefiroth*, or aspects of God, in the Cabala. The order claimed to be directed by 'secret and unknown Magi', who were 'shrouded and unapproachable to the profane' and possessed 'terrible superhuman powers'.

Temples were founded in Bradford, Edinburgh, Weston-super-Mare and Paris. Between 1888 and 1896 the Golden Dawn recruited 315 members, of whom 119 were women. Most of them came from 'conventional middle-class backgrounds'.[20] Quite a number joined from the Theosophical Society. Temples were also founded in the United States, including one in Chicago dedicated to Thoth-Hermes.

One of the earliest recruits was an art student, Moina Bergson (1865–1928), who married Mathers in 1890. She was the sister of Henri Bergson, the philosopher, whom Mathers tried unavailingly to convert to magic. They were married by the Reverend W. A. Ayton, another member of the Golden Dawn, who had an alchemical laboratory in the cellar of his vicarage. Other members included W. B. Yeats; Aleister Crowley; A. E. Waite; Maud Gonne, the Irish nationalist; Annie Horniman, the founder of the Abbey Theatre, Dublin; Florence Farr, the actress and mistress of Yeats and Bernard Shaw; Constance Wilde, the wife of Oscar Wilde; two thriller writers, Algernon Blackwood and Arthur Machen; the painter Gerald Kelly, afterwards President of the Royal Academy; and, very briefly, William Crookes, F.R.S., a distinguished scientist and well-known psychical researcher.

Conscientious members were kept busy. They studied for their examinations, took part in the sonorous and elaborate rituals, engaged in searching self-analysis and quelled disorderly elementals (minor 'spirits' or personality defects). They purified and exalted their spiritual natures. They made their own magical paraphernalia, prepared talismans, studied Dee's Enochian language and played Enochian chess, drew and examined their horoscopes and practised becoming invisible (meaning, to pass unnoticed). They cultivated clairvoyance and meditated on Tarot cards and other symbols, which induced experiences known as 'scrying on the astral plane', equivalent to the autohypnotic meditative explorations and ascents of earlier magicians. Some of them summoned and identified themselves with planetary 'spirits' and pagan 'gods', using the same imitative and power-inducing techniques which probably go back ultimately to prehistoric magicians.

Mathers and his wife settled in Paris in 1892. They founded a Golden Dawn temple there, to which Papus belonged. They also performed elaborate rites in honour of the goddess Isis, who was impersonated by Moina. A fondness for histrionics is a necessary characteristic of magicians, and so is power-hunger. By the end of the decade personal quarrels and jealousies in the Golden Dawn reached boiling point. The imperious behaviour of Mathers and his liking for Aleister Crowley, whom many members feared and detested, alienated a large group of initiates. In 1900 they rebelled against Mathers and expelled him from the order, specifically on the ground that he had put its authority in question by accusing Westcott (justly it seems) of forging its foundation documents. According to Crowley, the furious Mathers took a packet of dried peas and rattled them violently in a sieve, while calling on the demonic forces of Beelzebub and Seth-Typhon to smite and confound his adversaries. The adversaries were in considerable confusion in any case, but despite the pea-rattling and the dramatic incursion into their midst of Aleister Crowley in full Highland dress and a black mask, they refused to come to heel. Subsequent disagreements splintered the Golden Dawn still further and Mathers never succeeded in regaining control. He died in Paris in 1918.

Yeats took command of the rebel faction for a few months with the title of Imperator. Born in Ireland in 1865, William Butler Yeats was fascinated by magic, mythology, Celtic legend and folklore, and the Tarot. As an art student in Dublin in the 1880s, he joined the Theosophical Society and Anna Kingsford's Hermetic Society, with his friend 'AE' (George William Russell, 1867–1935), the mystical writer and painter. Yeats moved to London, left the Theosophists and joined the Golden Dawn in 1890. Two years later he told a friend that, next to his poetry, his magic was the most important pursuit of his life.

It was through Mathers that Yeats began experiments which convinced him that 'images well up before the mind's eye from a deeper source than conscious or subconscious memory'. He saw visions which recall the planetary 'images' of Ficino and Bruno, and found that by concentrating he could send a symbol into someone else's mind. The concept of the astral plane influenced his belief that in meditating on certain symbols he plumbed a cosmic well of memories, 'independent of embodied individual memories, though they constantly enrich it with their images and their thoughts'. This supported his conviction that the inspirations of great poets in their finest moments are 'literal truth'.[21] Yeats married a medium and remained a member of one of the Golden Dawn's offshoots, the Stella Matutina, or Order of the Morning Star, until the early 1920s. He died in 1939.

A. E. Waite took control of the Golden Dawn's London temple in 1903. More a mystic than a magician, he changed the society's name, significantly, from Hermetic Order to Holy Order. He rewrote the rituals in a Christian spirit, sent the Egyptian gods off to limbo and discouraged the practice of magic. Charles Williams, the novelist, and Evelyn Underhill, the writer on mysticism, were members of the Holy Order of the Golden Dawn, but it gained little support and Waite put an end to it in 1914. He founded another small group, the Fellowship of the True Rosy Cross, in 1916.

Arthur Edward Waite was born in Brooklyn, New York, in 1857, but spent almost all his life in London. He was brought up Roman Catholic, flirted briefly with Spiritualism and Theosophy, and joined the Golden Dawn in 1891. An enthusiastic Mason, he spent his life in pursuit of the 'secret tradition' of wisdom which had been handed down under cover for centuries. Like some ungainly whale he wallowed in the seven seas of occult literature, gulping down the plankton of alchemy, the Cabala, the grimoires, mysticism, mesmerism, Martinism, Rosicrucianism, Masonry and the Grail legends, to digest and distil the secret tradition's essence. He published his researches in ponderous tomes, lightened by bludgeoning sarcasm at the unscholarly fatuities of other authors. He also translated Lévi's *Doctrine and Ritual* in 1896, designed the best-known modern Tarot pack and wrote the standard introduction to the Tarot in English, *The Pictorial Key to the Tarot* (1910). It is impossible not to make fun of him, and he was mercilessly caricatured by Aleister Crowley as a drunken pedant and humbug; but his scholarship was not as defective as is sometimes claimed and he had a salutary impatience with the sillier varieties of occultism. He died in 1942.

Waite influenced another enthusiast for the Tarot, the American occultist Paul Foster Case (1884–1954), who was an official of the Thoth-Hermes temple in Chicago. Several American members of the Golden Dawn joined Case's School of Ageless Wisdom. This later turned into the Builders of the Adytum (the most sacred part of a temple), which continued after his death, with it headquarters in Los Angeles. But by this time the western world had witnessed with wonder, incomprehension and some alarm, the career of the most notorious magician of the century, Aleister Crowley.

Crowley and After

In native talent, penetrating intelligence and determination, Aleister Crowley was the best-equipped magician to emerge since the seventeenth century. He was a many-sided man, an expert chess-player and mountaineer, a seasoned traveller, a minor poet and painter, a satyriac and pornographer, and a gifted writer of prose, with a pleasing sense of humour, rare among magicians. The popular press in the 1920s proclaimed him 'the wickedest man in the world'. He was born Edward Alexander Crowley at Leamington, Warwickshire, in 1875, the year of Eliphas Lévi's death, and believed he was a reincarnation of Lévi. He had earlier been Cagliostro, Edward Kelley and Alexander VI, the Borgia pope.

Crowley's father was a wealthy brewer and Plymouth Brother. The boy rebelled against his strict, fundamentalist upbringing, preferred the evil characters in the Bible to the good ones, and when his mother told him that he was the Great Beast 666 of Revelation, he gladly accepted the identification. 'In his revolt against God', John Symonds says, 'he set himself up in God's place. It was not a temporary attitude, it stayed with him and set the whole course of his life.'[22]

Crowley joined the Golden Dawn in 1898, fresh from Cambridge, taking the magical name of Brother Perdurabo ('I will endure') and beginning his experiments with drugs. His voracious bisexuality and his interest in the darker forces in the human animal gave him a sinister reputation. Like his opposite numbers in Paris, Crowley was very much a figure of the 'decadence' of the *fin de siècle*, with its hymning of scarlet sins and purple passions, its loathing of Christianity and its romantic admiration for evil and Satan. Characteristically, he carried these tendencies to their limit. At first a devoted pupil of MacGregor Mathers, Crowley turned against him and attempted to oust him from the leadership of the rump of the Golden Dawn. A ferocious magical battle was waged between them, or so Crowley said. Mathers sent a beautiful vampire to seduce him, but Crowley 'smote the sorceress with her own current of evil'. The dramatic consequences were described by J. F. C. Fuller, the strategist and military historian, who for a time was the Beast's ardent disciple. The woman's hair turned white, her skin wrinkled, her eyes dulled. 'The girl of twenty had gone; before him stood a hag of sixty, bent, decrepit, debauched. With dribbling curses she hobbled from the room.'[23]

Mathers returned to the attack and struck Crowley's pack of bloodhounds dead from afar. In reply Crowley summoned up the great demon Beelzebub with forty-nine attendant fiends, all in singularly gruesome and disturbing forms, and ordered them off to chastise Mathers in Paris. The effects of this visitation on Mathers, if any, are not recorded.

Crowley and After

In 1904, in a mysterious episode in Cairo, a spirit named Aiwass, who was Crowley's own 'higher genius', dictated the brief and obscure *Book of the Law* to Crowley through his clairvoyant wife Rose, the sister of Gerald Kelly. A phrase from it became Crowley's tirelessly repeated maxim: 'Do what thou wilt shall be the whole of the law', meaning not 'do what you like' but 'be true to your real self'. The *Book of the Law* convinced Crowley that his mission in life was to destroy Christianity and build among its ruins his own religion of Thelema ('the will' in Greek). He was the Saviour of the World, the Logos of the Aeon, the Messiah of the new Age of Horus, as he called it, which had now replaced the Age of Osiris with its moribund Christian faith.

Crowley formed his own magical society, the Order of the Silver Star, in 1907, and from 1909 published a magazine, *The Equinox*. In 1912 he became head of the British section of a German group specializing in erotic magic, the Ordo Templi Orientis or Order of the Temple of the Orient, known for short as the O.T.O. Crowley took the title of Supreme and Holy King of Ireland, Iona and all the Britains within the Sanctuary of the Gnosis. He loved titles and liked to call himself Prince Chioa Khan, Count Vladimir Svareff, the Great Beast, or Baphomet, the name of the diabolical idol which the Knights Templar had been accused of worshipping.

Crowley spent the First World War in the United States, writing anti-British propaganda for the Germans, which did not endear him to his countrymen. In 1916, while living near Bristol, New Hampshire, he rose to the rank of Magus through a ceremony of his own devising, in which he baptized a frog as Jesus Christ and crucified it.

In 1920 Crowley went to Cefalu in Sicily and turned a villa into his Abbey of Thelema, with his current mistresses, the Scarlet Woman or Ape of Thoth, and Sister Cypris. In the following year he became Ipsissimus, in a flash of revelatory self-awareness, but he and his small band of followers attracted the unfavourable notice of the British popular press and the Italian government, which expelled the Beast from the country in 1923. He spent the next years as an unhappy wanderer, desperately in need of disciples and money, and making a gallant but unsuccessful effort to break his addiction to heroin. He finally returned to England, where he died in 1947.

It is only since his death that Crowley's prolific writings have become profitably publishable. His masterpiece is *Magick* or *Book Four* (the bulk of which came out in 1929 as *Magick in Theory and Practice*). The best of his other books are perhaps his occult thriller,

Moonchild (1929); his commentary on the Tarot pack, *The Book of Thoth* (1944); and his sardonic 'autohagiography' or *Confessions* (not published in full until 1969).

Though he was an almost forgotten man at his death, interest in Crowley has revived and he has more followers now than in his lifetime. This is largely the result of the glamour his 'wickedness' holds for those never unfortunate enough to experience it at first hand; but there are better reasons. Crowley reviewed and restated the theory of magic from a modern psychological point of view – owing something to Freud – with a forcefulness, intelligence and wit unmatched by any other writer. It is this achievement rather than his obsession with sex, of which so much is made, that is likely to be his monument.

Crowley's exaltation of man has appealed to people who feel themselves in danger of being reduced to ciphers in a dehumanized world. 'Man is ignorant of the nature of his own being and powers . . . Man is capable of being, and using, anything which he perceives, for everything that he perceives is in a certain sense part of his being.' Perhaps as a result of a psychological dilemma of his own, suggested by his fondness for aliases, he attached great importance to discovering the true self, the real person behind the masks on display to the outside world, and he believed the true self to have titanic potential, which he expressed in Paracelsian terms: 'Every man and every woman is a star.' In a society experiencing another identity crisis, the attraction of this belief is evident.[24]

Crowley's experiments with drugs and curious mental experiences 'on the astral plane' helped to draw attention to him when a wave of interest in psychedelic drugs and altered states of consciousness built up in the 1960s. The astral plane, rather than the older concept of the astral body, had been brought to the fore by Lévi, the Theosophical Society and the Golden Dawn, as a way of recovering the theory of macrocosm and microcosm which science had rejected. The astral plane is the realm in which thoughts, imaginings and desires have an independent reality, and in modern magical theory it is there that the traditional ascent of the spheres takes place.

Crowley learned magic in the Golden Dawn, but he also investigated Yoga and Tantrism, which seemed to justify his interest in sex as an ecstatic technique of transcending normal human limits and attaining the superhuman. Tantrism is an Indian religio-magical sexual cult. Knowledge of it was introduced to western occultists by Edward Sellon (1818–66), a minor pornographer and industrious lecher who wrote *Annotations*

Upon the Sacred Writings of the Hindus (1865), which influenced Hargrave Jennings.[25] The time was ripe, for a rebellion against conventional morality was already beginning. Given its ideal of 'the universal man', magic could hardly rest content with the depreciation of a powerful factor in human nature, and it was possible, as in Boullan's case, to go right to the other extreme and regard sex as sacred. The Golden Dawn taught that man's animal drives must be harnessed to his spiritual progress, but never officially countenanced erotic magic, though some of the inititiates were at least theoretically interested in it. Papus and Waite both made extensive use of sexual symbolism. Crowley put sex at the heart of his 'magick', the additional 'k' being the first letter of *kteis*, the Greek word for the female genitals.

The O.T.O., which also taught sexual magic, was a product of the German occult revival, which had been sparked off by the opening of the Berlin branch of the Theosophical Society in 1884. The Secretary-General of the Theosophical Society's German section, from 1902, was Rudolf Steiner (1861–1925), occultist, clairvoyant, mathematician, educational reformer and authority on Goethe. He broke away to found the Anthroposophical Society, which he hoped would fulfil the Rosicrucian ideal. Another, less reputable German Theosophist was a doctor, Franz Hartmann (1838–1912), who wrote an introduction to magic, *Magic White and Black*, a life of Paracelsus and several other books. Madame Blavatsky called him 'a bad lot'. Like the Golden Dawn, he emphasized that magic was, at least initially, a method of self-development. 'Magic means that divine art or exercise of spiritual power by which the awakened spirit in man controls the invisible living elements in the soul-substance of the universe; but above all, those in his own soul, which are the ones nearest to him.'[26]

Hartmann was involved in the founding of the O.T.O., in about 1902, though the prime mover was Karl Kellner (died 1905), a wealthy industrialist and Mason. Kellner had encountered Tantrism in his travels to India, or said he had, but he may have been more directly influenced by P. B. Randolph's disciples. The O.T.O. claimed to have rediscovered the 'great secret' of the Knights Templar, the magic of sex, which was not only the key to the ancient Egyptian and hermetic tradition but also explained 'all the secrets of Nature, all the symbolism of Freemasonry and all systems of religion'. In the light of this discovery, alchemy was reinterpreted as a method of erotic magic. The O.T.O. traced its pedigree through the Rite of Memphis and Misraim, an obscure fringe Masonic organization, possibly descended from Cagliostro's

Egyptian Rite and promoted by John Yarker (died 1913), an Englishman who ran an arcane periodical called *The Kneph*. He was unkindly described by A. E. Waite as 'a man of muddled information, with a mass of confused inferences from reams of undigested materials'.[27]

Steiner was briefly connected with the O.T.O. and Papus's Martinist Order was more closely linked with it. Aleister Crowley became head of the O.T.O. in 1922, but some of the members would not accept him and the German O.T.O. split into two factions, both of which were suppressed by the Nazi government in 1937. Groups claiming to be the true and authoritative O.T.O. now exist in Germany, Switzerland, the United States and Britain.

Other curious and sometimes sinister groups emerged in Germany before the First World War. An Order of New Templars was founded by Jörg Lanz von Liebenfels (Adolf Lanz, 1874–1954), an Austrian Anti-Semite and enthusiast for Aryan racial purity, astrology, phrenology and, paradoxically, the Cabala. The New Templars, one of whom was August Strindberg, the dramatist, celebrated Grail rituals in a romantic ruined castle on the Danube. Lanz's theories anticipated and influenced Nazi attitudes and policies, and Hitler was a reader of Lanz's magazine, *Ostara*. Hitler has been portrayed as passionately addicted to occultism by some writers, and as totally sceptical about it by others. The truth lies between these two extremes. He was interested in and swayed by occult theories which suited his own temperament and beliefs.[28]

Lanz was a friend of Guido von List (1848–1918), another Austrian, who was enraptured with Germanic mythology and folklore, worshipped Wotan and practised rune magic. Both men influenced the Germanen Order, a fiercely Anti-Semitic organization, founded in 1912 and concerned with the superiority of the German 'master race', the menace of 'international Jewry', Teutonic mythology, the cult of Wotan and the magic of the runes. Members wore bronze rings with runic inscriptions to ward off disease and ill luck. Some of them had connections with the early Nazi movement. A later group, the curiously named Association of Invisible Aryans, did runic exercises, twisting themselves into the shapes of runes while yodelling lustily to generate magical power.

The medieval belief in the demonic nature and evil magic of the Jews had reappeared in the nineteenth century as an outgrowth of the dread of secret societies. In 1869 Gougenot des Mousseaux published *Le Juif, le Judaisme et la Judaisation des Peuples Chrétiens*, in which he claimed to uncover a conspiracy against society by 'Kabbalistic Jews', who worshipped the Devil.

He imagined that there existed a secret demonic religion, a systematic cult of evil which had been established by the Devil at the very beginning of the world. The grand masters of this cult were the Jews . . . and those who had helped the Jews in spreading the reign of the Devil throughout the world included the medieval heretics, the Templars, and, more recently, the Freemasons. The cult itself centred on the worship of Satan, symbolized by a serpent and the phallus; and its ritual consisted of erotic orgies of the wildest kind, interspersed with episodes when Jews murdered Christian children in order to use their blood for magical purposes.[29]

The notorious forged *Protocols of the Elders of Zion* (1919), purporting to reveal a Jewish conspiracy against civilization, emerged from this background and fantasies of this kind, combined with nostalgia for heroic German paganism, had a powerful influence on the Nazi party and the course of history.

In the United States, Rosicrucian groups proliferated. Max Heindel (died 1919), a Danish immigrant who took much of his teaching from Rudolf Steiner, wrote several books on astrology and founded the Rosicrucian Fellowship at Oceanside, California, in 1909. A Rosicrucian Fraternity was founded by Reuben Swinburne Clymer, the heir of P. B. Randolph, though he knew nothing of Randolph's secret sexual teachings and would have disapproved of them if he had. Branches of the O.T.O. were established in Los Angeles and Vancouver before 1914 by Charles Stansfeld Jones (1886–1950), an accountant and follower of Crowley, who acclaimed him as his 'magical son' until they quarrelled over Jones's heretical reinterpretations of the Cabala.

The German O.T.O. independently authorized Harvey Spencer Lewis (died 1939) to run an American lodge. Lewis was an advertising man from New York, who had been a member of Péladan's Catholic Rosicrucian order. In 1915 he founded the well-known Ancient and Mystic Order Rosae Crucis (AMORC), which now does a massive business in correspondence courses from its headquarters in San Jose, California. It traces Rosicrucianism back to the 'mystery schools' of ancient Egypt and its administration building is a replica of an Egyptian temple. Lewis had no lasting interest in sexual magic. He was subsequently embarrassed by his early link with the O.T.O., which was used against him by Swinburne Clymer, his deadly rival and enemy, who denounced 'the boastful pilfering Imperator with his black-magic, sex-magic connections'.[30]

Attitudes to magic were affected by the rise of interest in clairvoyance, telepathy, precognition and psychokinesis, or 'mind over matter'. Spiritualism had dramatically drawn attention to human abilities which in the past had been regarded as magical and which orthodox science adamantly denied, and the Theosophical Society had set out to explore them. They were investigated in a scientific spirit by psychical researchers and parapsychologists. The Society for Psychical Research was founded in London in 1882, and its American counterpart three years later. Experimental research under controlled laboratory conditions was pioneered by J. B. Rhine at Duke University, North Carolina, from 1927 onwards. The results of scientific research gained increasing attention and, gradually, increasing acceptance. The effect of this development was double-edged. It made inroads into magic's territory by planting the flag of science on a substantial area of it. But on the other hand, sympathetic interest in magic was stimulated by evidence that some of its traditional claims were founded on fact: the claim to observe events far beyond sight, to have direct access to other people's minds, to see into the future, and even to exert mental influence on matter.

General acceptance of the existence of the unconscious mind, following Freud's work, and a growing realization that mind and body interact similarly cut both ways. Psychology carved out its own principality on religio-magical ground. Much of what had once been considered supernatural was now explained in natural, psychological terms. The effects of a curse, for instance, could now be satisfactorily put down to the victim's own psychosomatic response to it. If a man called up spirits and claimed to see and hear them, they could be explained as projections from his own mind, and it was even possible that other people in a highly suggestible condition might see and hear them too. There were no longer only two alternatives, either to believe in magic or to dismiss quantities of human experience as unreal.

On the other side of the coin, however, magic had always condemned reason as an inadequate guide to reality and the new recognition of immensely powerful irrational drives in human nature helped to make magic less of a pejorative term. A primitive realm of dark, mysterious forces, remote from conscious and rational control, had been rediscovered and was excitedly reconnoitered. From the First World War onwards, for example, the Dada and Surrealist movements in art, which were influenced by both Freud and the French occult revival, explored the hinterland of the mind in an anti-rational and magical spirit which foreshadowed the later interest in ways of expanding consciousness and penetrating the labyrinths of 'inner space'.

Meanwhile, the weakening of Christianity's hold on the

intelligentsia was a factor in the growth of academic interest in magic among anthropologists and writers on comparative religion, mythology and folklore. Sir James Frazer's masterpiece, *The Golden Bough*, came out in 1890 and was reissued, much enlarged, in twelve volumes between 1907 and 1915. Directly and indirectly, Frazer reached an audience far beyond academic circles and his influence on poets, novelists and intellectual trends would make a study in itself. Scholarly investigation of magic as a historical and social phenomenon also helped to stimulate sympathetic interest in it. So did a reaction against the self-confident Victorian tendency to scoff at the beliefs of 'lesser breeds without the law'. The new researches, inevitably, added to the general pool of occultists' ideas. Frazer's own sardonic treatment of Christianity and his central theme of the divine king attracted magicians like Crowley, who commended *The Golden Bough* to students of 'magick'.

Magicians also drew heavily on pseudo-scholarship which suited them. The romantic allure of the land of the Pharaohs, for instance, was strengthened by the later writings of Gerald Massey (1828–1907), an English poet and Christian Socialist, who became interested in mesmerism, Spiritualism and psychic phenomena. He pursued his interests back in time to Egypt and wrote massive books, including *A Book of the Beginnings* (1881) and *Ancient Egypt the Light of the World* (1907), which have been described as 'copious, rambling and valueless compilations', but which influenced occult groups. Massey is said to have succeeded E. V. H. Kenealy as head of the Druid Order.

In the 1920s and '30s there were signs of a mounting interest in the occult on a much broader popular front, largely in direct response to the appalling slaughter of the First World War and the misery of the Depression, which undermined confidence in western society's values and deepened concern about its spiritual malaise. Spiritualism reached the peak of its popular appeal and there was an explosion of newspaper astrology. In 1930 the London *Sunday Express* began to run a regular column by a professional astrologer, R. H. Naylor (1889–1952). It is typical of the genre that the first article archly interpreted the horoscope of the baby Princess Margaret. The enthusiasm of readers was such that the example was soon followed by other British papers and the French and American press. By 1969, according to *Newsweek* magazine, astrology had ten million committed adherents in the United States, with perhaps four times as many dabblers.

With astrology in the van and a growing popular interest in

psychic powers as its ally, publishers were able to exploit other types of fortune-telling on an unprecedented scale. Louis Hamon (1866–1936) made a name for himself as Cheiro with popular books on palmistry and numerology, full of vague, high-toned spiritual uplift of a debased Theosophical variety. Dream interpretation had been given a new intellectual respectability by Freud, though the popular dream guides continued to mine traditional seams.

In Germany, until 1945, astrology was kept out of the newspapers by the Nazi government, whose attitude to it recreated that of the Roman emperors: it was useful in their own hands and dangerous in anyone else's. Probably as a direct result, there was a thriving interest in it of a more sophisticated kind than elsewhere. A French soldier, Paul Choisnard (1867–1930), had made serious attempts, early in the century, to test the validity of astrological character analysis statistically by comparing people with their horoscopes. More thorough efforts to put astrology on a firm factual base were made in Germany, notably by Karl Ernst Krafft (1900–45), a Swiss astrologer employed by the Nazis. Krafft's findings were subsequently demolished by a French statistician, Michel Gauquelin, but Gauquelin went on to discover correlations between people's occupations and the planetary positions at birth which have recently begun to impress initially sceptical observers.[31]

The period between the World Wars saw a major vogue, especially in the United States, for the system of self-development invented by Emile Coué (1857–1926), who coined the phrase 'Every day and in every way I am getting better and better', to be repeated while gazing commandingly at oneself in a mirror. Coué was a French psychotherapist who believed in the power of imagination and auto-suggestion over both the human character and the human body. He was not a magician, but self-improvement through appropriate thoughts is an old magical technique: Paracelsus said that a man is what he imagines himself to be, and Coué catered to a longing for power in a world which hemmed the individual in. Various other groups dedicated to mental and spiritual healing were flourishing and in France, from 1922 until his death in 1949, Georgei Ivanovich Gurdjieff imparted his own complex system of self-mastery to select disciples at his Institute for the Harmonious Development of Man. Gurdjieff had taught in Moscow before fleeing from the Russian Revolution. He again was concerned with untapped human potential and was influenced by his studies of Yoga and hypnosis and his meetings with fakirs and dervishes in the East as a young man.

Apart from Crowley, the best-known magician in Britain between the wars was Dion Fortune (Violet Mary Firth, 1891–1946), a prolific writer of books, including *Psychic Self-Defence* (1930) and *The Mystical Qabalah* (1935). The sales of the former title, which reached its thirteenth impression in 1971, say something about the mood of the time. The latter is an excellent introduction to the Golden Dawn's interpretation of the Cabala. Dion Fortune was an orphan, brought up as a Christian Scientist. In 1920 she joined an Alpha Omega lodge of the Golden Dawn founded by Moina Mathers, who had moved back to England after her husband's death. The two women fell out and engaged in a magical battle, or so Dion Fortune reported. She found herself plagued by an infestation of evil-smelling black tom-cats of licentious habit, and eventually fought and routed her enemy – who took the form of a gigantic tabby – on the astral plane. In 1922 she formed her own society, the Fraternity of the Inner Light, for the study of the western esoteric tradition.

Druidry gained an energetic organizer and recruiting sergeant in Lewis Spence (1874–1955), a Scots journalist who published an *Encyclopaedia of Occultism* (1920), *The Origins of Druidism* (1949), several books on Atlantis and many others on mythology and folklore. The Druid Order subsequently split into two antagonistic factions, in 1964. An obscurer figure was Austin Osman Spare (1886–1956), a youthful prodigy as a painter and a pupil of Aleister Crowley, whose weirdly powerful work has recently become fashionable. As a boy in London, Spare was the protégé of an old woman who claimed to be a hereditary witch, descended from a long line of witches in Salem, Massachusetts. Inspired by her, Spare worked out his own methods of 'atavistic resurgence', the evocation of strange and terrifying beings from the most primitive and ancient depths of the mind. He drew and painted these atavisms and other 'spirits' which he summed up to visible appearance, but found himself unable to depict his experiences of being suddenly propelled into 'spaces beyond space'.[32]

During the Second World War, Karl Krafft and other astrologers in Germany were put to work analyzing the horoscopes of German and Allied commanders and leaders. Krafft incautiously decided that General Montgomery's birth chart was stronger than General Rommel's, and was packed off to a concentration camp. He had come to Nazi notice in 1939, when he forecast an attempt on Hitler's life between the seventh and tenth of November, and an assassination attempt duly occurred in Munich on the eighth. He was soon employed to produce rehashed

Nostradamus prophecies predicting the inevitable triumph of the Third Reich, which were distributed as propaganda. Krafft's masters seem to have been entirely cynical about this exercise in psychological warfare. So were their British opponents, who hired an astrologer and refugee from Germany, Louis de Wohl, to deduce what astrological advice Krafft might be giving Hitler, and later to fabricate bogus Nostradamus quatrains for their own propaganda purposes.

Some of the Nazi leaders were less cynical. Himmler believed in the magical power of concentrated thought, kept a band of clairvoyants and mediums on tap and retained a professional astrologer, Wilhelm Wulff, to advise him. He was also addicted to Spiritualism, fringe medicine and strange cosmological theories. In a locked safe his staff kept two horoscopes, Hitler's and the Reich's, both of which suggested that April 1945 would be a turning point in Germany's favour in the war. Hitler and Goebbels at first believed that the death of President Roosevelt was the fulfillment of this prophecy. Earlier, in 1942, a Pendulum Institute was set up in Berlin. It recruited psychics and astrologers in an effort to counter the pendulum aces of British naval intelligence, who were believed to be divining the positions of German submarines at sea by dangling pendulums over maps of the Atlantic.

By the end of the war, eccentric sages, curious cults and unusual enthusiasms were blossoming in profusion in southern California, the last frontier of nonconformity before the Pacific. A Church of Thelema, or Agape lodge, of Crowley's O.T.O. had been formed in Pasadena and was now headed by Jack Parsons, a young and dynamic scientist. In 1946, inspired by Crowley's *Moonchild*, Parsons performed an elaborate magical operation to produce a child who would be an incarnation of Babalon, the Crowleyan name of the great mother goddess or feminine principle. To bear the child, he conjured up an elemental, who appeared in the form of a green-eyed girl from New York. L. Ron Hubbard, later the founder of Scientology, was involved in the experiment and afterwards explained that he had made friends with Parsons in order to frustrate his evil designs. No Babalon was conceived, but Parsons continued his magical career, changed his name to Belarion Armiluss Al Dajjal Antichrist, and died in a laboratory explosion in 1952.[33]

Crowley directly influenced the modern witchcraft movement, which has burgeoned in Britain and the United States since the 1950s. It is based on the theories of Margaret Murray (1863–1963), a British academic who published *The Witch-Cult in Western Europe* in 1921. This book and its later, more popular version, *The God of the Witches*, have made a remarkable impression, not limited only to would-be witches. Margaret Murray was influenced by both Frazer and Hargrave Jennings. She reinterpreted the evidence from the witch trials to show that the witches had worshipped, not Satan, but the 'horned god' and the great goddess of a pagan nature religion: 'Underlying the Christian religion was a cult practised by many classes of the community, chiefly, however, by the more ignorant or those in the less thickly inhabited parts of the country. It can be traced back to pre-Christian times and appears to be the ancient religion of western Europe.'[34]

This brilliant and ingenious theory is unfortunately full of holes and has been demolished time and again, without in the least deterring those drawn to it. That so many have been drawn to it is a sign of the times. Its great attractions are its anti-Christian and anti-establishment spirit and its elevation of witchcraft into an ancient, pagan and sensuous nature cult, springing from a deep, instinctive folk wisdom alien to modern science and technology. This fiction has been brought to life by groups practising Wicca, the pagan 'old religion'. There are thought to be anything from 10,000 to 20,000 witches now in the United States and half as many in Britain.

The chief publicist and organizer of modern witchcraft, Gerald Brosseau Gardner, was born in England in 1884, the son of a prosperous merchant. He spent most of his life in the Far East as a rubber planter and customs official, returning home in 1937. He was interested in magic, Spiritualism, folklore, edged weapons and flagellation. In 1940 he joined a Rosicrucian group in Hampshire, through which he met a small coven of Murrayite witches. Gardner took up witchcraft with enthusiasm. He was an initiate of Crowley's O.T.O. and hired the Beast to write witchcraft rituals for him. Crowley welcomed what he saw as a popularized form of his own creed. As far back as 1915 he had written to Charles Stansfeld Jones, urging him to start such a cult. 'The time is just ripe for a natural religion. People like rites and ceremonies, and they are tired of hypothetical gods. Insist on the real benefits of the Sun, the Mother-force, the Father-force and so on ... In short, be the founder of a new and greater Pagan cult....'[35]

If the time was not quite ripe in 1915, it was in 1954, when Gardner revealed the existence of witch covens in his book *Witchcraft Today*. People who wanted to be Murrayite witches wrote to him and he formed many new groups. The Witchcraft Act had been repealed in 1951, so that it was no longer illegal to practise, or purport to practise, witchcraft. Americans initiated in Britain took the new religion across the Atlantic and it was also exported to France and Germany. Covens were organized in three grades: Priest and Witch of the Great Goddess; Witch Queen or Magus; and at the top, High Priestess or High Priest. There were supposed to be thirteen members in a coven, though many were smaller. The principal instructions and rituals were included in a Book of Shadows, which mingled Crowleyan magic with Masonic symbolism and ingredients from *Aradia, the Gospel of the Witches,* published in 1899 by an American folklorist, C. G. Leland, who on his travels in Italy gathered material from a Tuscan fortune-teller claiming to be a hereditary witch.

Each coven tended to go its own way under its leader, and since Gardner's death in 1964 there have been various claimants to supremacy in the movement. Some covens have dropped the flagellatory and sexual rituals which Gardner enjoined, others have emphasized them. Some concentrate on healing through spells and herbal remedies. Some have added elements drawn from the Golden Dawn, including Enochian magic and meditation on Tarot cards, from Druidry, Robert Graves's book *The White Goddess,* Welsh traditions and 'Celtic mysteries' in general. Some leaders have turned themselves into full-blown ceremonial magicians. The witchcraft and liberation movements have met at their edges and there are covens of 'gay' witches in the United States.

Another startling development has been a resurgence of belief in demonic possession and a consequent sharp rise in the demand for exorcism. Clergymen and laymen who have begun to specialize as exorcists have found themselves swamped by the need for their services. In Switzerland in 1966 a girl was beaten to death in a frantic attempt to drive the Devil out of her. In 1974, a man on trial at the Old Bailey in London for attempted rape claimed that he was not responsible for his actions because he had been possessed by the Devil at the time. The judge did not take kindly to this plea and it was withdrawn.

In 1966 a new organization called the Church of Satan, spiritually descended from Crowley and dedicated to the worship of the Devil as a symbol of the pleasure principle, was founded in San Francisco under the leadership of Anton Szandor La Vey, author of *The Satanic Bible* (1969). It attracted feverish attention from the press and in 1974 claimed to have 25,000 members in its 'grottos' or branches in the United States and abroad. An anthropologist who did his fieldwork as a member of its First Church of the Trapezoid, San Francisco, came to the conclusion that, like the modern witchcraft movement, its appeal was to the frustration and envy felt by people unable to achieve their goals by conventionally acceptable methods. Its recruits, he said, 'desire successes denied them – money, fame, recognition, power – and with all legitimate avenues apparently blocked, with no apparent means by which legitimate effort will bring reward, they turn to Satanism and witchcraft'.[36]

Satanist witches hundreds of years ago, assuming there were some, were probably driven by the same motives, and magic's great attraction all through the centuries has been as a road to power and success unattainable by ordinary approaches. But since the 1960s there has been an upsurge of interest in magic and the occult on a scale which suggests resentment on a broader front than disappointed individual ambiton. This upsurge has been part of a gathering tide of rebellion against rationalism, materialism, science and technology. Especially at the more popular levels, the demand is less for 'occult science' than for an alternative to science.

The rebellion has been most evident in middlebrow and middle-class circles, though not confined to them. It is associated with a feeling that man has fallen out of harmony with the right order of things; anti-materialist attitudes and hostility to established authority; opposition to the destructiveness and wastefulness of modern technology; abandonment of the nineteenth-century belief in progress and a search for value in traditions alien to western rationalism; enthusiasm for oriental spiritual techniques, such as Yoga; exploration of drugs and meditation as methods of perceiving otherworldly reality; a longing to return to nature, with a hankering for the pre-industrial age and a nostalgia for paganism; admiration for primitive or 'simpler' societies as being closer to nature; and a general appetite for the spiritual and the psychic, though not for Christianity, which tends to be dismissed as a discredited prop of the old rationalist and materialist order.

C. G. Jung (1875–1961) was an important influence on this whole trend of thought and feeling. Unlike Freud, whose attitude to the paranormal swung between attraction and repulsion, Jung experienced visions and psychic phenomena himself, and in his psychiatric work found that 'loss of religious faith' was a common cause of nervous breakdown. From an early interest in mediumistic powers and Swedenborg, he went on to investigate gnosticism and the hermetic tradition, dreams, alchemy, astrology, mysticism, myths and legends. His concept of the collective unconscious as a reservoir of primordial 'images' or ways of thinking which find expression in religion, philosophy, science, art, symbolism, visions and fantasies, recalls the speculations of Yeats and the astral plane of occult theory. His respect for the I Ching, an old Chinese system of divination, helped to inspire the present enthusiasm for it. The I Ching was translated into English in 1882 and into German in the 1920s by Richard Wilhelm, an orientalist and friend of Jung. Aleister Crowley valued it and it now rivals the Tarot as a fashionable oracle.

Jung's sympathetic approach to astrology fostered sophisticated interest in it as a system of character analysis. It was largely through his work that alchemy was rescued from the garbage dump of pseudo-science and recognized as a spiritual technique. Jung's goal of 'individuation', the construction of an integrated personality through the reconciliation of warring psychological factors, is directly related to the magical concept of the true self and the principle of the harmonious synthesis of opposites. But Jung's chief importance lies in his influence, not on magicians, but on the far larger number of people who are not magicians and never intend to be. He built yet another bridge between the rational and scientific on one side and the spiritual and magical on the other, a bridge which restless dwellers in the former camp could cross to explore the latter without feeling embarrassed.

The causes of the occult revival since the later eighteenth century must be numerous and complicated, but it seems likely that, as in the Roman Empire, they have much to do with an identity crisis. The old agricultural order, with its stratified society, provided a role and a station in life for each person born into it. The destruction of this order brought many advantages, but industrialization, urbanization, the growth of large communities and organizations, the spread of education and increased physical and social mobility, with a loosening of family and neighbourhood ties, all caused on their debit side confusion of roles, rootlessness, anxiety and a sense of not being identifiable and not belonging anywhere. Science and technology, which appeared to be steeds to ride, turned out to be tigers. Life seemed alarmingly complex, inhuman and uncontrollable, and the individual as powerless as a rat in a laboratory maze. Rationalist and agnostic philosophies and the decay of Christianity's authority contributed to uncertainty and lack of self-confidence.

The solutions, it seemed to many, must lie along paths from

which the rational man had turned away. One of them was magic, whose central concerns were identity and power, achieved by non-rational means. W. B. Yeats summed up the occult renaissance of his day in a telling phrase as 'the revolt of the soul against intellect'. Society, philosophy and science since the seventeenth century have valued reason and intellect at the expense of the rest of human nature. Though the revival of magic has been liberally embellished with lunacy, there is something of worth at its centre in its effort to restore 'the universal man' to his lost throne.

NOTES

PROLOGUE : THE BEGINNINGS

1. Dodds, *The Greeks and the Irrational*, p. 13.
2. Maringer, *The Gods of Prehistoric Man*, p. 106.
3. Aldred, *The Egyptians*, pp. 69, 157–9.
4. Peter Brown in *Witchcraft Confessions and Accusations*, pp. 21–2.

CHAPTER ONE : ROME AND THE EAST

1. Tarn and Griffith, *Hellenistic Civilisation*, p. 352.
2. Pliny *Natural History* 30.1; cf. 2 Timothy 3:8.
3. Empedocles, fragment 117, quoted in Burnet, *Early Greek Philosophy*.
4. Philostratus *Life of Apollonius* 4.25.
5. *Corpus Hermeticum*, 11.20, quoted in Dodds, *Pagan and Christian in an Age of Anxiety*, p. 82.
6. For theurgy see Dodds, *The Greeks and the Irrational*, Appendix 2.
7. Livy *Ab Urbe Condita* 22.9.9.
8. Ibid. 22.57.4.
9. Petronius *Satyricon* p. 71.
10. Rose, *Ancient Roman Religion*, pp. 35–6.
11. Pliny *Natural History* 28.3.10.
12. Guthrie, *The Greeks and Their Gods*, pp. 270–4.
13. Tacitus *The Annals of Imperial Rome* 2.69.
14. Theophrastus *Enquiry into Plants* 9.8.8.
15. 1 Kings 3:4.
16. Mackenzie, *Dreams and Dreaming*, p. 28.
17. Ovid *Fasti* 6.131; Horace *Epodes* 5.
18. Petronius *Satyricon* p. 63; Augustine *City of God*, 21.6.
19. Homer *Odyssey* 10.
20. Horace *Satires* 1.8.
21. Lucan *Pharsalia* 6.
22. Juvenal *Satires* 6.548, 610.
23. Cumont, *Astrology and Religion among the Greeks and Romans*, p. xi.
24. Hooke, *Babylonian and Assyrian Religion*, p. 95.
25. Herodotus *The Histories* 2.82; McIntosh, *The Astrologers and Their Creed*, p. 9.
26. Ptolemy *Tetrabiblos* 1.2.
27. Ammianus Marcellinus *Works* 29.1.27; see also Dodds, 'Supernormal Phenomena'.
28. Aldred, *Egyptians*, p. 119.
29. Ammianus Marcellinus *Works* 19.12.19.

30. Acts 16:16.
31. *De Anima Mantissa*, quoted in Cumont, *Astrology and Religion*, p. 87.

CHAPTER TWO: CHRISTIANITY AND THE MIDDLE AGES

1. Acts 9:42, 14:8, 19:11.
2. Acts 2:14–15.
3. 1 Corinthians 3:16–17.
4. Lea, *Materials Towards a History of Witchcraft*, vol. i, p. 113.
5. Jungmann, *The Early Liturgy*, pp. 182–3.
6. Geoffrey Ashe in *Man, Myth & Magic*, vol. vi, p. 2353.
7. Lea, *A History of the Inquisition*, vol. iii, p. 400.
8. Caesar *Gallic War* 6.33.
9. Tacitus *Annals* 14.30.
10. Deuteronomy 18:10; Isaiah 8:19.
11. 1 Samuel 28:12–19.
12. *Key of Solomon*, 1.7.
13. Scholem, *Major Trends in Jewish Mysticism*, p. 49.
14. Quoted in Blau, *The Christian Interpretation of the Cabala in the Renaissance*, p. 69, my italics; for Abulafia see Scholem, *Major Trends*, chapter 4.
15. Trachtenberg, *Jewish Magic and Superstition*, p. 22.
16. Seznec, *The Survival of the Pagan Gods*, p. 53.
17. Quoted by Allan Macfarlane in *Witchcraft Confessions and Accusations*, p. 91.
18. See H. R. Ellis Davidson in *The Witch Figure*, pp. 20–39.
19. Cohn, *Europe's Inner Demons*, chapter 7.
20. *Malleus Maleficarum* 1.1.
21. Ibid., 2.1.
22. Lea, *Materials*, vol. i, p. 89.
23. Russell, *Witchcraft in the Middle Ages*, p. 227.

CHAPTER THREE: THE RENAISSANCE AND THE WITCH MANIA

1. Wind, *Pagan Mysteries in the Renaissance*, pp. 48, 110.
2. Seznec, *The Survival of the Pagan Gods*, p. 91.
3. Walker, *Spiritual and Demonic Magic from Ficino to Campanella*, pp. 32–3.
4. Wind, *Pagan Mysteries*, p. 62; see also Yates, *Giordano Bruno and the Hermetic Tradition*, p. 127.
5. Agrippa *Occult Philosophy* 1.66.
6. Scholem, *Major Trends in Jewish Mysticism*, p. 142.
7. Agrippa *Occult Philosophy* 2.50, 3.36.
8. Thorndike, *A History of Magic and Experimental Science*, vol. iv, pp. 370–1, 442.
9. Seznec, *The Survival of the Pagan Gods*, p. 59.
10. Cheetham, *The Prophecies of Nostradamus*, 1.23.

11. Rowse, *Simon Forman*, p. 186.
12. See Yates, *Giordano Bruno*.
13. Yates, *The Rosicrucian Enlightenment*, p. 40.
14. See Yates, *Giordano Bruno*, pp. 416–23.
15. Piggott, *The Druids*, p. 119.
16. Waite, *The Brotherhood of the Rosy Cross*, p. 369.
17. Russell, *Witchcraft in the Middle Ages*, p. 203.
18. Lea, *Materials Towards a History of Witchcraft*, vol. ii, p. 422.
19. Boguet, *An Examen of Witches*, see the dedication.
20. Lea, *Materials*, vol. iii, p. 1125.
21. Baroja, *The World of Witches*, pp. 183, 188.
22. Robbins, *The Encyclopedia of Witchcraft and Demonology*, p. 555.
23. Ewen, *Witch Hunting and Witch Trials*, p. 113.
24. Remy, *Demonolatry*, 1.1; Boguet, *Examen*, chapter 8.
25. Thomas, *Religion and the Decline of Magic*, pp. 493ff.
26. Trevor-Roper, *European Witch Craze of the 16th and 17th Centuries*, p. 110.

CHAPTER FOUR: THE MODERN REVIVAL

1. Howe, *Urania's Children*, pp. 21–2.
2. Ewen, *Witch Hunting and Witch Trials*, p. 45.
3. Waite, *The Brotherhood of the Rosy Cross*, p. 504; for these eighteenth-century groups see also Roberts, *The Mythology of the Secret Societies*.
4. For the full, highly entertaining story see Masters, *Casanova*.
5. Lévi, *The History of Magic*, p. 437.
6. Mackenzie, *Dreams and Dreaming*, p. 80.
7. Howe, *Urania's Children*, p. 29.
8. McIntosh, *The Astrologers and Their Creed*, p. 94.
9. Webb, *The Flight From Reason*, chapter 7.
10. McIntosh, *Eliphas Lévi and the French Occult Revival*, pp. 131–2.
11. Lévi, *The Key of the Mysteries*, p. 171.
12. Lévi, *Transcendental Magic: Its Doctrine and Ritual*, pp. 4–5.
13. Yeats, *Autobiographies*, pp. 173–5.
14. Huysmans's letters from Lyons are quoted in Baldick, *Life of Huysmans*, pp. 186–9; see also *Man, Myth & Magic*, vol. i, pp. 228–9.
15. Webb, *The Flight from Reason*, chapter 5.
16. Crowley, *The Confessions of Aleister Crowley*, p. 194; Yeats, *Autobiographies*, pp. 182–3.
17. For the Golden Dawn and its offshoots see: Howe, *Magicians of the Golden Dawn*; King, *Ritual Magic in England*; and Colquhoun, *Sword of Wisdom*; for the rituals and documents see Regardie, *The Golden Dawn* and King, ed., *Astral Projection, Ritual Magic and Alchemy*.
18. Regardie, *The Golden Dawn*, vol. ii, p. 214.

19. Ibid., vol. iii, pp. 259–65.
20. Howe, *Magicians*, pp. 49–50.
21. Yeats, *Autobiographies*, pp. 90, 183, 262.
22. Symonds, *The Great Beast*, p. 10.
23. Crowley, *Confessions*, p. 336.
24. Crowley, *Magick*, pp. 132–4.
25. King, *Sexuality, Magic and Perversion*, chapter 2.
26. Hartmann, *Magic White and Black*, p. 9.
27. Waite, *The Brotherhood of the Rosy Cross*, p. 437; for the O.T.O., see King, ed., *Secret Rituals of the O.T.O.*
28. For the Nazis and the occult, see: King, *Satan and Swastika*; Howe, *Urania's Children*; and relevant articles in *Encyclopedia of the Unexplained*.
29. Norman Cohn in *Witchcraft Confessions and Accusations*, pp. 14–15.
30. King, *Sexuality*, p. 144.
31. On this subject, see Howe, *Urania's Children*.
32. See Kenneth Grant's article in *Encyclopedia of the Unexplained*, p. 224.
33. Symonds, *The Great Beast*, pp. 393–5.
34. Murray, *The Witch-Cult in Western Europe*, pp. 11–12.
35. Quoted by Francis King in *Encyclopedia of the Unexplained*, p. 276; see also Mr King's article in *Fate and Fortune*, Issue 9, and his *Ritual Magic*, pp. 176–81.
36. Edward J. Moody in *Religious Movements in Contemporary America*, p. 358; see also Freedland, *The Occult Explosion*.

BIBLIOGRAPHY

Agrippa, *Three Books of Occult Philosophy*, London, 1651.

Aldred, Cyril, *The Egyptians*, Thames & Hudson, London, 1961.

Ammianus Marcellinus, *Works*, trans. J. C. Rolfe, 3 vols, Loeb, revised edn, Heinemann, London, 1950–2.

Apuleius, *The Golden Ass,* trans. R. Graves, Pocket Library, New York, 1954.

Augustine, St, *The City of God*, 2 vols, Everyman's Library, London, 1945.

Baldick, Robert, *The Life of J. K. Huysmans*, Clarendon Press, Oxford, 1955.

Baroja, J. C., *The World of Witches*, Weidenfeld & Nicolson, London, 1964.

Barrett, Francis, *The Magus, or Celestial Intelligencer*, University Books, New York, 1967 reprint.

Blau, J. L., *The Christian Interpretation of the Cabala in the Renaissance*, Columbia University Press, 1944.

Boguet, Henri, *An Examen of Witches (Discours des Sorciers)*, trans. E. A. Ashwin, Muller, London, 1971 reprint.

Brown, Peter, *The World of Late Antiquity*, Thames & Hudson, London, 1971.

Burnet, John, *Early Greek Philosophy*, Black, London, 4th edn., 1930.

Butler, E. M., *The Myth of the Magus*, Cambridge University Press, 1948.

Ritual Magic, Cambridge University Press, 1949.

Caesar, Julius, *The Conquest of Gaul*, trans. S. A. Handford, Penguin, 1951.

Cavendish, Richard, *The Black Arts*, Routledge & Kegan Paul, London, 1967; Putnam, New York, 1967.

The Tarot, Michael Joseph, London, 1975; Harper & Row, New York, 1975.

Cheetham, Erica, *The Prophecies of Nostradamus*, Putnam, New York, 1972; Spearman, London, 1973.

Cohn, Norman, *Europe's Inner Demons*, Sussex University Press, 1975.

Colquhoun, Ithell, *Sword of Wisdom*, Spearman, London, 1975.

Crowley, Aleister, *The Confessions of Aleister Crowley,* ed. J. Symonds and K. Grant, Jonathan Cape, London, 1969; Hill & Wang, New York, 1970.

Magick, ed. J. Symonds and K. Grant, Routledge & Kegan Paul, London, 1973.

Cumont, Franz, *Astrology and Religion Among the Greeks and Romans*, Dover, New York, 1960 reprint.

Dodds, E. R., *The Greeks and the Irrational*, University of California
    Press, 1968 reprint.
    Pagan and Christian in an Age of Anxiety, Cambridge University
    Press, 1965.
    'Supernormal Phenomena in Classical Antiquity', *Proceedings of the
    Society for Psychical Research*, March, 1971.
Elliott, R. W. V., *Runes*, Manchester University Press, 1959.
Encyclopedia of the Unexplained, ed. R. Cavendish, Routledge & Kegan
    Paul, London, 1974; McGraw Hill, New York, 1974.
Ewen, C. L'E., *Witch Hunting and Witch Trials*, Kegan Paul, London,
    1929.
Ferguson, John, *The Religions of the Roman Empire*, Thames & Hudson,
    London, 1970.
Frazer, J. G., *The Golden Bough*, abridged edn., Macmillan, London,
    1922.
Freedland, Nat, *The Occult Explosion*, Putnam, New York, 1972;
    Michael Joseph, London, 1972.
Guazzo, F. M., *Compendium Maleficarum*, trans. E. A. Ashwin, Muller,
    London, 1970 reprint.
Guthrie, W. K. C., *The Greeks and Their Gods*, Methuen, London, 1950.
Hartmann, Franz, *Magic White and Black*, Kegan Paul, London, 1893.
Herodotus, *The Histories*, trans. A. de Selincourt, Penguin,
    Harmondsworth, 1954.
Holmyard, E. J., *Alchemy*, Penguin, Harmondsworth, 1957.
Homer, *The Odyssey*, trans. E. V. Rieu, Penguin, Harmondsworth, 1946.
Hooke, S. H., *Babylonian and Assyrian Religion*, Hutchinson, London,
    1953.
Horace, *Works*, ed. E. C. Wickham, Clarendon Press, Oxford, 1896.
Howe, Ellic, *Urania's Children*, Kimber, London, 1967.
    The Magicians of the Golden Dawn, Routledge & Kegan Paul, London,
    1972.
Jung, C. G., *Psychology and Alchemy*, trans. R. F. C. Hull, Routledge &
    Kegan Paul, London, 1953.
Jungmann, J. A., *The Early Liturgy*, University of Notre Dame Press,
    1959.
Juvenal, *Satires*, trans. G. G. Ramsey, Loeb, revised edn., Heinemann,
    London, 1940.
The Key of Solomon, ed. S. L. M. Mathers, Routledge & Kegan Paul,
    London, 1972 reprint.
King, Francis, *Ritual Magic in England*, Spearman, London, 1970.
    Sexuality, Magic and Perversion, Spearman, London, 1971.
    ed., *Astral Projection, Ritual Magic and Alchemy*, Spearman, London,
    1971.
    ed., *The Secret Rituals of the O.T.O.*, Daniel, London, 1973.
    Satan and Swastika, Mayflower, London, 1976.
Lea, H. C., *A History of the Inquisition*, 3 vols, Russell & Russell, New
    York, 1955 reprint.

Materials Towards a History of Witchcraft, 3 vols, Yoseloff, New York, 1957 reprint.

Lemegeton or Lesser Key of Solomon, Sloane MS. 2731, British Museum.

Lévi, Eliphas, *Transcendental Magic: Its Doctrine and Ritual*, trans. A. E. Waite, Redway, London, 1896.

    The History of Magic, trans. A. E. Waite, Dutton, New York, 3rd edn., n.d.

    The Key of the Mysteries, trans. A. Crowley, Rider, London, 1959.

Lilly, William, *The Last of the Astrologers* (Lilly's autobiography), ed. K. M. Briggs, Mistletoe Books, Folklore Society, London, 1974.

Livy, *Ab Urbe Condita*, trans. B. O. Foster, vol. 5, Loeb edn., Heinemann, London, 1949.

Lucan, *Pharsalia*, trans. R. Graves, Penguin, Harmondsworth, 1956.

Mackenzie, Norman, *Dreams and Dreaming*, Aldus, London, 1965.

Malleus Maleficarum, trans. M. Summers, Pushkin Press, London, 1951 reprint.

Man, Myth and Magic, ed. R. Cavendish, 7 vols, Purnell, London, 1970–2.

Maringer, Johannes, *The Gods of Prehistoric Man*, Weidenfeld & Nicolson, London, 1960; Knopf, New York, 1960.

Masters, John, *Casanova*, Michael Joseph, London, 1969.

McIntosh, Christopher, *The Astrologers and Their Creed*, Hutchinson, London, 1969; Praeger, New York, 1970.

    Eliphas Lévi and the French Occult Revival, Rider, London, 1972.

Murray, Margaret A., *The Witch-Cult in Western Europe*, Clarendon Press, Oxford, 1921.

Oppenheim, A. Leo, *Ancient Mesopotamia*, University of Chicago Press, 1964.

Ovid, *Fasti*, ed. J. G. Frazer, Loeb edn., Heinemann, London, 1931.

Paracelsus, *Selected Writings*, trans. N. Guterman, Routledge & Kegan Paul, London, 1951; Princeton University Press, 1958.

Petronius, *Satyricon*, trans. W. Arrowsmith, University of Michigan Press, 1959.

Philostratus, *Life of Apollonius*, trans. C. P. Jones, Penguin, Harmondsworth, 1970.

Piggott, Stuart, *The Druids*, Penguin, Harmondsworth, 1974.

Pliny, *Natural History*, 9 vols, Loeb edn., Heinemann, London, 1949–63.

Ptolemy, *Tetrabiblos*, trans. F. E. Robbins, Loeb edn., Heinemann, London, 1940.

Regardie, Israel, *The Golden Dawn*, 3rd edn., 4 vols, Llewellyn, St Paul, Minnesota, 1970.

Religious Movements in Contemporary America, ed. I. I. Zaretsky and M. P. Leone, Princeton University Press, 1974.

Remy, Nicolas, *Demonolatry*, trans. E. A. Ashwin, Muller, London, 1970 reprint.

Rhodes, H. T. F., *The Satanic Mass*, Rider, London, 1954.

Robbins, R. H., *The Encyclopedia of Witchcraft and Demonology*, Crown, New York, 1959.

Roberts, J. M., *The Mythology of the Secret Societies*, Secker & Warburg, London, 1972.

Rose, H. J., *Ancient Greek Religion*, Hutchinson, London, 1946.
Ancient Roman Religion, Hutchinson, London, 1948.

Ross, Anne, *Pagan Celtic Britain*, Routledge, London, 1967.

Rowse, A. L., *Simon Forman*, Weidenfeld & Nicolson, London, 1974.

Russell, J. B., *Witchcraft in the Middle Ages*, Cornell University Press, 1972.

Scholem, G. G., *Major Trends in Jewish Mysticism*, Thames & Hudson, London, 1955; Schocken Books, New York, 1961.

Seznec, Jean, *The Survival of the Pagan Gods*, Harper Torchbooks, New York, 1961 reprint.

The Sword of Moses, ed. M. Gaster, Weiser, New York, 1970 reprint.

Symonds, John, *The Great Beast*, revised edn., Macdonald, London, 1971.

Tacitus, *The Annals of Imperial Rome*, trans. M. Grant, Penguin, Harmondsworth, 1956.
The Agricola and the Germania, revised edn., Penguin, Harmondsworth, 1970.

Tarn, W. and Griffith, G. T., *Hellenistic Civilisation*, 3rd edn., Edward Arnold, London, 1952.

Theophrastus, *Enquiry into Plants*, 2 vols, trans. A. Hort, Loeb edn., Heinemann, London, 1916.

Thomas, Keith, *Religion and the Decline of Magic*, Weidenfeld & Nicolson, London, 1971.

Thorndike, Lyn, *A History of Magic and Experimental Science*, 8 vols, Columbia University Press, 1923–58.

Trachtenberg, J., *Jewish Magic and Superstition*, Meridian Books, New York, 1961 reprint.

Trevor-Roper, H. R., *The European Witch-Craze of the 16th and 17th Centuries*, Penguin, 1969; Harper & Row, New York, 1969.

Virgil, *The Pastoral Poems*, trans. E. V. Rieu, Penguin, Harmondsworth, 1954.

Waite, A. E., *The Book of Ceremonial Magic*, University Books, New York, 1961 reprint.
The Brotherhood of the Rosy Cross, University Books, New York, reprint, n.d.

Walker, D. P., *Spiritual and Demonic Magic from Ficino to Campanella*, Warburg Institute, London, 1958.

Webb, James, *The Flight From Reason*, Macdonald, London, 1971.

Wind, Edgar, *Pagan Mysteries in the Renaissance*, Penguin, Harmondsworth, 1967.

Witchcraft Confessions and Accusations, ed. M. Douglas, Tavistock, London, 1970.

The Witch Figure, ed. V. Newall, Routledge & Kegan Paul, London, 1973.

BIBLIOGRAPHY

Yates, Frances A., *Giordano Bruno and the Hermetic Tradition*,
    Routledge & Kegan Paul, London, 1964; University of Chicago Press,
    1964.
    The Rosicrucian Enlightenment, Routledge & Kegan Paul, London,
    1972.
Yeats, W. B., *Autobiographies*, Macmillan, London, 1955.

ACKNOWLEDGMENTS

The illustrations in this book are supplied or reproduced by kind
    permission of the following:

Bayerischen Staatsgemäldesammlungen, Munich, 10
Bibliothèque Nationale, Paris, 9
The British Library, London, 16
The British Museum, London, 3, 4, 5, 11, 14, 18, 20
The Courtauld Institute of Art, London, 6, 15
The Danish National Museum, Copenhagen, 12
The Dean and Chapter, Winchester, 8
Fotomas Index, London, 17
Sonia Halliday, 8
Keystone Press Agency, London, 32
Librarie Larousse, Paris, 1
The Mansell Collection, London, 7, 21, 22, 25, 26
The National Portrait Gallery, London, 31
Picturepoint, London, 2, 27
Popperfoto, London, 23, 28, 33
Radio Times Hulton Picture Library, London, 30
Riksantikvarieämbetet och Statens Historiska Museer, Stockholm, 13
The Warburg Institute, London, 24
Weidenfeld & Nicolson Archives, 29
The Wellcome Trustees, The Wellcome Institute for the History of
    Medicine, London, 19

Picture Research by Debbie Beevor

INDEX

Abulafia, Abraham, 60–1, 88
Adam, 18, 56, 100, 127
Aesculapius (Asklepios), 30–1, 47
Agnus Dei, 50
Agrippa (Heinrich Cornelius), 83,
   89–90, 91, 92, 95, 97, 101, 110, 128,
   132, 133, 136
Albertus Magnus, 58
Albumazar, 65
alchemy, 62–5, 66, 77, 86, 89, 90, 94,
   95, 96, 98–9, 101, 103, 105; origins,
   19, 63; purposes, 62–3, 99, 162;
   symbolism, 63, 64, 151; bridge
   between scientific and spiritual,
   100, 123; and fringe Masonry, 126,
   127, 128, 129, 130; and modern
   magic, 132, 133, 136, 143, 145, 147,
   151; Jung on, 162
Alexander of Aphrodisias, 42
Alexander the Great, 9–10, 16
almanacs, 93, 94, 123, 133, 134
Almandel, 58
altered states of consciousness, 3, 4, 5,
   9, 17, 19, 22, 31, 37, 45–6, 55–6,
   59–61, 63, 71, 87, 88, 89, 122, 144,
   150 *see also* astral body, oracles,
   prophecy
Ammianus Marcellinus, 40
amulets and talismans, 6, 7, 9, 12, 30,
   41, 49, 50, 51, 59, 61, 67, 96, 133,
   145, 152; for astrological 'images',
   see astrology
Ancient and Accepted Rite, 126
Ancient and Mystic Order Rosae
   Crucis, 153
Andreae, J. V., 100, 101
angels, 17, 57, 61, 66, 67, 77, 88, 89,
   90, 92, 95, 96, 97, 103, 104, 120, 128,
   140
animal magnetism, *see* hypnosis
ankh, 41, 47
Anthony, St, 47
Anthroposophical Society, 151
antisemitism, 62, 152–3
Apollo, 13, 39, 40, 41
Apollonius of Tyana, 14–16, 17, 101,
   103, 110, 135
Apuleius, 33, 34

Aquinas, St Thomas, 66, 67, 81
Arab influence, 62, 63–4, 65, 99
Aradia, 160
Arbatel, 92
Arnald of Villanova, 64, 67
art, magic and, *see* magic (general);
   music
Artemidorus, 32, 92
Ashmole, Elias, 103, 104
Asklepios, *see* Aesculapius
Assurbanipal, 32, 37
Assyria, *see* Mesopotamia
astral body, plane, 87, 89, 135–6, 137,
   140, 145, 146, 150, 157, 162
astrology, 9, 10, 11, 14, 17, 36–9, 54,
   61, 65–8, 74, 80, 90, 93, 94, 95, 96,
   101–2, 103, 104–5, 117, 123, 129,
   130; Mesopotamian origins, 12,
   36–8; high and low, 38–9, 134; and
   Christianity, 50, 65–8; and
   alchemy, 62–3; astrological
   'images', talismans, 64, 67, 68, 78,
   86, 87–8, 89, 97, 133, 140; modern
   revival, 133–4, 135, 142, 143, 145,
   152, 153, 155, 156, 157–8, 162
Attis, 17, 47
Aubrey, John, 102
augury, 40, 53, 55
Augustine, St, 34, 49, 66
Augustus, 16, 39, 41
Avicenna, 67

Babylonia, *see* Chaldea; Mesopotamia
Bacchus, *see* Dionysus
Bacon, Francis, 101, 130
Bacon, Roger, 58, 64, 67
Balsamo, Giuseppe, *see* Cagliostro
Baphomet, 72, 149
Barrett, Francis, 133, 139
beating the bounds, 52
Berosus, 38
Bes, 41
Binsfeld, Peter, 111
Black Death, 65, 81
Black Mass, 51, 79, 113, 115, 116, 140
Blavatsky, Mme H. P., 126, 139, 142,
   143, 151
Bodin, Jean, 111, 119

173

ARKANA – NEW-AGE BOOKS FOR MIND, BODY AND SPIRIT

With over 150 titles currently in print, Arkana is the leading name in quality new-age books for mind, body and spirit. Arkana encompasses the spirituality of both East and West, ancient and new, in fiction and non-fiction. A vast range of interests is covered, including Psychology and Transformation, Health, Science and Mysticism, Women's Spirituality and Astrology.

If you would like a catalogue of Arkana books, please write to:

Arkana Marketing Department
Penguin Books Ltd
27 Wright's Lane
London W8 5TZ

ARKANA – NEW-AGE BOOKS FOR MIND, BODY AND SPIRIT

A selection of titles already published or in preparation

Being Intimate: A Guide to Successful Relationships
John and Kris Amodeo

This invaluable guide aims to enrich one of the most important – yet often problematic – aspects of our lives: intimate relationships and friendships.

'A clear and practical guide to the realization and communication of authentic feelings, and thus an excellent pathway towards lasting intimacy and love' – George Leonard

The Brain Book Peter Russell

The essential handbook for brain users.

'A fascinating book – for everyone who is able to appreciate the human brain, which, as Russell says, is the most complex and most powerful information processor known to man. It is especially relevant for those who are called upon to read a great deal when time is limited, or who attend lectures or seminars and need to take notes' – *Nursing Times*

The Act of Creation Arthur Koestler

This second book in Koestler's classic trio of works on the human mind (which opened with *The Sleepwalkers* and concludes with *The Ghost in the Machine*) advances the theory that all creative activities – the conscious and unconscious processes underlying artistic originality, scientific discovery and comic inspiration – share a basic pattern, which Koestler expounds and explores with all his usual clarity and brilliance.

A Psychology With a Soul: Psychosynthesis in Evolutionary Context Jean Hardy

Psychosynthesis was developed between 1910 and the 1950s by Roberto Assagioli – an Italian psychiatrist who, like Jung, diverged from Freud in search of a more spiritually based understanding of human nature. Jean Hardy's account of this comprehensive approach to self-realization will be of great value to everyone concerned with personal integration and spiritual growth.

ARKANA – NEW-AGE BOOKS FOR MIND, BODY AND SPIRIT

A selection of titles already published or in preparation

Encyclopedia of the Unexplained
Edited by Richard Cavendish Consultant: J. B. Rhine

'Will probably be the definitive work of its kind for a long time to come' – *Prediction*

The ultimate guide to the unknown, the esoteric and the unproven: richly illustrated, with almost 450 clear and lively entries from Alchemy, the Black Box and Crowley to faculty X, Yoga and the Zodiac.

Buddhist Civilization in Tibet Tulku Thondup Rinpoche

Unique among works in English, *Buddhist Civilization in Tibet* provides an astonishing wealth of information on the various strands of Tibetan religion and literature in a single compact volume, focusing predominantly on the four major schools of Buddhism: Nyingma, Kagyud, Sakya and Gelug.

The Living Earth Manual of Feng-Shui Stephen Skinner

The ancient Chinese art of Feng-Shui – tracking the hidden energy flow which runs through the earth in order to derive maximum benefit from being in the right place at the right time – can be applied equally to the siting and layout of cities, houses, tombs and even flats and bedsits; and can be practised as successfully in the West as in the East with the aid of this accessible manual.

In Search of the Miraculous: Fragments of an Unknown Teaching P. D. Ouspensky

Ouspensky's renowned, vivid and characteristically honest account of his work with Gurdjieff from 1915–18.

'Undoubtedly a *tour de force*. To put entirely new and very complex cosmology and psychology into fewer than 400 pages, and to do this with a simplicity and vividness that makes the book accessible to any educated reader, is in itself something of an achievement' – *The Times Literary Supplement*